MURDER AT THE CAFE BONBON

Andrea Hicks

This book is a work of fiction. The names, characters, places, and incidents are products of the writer's imagination, or have been used fictitiously. Any resemblance to persons, living or dead, actual events, locales or organisations is coincidental.
All rights reserved. No part of this book may be stored
in a retrieval system or transmitted, or reproduced in any form
except for the inclusion of brief quotations in review without permission in writing
from the author at
info@andreahicks-writer.com

Copyright Andrea Hicks©2024

CHAPTERS

Prologue..1
Chapter 1..3
Chapter 2..9
Chapter 3..13
Chapter 4..19
Chapter 5..23
Chapter 6..31
Chapter 7..37
Chapter 8..44
Chapter 9..51
Chapter 10..58
Chapter 11..64
Chapter 12..71
Chapter 13..75
Chapter 14..85
Chapter 15..92
Chapter 16..100
Chapter 17..111
Chapter 18..116
Chapter 19..127
Chapter 20..134
Chapter 21..138
Chapter 22..154
Chapter 23..161
Chapter 24..166
Chapter 25..168
Chapter 26..176
Chapter 27..184
Chapter 28..189
Chapter 29..195
Chapter 30..203
Chapter 31..220
Chapter 32..229
Chapter 33..231
Chapter 34..249
Chapter 35..255
Chapter 36..260
Chapter 37..262
Chapter 38.. 266
Chapter 39..270
Chapter 40..273
A Note from the Author.. 277

For my mum…who loved to sing

Prologue

Detective Inspector Richard Owen fixed his tie as he stared at his reflection in the mirror on his walnut wood dresser. He hated ties, either tying them when he was all fingers and thumbs, or feeling required to wear them. Of course it was expected in his work, there were standards to maintain, and he was observant of all the standards expected of him. One didn't see anyone on the force without a tie, but it was rare for him to wear a tie on an off day. Today was one of those days; the evening to be exact. One he had given much thought to. In fact it had occupied his thoughts for most of the previous two months.

He had been careful about his appearance that evening. The tie he'd chosen was the colour of a peacock's feathers, a stunning royal blue, which he knew was a favourite colour of Camille's. He was quite sure it wouldn't make a ha'porth of difference to the outcome of his meeting with Camille Divine, but he needed to feel confident, more than confident in fact; assured of himself if possible, and determined in his state of mind for what he was about to do.

They had left each other in Paris in a hurry. No one's fault of course, simply life getting in the way. He and Camille had planned a last lunch before she had returned to London, and he to go on a visit to his deceased wife's relatives in the South of France, but her cook and close friend,

Knolly, had been taken ill at Camille's house in Duke Street and Camille had been desperate to get home to be by her side.

Her hurry to return to her friend had not surprised him. Camille was the most caring woman he had ever known. It was one of the things that had attracted him to her when he had first met her, an inauspicious occasion it was true, but he had learnt so much about her since. He tried his best not to think about the other things, her obvious attributes. He knew it was shallow of him, but she was undoubtedly beautiful, elegant, and accomplished, yet there was a vulnerability about her, making him want to take care of her. Of course, she was more than capable of taking care of herself, and would have been astonished if he ever admitted as much to her. She was indeed 'divine' in his eyes.

Richard took one last look at himself in the mirror and sighed, knowing this could be the night to seal or divide the relationship they had found. He chuckled at the word relationship.

'We solve murders and mysteries together,' he said aloud, shrugging on his jacket. 'Can it be called a relationship?' He shook his head, and although wasn't religious in any way said a quiet prayer. 'Let her understand,' he said to his reflection. 'To understand and realise I am my father's son, but not his disciple. I'm me, the Richard she has known for the last year or more…and I follow my own path.' He nodded to himself in the mirror. 'Good luck, Richard. I think you're going to need it.'

Chapter 1

'Now you will be all right, Knolly, won't you? I'd rather not leave you, but Chief Inspector Owen made it sound so important I felt I couldn't refuse.'

Knolly chuckled. 'Madam, you're beginning to fuss. I'm perfectly all right as well you know. The doctor has given me a clean bill of 'ealth and I've never felt better. And anyway, Cecily's 'ere…and Phillips. They know how to take care of an old girl like me.'

'You're hardly old, Knolly, but you heard what Doctor Rathbone said…you've been overdoing things. I wish you'd taken up the offer of a holiday. I think it would do you the world of good.'

'And where would I go, Lady Divine? And on me own too. That's no 'oliday as far as I'm concerned, more like a penance. I'd feel like I was bein' sent away as a punishment.'

She folded her hands in her lap as she sat at the kitchen table and looked more determined than Camille had ever seen her.

'No, I'm better off with my family and in me 'ome where I feel safe. And anyway, 'e said it was that change of life thing what 'ad made it all worse. I'd noticed things were changing somewhat, yer know, I felt a bit different, an' other things,' she looked slightly embarrassed, 'but I never knew it would make me feel like that. Proper dizzy and 'ot I was. Thought it was the end of me. And poor Phillips, 'e didn't know what ter do. The man was running around like a chicken what 'ad 'ad its 'ead chopped off. Kept getting' me glasses of water, then sayin' I wasn't eatin' enough.' She threw back her head and laughed. 'Well, we all know that ain't true. I love me food I do. Never say no to anythin'.'

Camille sighed then giggled. 'I have to agree with you there, Knolly, but then your cooking is hard to resist.'

Knolly flushed looking pleased. 'Thank you, Madam. I takes pride in me work as you know. Go on upstairs now and get ready. Cecily's up in your room, layin' out yer clothes. We know 'ow much you like the Chief Inspector…' she cleared her throat, 'and we know 'ow much he likes you.' She glanced at Camille with a twinkle in her eye and a wry smile. Camille laughed and made her way upstairs.

'She's right yer know, Madam,' said Cecily as she ran about the bedroom, straightening up the room so Camille could try on her outfits at her leisure, and apply her cosmetics. 'She'll be perfectly all right with me and Phillips. You 'aven't been out for ages. You deserve a treat.'

'I've been very worried, Cecily. You know what the doctor said. It could be her heart.'

'Could be, he said, but until the tests come back, we won't know will we? And don't yer think she seems all right?'

Camille nodded. 'Well, yes, yes I do. She seems just like her old self with no sign of the previous problem. I think the rest has done her good.'

Cecily giggled. 'Yeah, well she won't let that go on much longer. She says she's fed up wiv eating restaurant food. She says it ain't the same.'

'She's right.'

'I fink she's right too. It just don't taste the same. Seems like a luxury at first, but to tell the truth, I'm a bit fed up wiv it. All them sauces and whatnot. I'm sure they're not good for yer. Knolly's food is so wholesome…and well, tasty, without no fancy stuff. I fink they use the sauces to cover fings up.'

Camille nodded. 'Knolly has told me she's back to work tomorrow. I've tried to dissuade her but…' Camille shook her head, 'she's having none of it.'

'Course she ain't. She told me she's bored witless.'

Camille went over to the bed and picked up one of the dresses, an apricot-coloured chiffon shift, feeling the fabric between her fingers. 'I wonder what Richard wants to see me about?'

'P'raps it's a new investigation, Madam. Needs you on the case as it were.'

Camille shook her head. 'I'm not sure it is. If it were he could have telephoned. No,' she frowned. 'My instincts are telling me there's more to it.'

'Somethin' dangerous, Madam?'

'I don't know, Cecily, and I'm not sure what to wear to fit the occasion.'

'Where are yer going?' asked Cecily as she bent down to retrieve the matching shoes to the apricot dress from the shoe closet.

'The Café Bonbon.'

Cecily straightened up and stared at her. 'Ooh, Madam, that new place?'

'Yes. I hear it has a bit of a reputation for high jinks. Sounds fun doesn't it?'

'I s'pose it does if yer fink high jinks is fun. I've never 'ad any so I can't really say.'

Camille raised her eyebrows and smiled. 'Perhaps it's time you did.'

'Sounds a bit scary if you ask me, Madam.'

Camille looked surprised. 'Scary? Why would having fun be scary, Cecily?'

Cecily shrugged. 'Oh, I dunno. I s'pose it's cos I'm not used to that kind of thing.' She shrugged again. 'And the apricot chiffon ain't right, Madam, not for Café Bonbon.' She reached into the wardrobe and pulled out another dress. 'This is it, Madam, much more like it.' She held up a deep navy fitted dress split to the thigh. It had silver bugle beads on the bodice and came with a navy headband complete with a long silver feather.

Camille's eyes widened. 'It's a bit racy isn't it?' She folded her arms in front of her. 'I bought that for a New Years Eve party. The theme was Glitz and Glamour. I'm not sure it's suitable for an ordinary night out in London.'

'It's more proper than the apricot shift, Madam, for where you're goin'. I've 'eard Café Bonbon ain't nothin' like an ordinary night out in London. I read it was, now what was the word?' She tapped her chin with her fingers. 'Began wiv a h'aich. Hed…hed…'

'I think you mean hedonistic, Cecily. It means decadent, riotous, a bit wild.'

'Yeah, that's it. I'm wondering if Chief Inspector Owen knows what 'e's lettin' 'imself in for.'

'Perhaps he's looking for some fun.' chuckled Camille. 'I'm sure there's a funny bone inside him somewhere, although he can be quite serious I grant you.'

'He's a dreamy dancer though.'

Camille turned to Cecily and grinned. 'And how would you know that, pray?'

'When we was at Antonella Toignton's Summer Ball.' She giggled. 'I sneaked in an' watched for a minute,' she turned and picked something off the bed to fold, although it was already folded, 'although I missed all the excitement, what I was glad about I can tell yer. Not the sort of excitement I want ter see thank you very much.'

Camille inhaled. 'Yes, well, it's not what I expected to see either, but there we are. Thank goodness it's all behind us.'

Cecily nodded. 'Did yer say Chief Inspector Owen wanted to speak wiv yer about something? I wonder what it is?'

'I'm just hoping it isn't anything to do with investigating. I'd like to begin the season without bloodshed or murders, or…anything like it. It would be nice to have some quiet time.'

'I agree, Madam.'

'Ta da! How do I look, Cecily.'

Camille stood with her arms in the air, one foot forward, as though she were about to go on stage. The feather in her headband swayed as she moved.

Cecily clapped her hands. 'Ooh, Madam, it's perfect. That dress…it's gorgeous. You should wear things like it more often.'

Camille grabbed her tiny bag from the dresser and put the chain over one shoulder. 'I don't think so. Whatever would Lord Divine say?'

Cecily humphed. 'Shouldn't think you could give too 'oots what he'd say.'

Camile smiled gently. 'You haven't forgiven him yet, have you?'

'No, Madam, I ain't, and I don't think I ever will. What he done was awful. He treated you very shabbily, if yer don't mind me sayin'.' She cleared her throat. 'Not my place a course. Nuffin to do with me.'

'Best to forget about it, Cecily,' Camille said, patting Cecily's shoulder. 'I'm extremely happy. In fact, I rather think Lord Divine did me a service. I cannot imagine living in that stuffy old house now. I like it here, and I like being with you, and Knolly, and Phillips.'

'And you like Chief Inspector Owen.'

'Yes. Yes I do rather.'

'What time will 'e call for yer?'

'About now, I should think. I feel rather nervous. He's never seen me dressed like this.' Camille pulled a face. 'I can't imagine what he'll make of it.'

Cecily chuckled. 'Oh, I can, Madam. I definitely can.'

Chapter 2

'Camille!'

Richard stood on the front pavement outside of Camille's house in Duke Street and stared.

'Is it too much?' She asked him, uncertain now. 'Should I change, d'you think?'

He held out his arm for her. 'Not at all. You look ravishing.' Camille heard Cecily giggling behind her. 'You know where we're going?'

'You said The Café Bonbon. Not long opened I understand.'

'That's right. One of my colleagues said I should give it a whirl, and I could think of no better person than you to accompany me.'

Camille stepped out onto the pavement and closed the door behind her. 'I can whirl, Richard,' she said, slipping an arm through his.

'Of that I'm in no doubt,' he murmured.

The Café Bonbon was situated just off Leicester Square in Bear Street. The taxicab pulled up outside and Richard got out first, helping Camille onto the pavement by offering her his hand.

'Are you warm enough?' he asked her.

She smiled. 'Am I showing too much flesh, Richard?'

'Not as far as I'm concerned,' he said, giving her a sideways look. He pulled her chiffon shawl around her shoulders. It gave no warmth but looked sensational. He felt proud to be with her.

Camille giggled, feeling more girlish than she had for a long time. She couldn't put her finger on why she felt the way she did about Richard, but it had occurred to her that he reminded her of her father. Her Papa was a quiet, contemplative man with beautiful manners. He knew how to treat women, with respect, and sometimes, with deference. Her Mama had always been besotted with him, and to Camille's knowledge, still was.

Richard made her feel safe. She had chuckled to herself when she had thought about it. Was it because he was a policeman? It wasn't this which drew her to him. Sharing her life with a policeman had never occurred to her. No, it was much more than that. He was kind, thoughtful, caring…and he looked at her as though she were the only woman on earth. Any woman would love his exquisitely long fingers, his manicured fingernails, the perfume from his cologne, heady and musky, and of course, the way he dressed. Richard always knew the correct things to wear wherever they had been together. He looked just as dashing on any occasion, whether they were at a restaurant or simply walking in the park.

Of course, she had wondered about him. Like her father he gave nothing away. Her Papa had not told her of his heritage until she was much older, and as a young woman she had felt so very proud of him. She imagined Richard had come from a similar background, not aristocratic of course, but one where he had been raised in a comfortable home with servants. His beautiful manners gave him away. His being part of the police force had perhaps been a step away from his middle-class upbringing. She wondered what his family had thought when he had told them he was to join the Metropolitan Police.

Once inside Café Bonbon they made their way into the foyer which was decorated rather like the night sky. The walls were decorated in a deep blue, almost indigo, with myriad lights scattered across the walls. They looked like stars, and twinkled on and off, which Camille found enchanting. It was like being cast into the universe.

'This is stunning,' she breathed.

'A good start,' said Richard.

'Oh, yes. I can't wait to get further inside.'

Above them was an illuminated crescent moon on which a young women lay in the curve. She had long slim legs, and one arm was folded under her head as though she was sleeping. She was scantily dressed, as though a chiffon ribbon had simply been wound around her lithe body. Camille turned to Richard and raised her eyebrows.

'I don't know about showing too much flesh?' she laughed. 'I think I'm over-dressed.' Richard grinned and put a hand on her back, steering her through an archway which had a set of wrought-iron double doors, leading them into the main nightclub.

Inside, on the nightclub floor, the atmosphere was dark and smoky. The floor was chequered black and white like a chess board, and there were different coloured flashing lights and dancers on podiums, similarly dressed to the young woman reclining on the crescent moon in the foyer. Small tables had been placed in the centre of the room, each one with a tiny table lamp in the middle which illuminated the guests faces.

'Did you have to book, Richard?' asked Camille.

He nodded. 'Yes. Perhaps we should find our table.' Before they could move into the main arena, a young woman approached them.

'You've booked, sir?' she asked Richard.

'I have. Mr. Owen and guest.'

She ran her finger down the list of guests, then smiled. 'Yes, here we are. You have a table at the front, Mr. Owen. Please follow me.'

Chapter 3

The young woman led them to the front of the club, stepping down one narrow step onto the chequered floor. The table was in the centre and in front of the stage.

'Would you like me to send Emma over to you, sir, madam?' asked the vendeuse who was there to sell all that the nightclub had to offer as well as directing guests to their seats. 'And the waiter? You would like some drinks, yes?' Richard nodded and thanked her.

'How wonderful,' cried Camille. 'We're near the dancefloor and the band.'

'I know you like to dance,' he murmured in her ear as he pulled out a chair for her to sit.

'And so do you,' she said, smoothing the skirt of her dress and sitting on the chair he proffered. She glanced up at him. 'Cecily says you dance like a dream.'

He laughed as he joined her at the table. 'And how would Cecily know?'

'She was watching us at the Summer Ball at Antonella Toignton's. I think she sneaked into the ballroom for a few moments. She said you were dreamy.'

He frowned. 'Dreamy, eh? He nodded and turned his frown into a smile as Camille gave her drinks order to a waiter. Let's hope it doesn't turn into a nightmare, he thought.

They chatted for a few moments about this and that. He asked about Knolly and Camille smiled, so he knew he was on safe ground.

'She's all right…perhaps a little vulnerable. Poor Phillips, he didn't know what to do.'

'Is it serious?'

'Not exactly.' She leaned into him to whisper. 'The change of life. It can be difficult for a woman.' He nodded. 'And she had a little heart arrythmia which was the most frightening aspect. She was in hospital for three days and was then allowed home. We're awaiting the results of some tests with our fingers firmly crossed. I've been very careful with her but she's not the easiest patient in the world. She wants to get back into the kitchen where she's happiest, but I've rationed the amount of times she's allowed to cook. Just a little supper, nothing too taxing.'

They were interrupted by an attractive girl, as scantily dressed as the other female employees, but holding a tray of cigarettes which was suspended from a strap around her neck.

'Sir,' she said in a rather high-pitched voice which made her sound younger than she looked. 'I'm Emma. Yvette said you wanted some cigarettes.'

Richard smiled up at her. 'Yes, I do.' He pointed to his favourite brand and Emma took one from the tray and handed it to him. He paid for the cigarettes, then added some more to it as a tip. Emma bounced a small curtsey.

'Why, thank you, sir.'

Richard nodded and Emma went to another table, where there was a rather rowdy party. 'What have you been doing for food?' Richard grinned at Camille. 'Don't tell me you've been cooking for the family.'

Camille picked up her martini and took a sip, then laughed. 'Don't be silly. I want Knolly to get better, not make her worse, and I would rather like the others to survive. No, we've been getting food from a restaurant in Oxford Street. Knolly is right though…when she says it's not the same. It really isn't.'

'She's the mistress of her art.'

'I always knew it, but of course eating from a restaurant every day is not good for anyone. It was necessary though. I can barely boil an egg, and Cecily is the same unfortunately.'

'Perhaps some classes for Cecily. She could take some of the work from Knolly's shoulders.'

Camille stared at him. 'That's a marvellous idea. Wish I'd thought of it. Yes, yes I'll book her some classes.'

'And is she driving?'

'She is, and she loves it. Of course Harry wasn't impressed. She insisted I tell him in case he saw her out in the car on her own, but he had no choice in the matter. I send her on little errands so she can drive regularly and she is quite the proficient.'

'You've changed her life.'

Camille sighed. 'I suppose so…but only because she wanted it. She's so loyal and willing to learn new things. It makes things easier for me too. I'm glad I've been able to provide her with the means to widen her horizons. She deserves it.'

'Do you think a person's upbringing, their start in life dictates what happens to them when they're older. Cecily had a rough start, didn't she, being born to a poor couple who lived in the St Giles rookery?'

'She had a terrible beginning, but sadly she's not alone in that. Many people have unfortunate beginnings. I think it's how they lift themselves out of it that's the important thing.'

Richard leant towards her and stared directly into her eyes. 'So you think people can overcome their start in life?'

Camille nodded.' As long as they're willing to follow another path, yes, I do.' She frowned and returned his steady gaze. 'Is this leading somewhere, Richard? Since we were in Paris together I've felt something is bothering you? You didn't look comfortable, and I wasn't the only one who noticed it.' She reached for his hand, laying hers gently over his. 'Is it our friendship? Do you think it's inappropriate?'

He squeezed her hand. 'It's not that it's…' He was stopped in his tracks by a Master of Ceremonies who arrived on the stage to announce the entertainment.

The MC was a flamboyant character who would give the guests a look which would curdle milk if they dared to have conversations while he was speaking. Richard leant away from Camille with a sigh and lit a cigarette, seemingly thwarted again. I must speak with her, he thought. It's important this is all brought out into the open. What happens afterwards is something I'll have no control over.

He watched Camille as she laughed at the MC's risqué jokes and asides, his stomach rolling. He had thought about this moment from when she had left him at the Hotel Narcisse Blanc in Paris, and would have spoken to her at that time had she not been called away because of Knolly's illness. He was aware the evening at Café Bonbon could be the last time he would see her, at least socially. If she decided he was too hot to handle, because of her upbringing as an aristocrat, because of her daughter, because of her previous life, he would have to accept it. The thought of losing her took his breath away. To him it was unthinkable, yet he also knew it was a real possibility.

He was suddenly brought back to the ambiance of the nightclub when a member of the band hit a cymbal to announce the arrival of the singer. He squinted as he lifted his eyes to the stage. Into the spotlight sashayed a young woman. She wore a red dress, cut to flatter, and which left nothing to the imagination. Her hair was almost black, and pulled into a tight chignon at the nape of her neck. Her skin was the colour of a ripe olive, her lips painted the same red as her dress. She looked exotic and unusual and when she began to sing, her voice was as dusky as a hot summer night.

'Isn't she beautiful?' sighed Camille. 'And that voice. She's sensational.'

Richard nodded and stubbed his cigarette out in the ashtray. 'Shall we start the dancing?'

'You don't mind?'

'Why would I mind? I'll be dancing with the most beautiful woman in the room. All eyes will be on her…and I'm going to feel rather smug.'

Camille smiled and flushed slightly. 'You say the loveliest things.'

'Only when they're true.'

He took her hand and led her onto the sparkly dance floor. He pulled her close and allowed her hair to brush against his face. She smelt of the most exquisite perfume, a musky scent with floral undertones. It was heavenly.

'There was a reason I asked you here this evening,' he said.

She drew back a little and gazed up at him. 'Oh? Is it serious?'

He bit his lip and pulled her to him again. 'I don't know. I think it rather depends on you.'

Again she drew back. 'On me? Why would it depend on me?'

He shook his head. 'I need to speak with you. In hindsight this was not the best place to invite you for a conversation…an important conversation, but I wanted you to have some fun. I know you've been cooped up in Duke Street while you cared for Knolly. I met Cecily in Great Russell Street when she was out on an errand. She said you seemed a little down. I thought Café Bonbon would cheer you up.'

She tried to smile. 'And so it has, but I must confess, I'm a little worried, Richard.'

He lifted her chin and looked into her eyes. 'There's nothing to worry about. Not for you at least.'

'You're ill?'

'No…not that.'

She looked relieved. 'Thank goodness. My heart nearly stopped.'

'It's not serious, but it is important. Perhaps when dinner is served. It could be a topic for discussion then.'

Camille frowned. 'Does it need discussion?'

He nodded. 'I rather think it does.'

Chapter 4

Camille nodded and swallowed hard. She had known there was something bothering Richard during their stay in Paris but had thought perhaps he was unhappy with his room or the rather rich food hadn't suited him. His mind had seemed miles away, as though his thoughts were not with them. Occasionally she had seen the Richard she was used to, when they had had dinner together, or when they were discussing police matters; he was always professional when it came to matters of crime or an investigation, but his mask had slipped sometimes. Elsie had also noticed it. His nibs, as she affectionately called him, was not at his best.

They returned to their table. The beautiful songstress had changed the tempo, and Camille was certain it did not match Richard's mood. It was upbeat, and the other guests were dancing in lines across the dance floor which she was sure was something of which he didn't want to be part.

They chatted about inconsequential things; Ottilie's schooling, Knolly's recovery, and how much Camille's staff meant to her.

Her divorce came into the conversation. She knew it would not be long before it was finalized. It didn't mean she was a totally free woman. Divorcees were expected to leave a respectful amount of time before they considered restarting their lives with other men. Many didn't at all, mostly because it had been the husband who had wanted the divorce, usually because, as in Lord Harry Divine's case, they had taken up with another woman and wanted nothing more than to be rid of their previous wife. Camille realised it was all so terribly unfair for the wife, who had simply done what was expected of her, which was make life as comfortable and as easy as was possible for her husband. Boredom had often set in, and the husband had either visited brothels and kept everything secret, or, like Harry, had fallen for an actress and invited her into his bed.

Camille had mixed feelings about her divorce from her husband. Although part of her looked forward to being free of the restraints Harry insisted on placing on her, she had already begun to feel rather untethered, almost like a boat that had slipped its anchor. Sometimes she found herself slipping into melancholy, particularly if she had not had other things to occupy her.

Although she had never intended to become embroiled in private investigations and had not looked for them, it was rather as though they had looked for her, and she'd acknowledged they had helped her by allowing her to forget about the past. Her parents had advised her to look towards the future and not to look back.

'Nothing good can come from ruminating on what might have been, darling,' Camille's mother had said to her on one of her rare visits to Duke Street. 'Harry has behaved appallingly, of course, one would not disagree, and I am surprised he still pushes for divorce even though the lady of his affections is no longer with us. However, it will free you to be who and what you wish without a man telling you how to live. You are no longer a child. You are a grown woman with a child of your own. You make your own decisions about how you wish your life, and hers, to be.' Camille had nodded, knowing her Mama was a woman of the world and could easily fend for herself if she was forced to. 'But don't break the rules,' cautioned her mother. 'At least, do not break them in plain sight. The rules are there, set by men to subjugate women, but there are always ways around them. You must find them and make them work to suit the life you want.'

Camille nodded again, feeling more like a child than ever. Her mother had risen from her chair in the sitting room and crossed to the window, staring out onto the rather grey street with its austere buildings and the traffic noise from Oxford Street, an alien environ for such a gracious lady.

'If you want a man, have him.' She'd turned to face Camille, a plume of smoke curling from her lips as she drew on her cigarette holder. 'But don't flaunt him, darling. Be proud, yes, and discerning of course. One must be judicious about whom one gives ones heart to, particularly as a divorcee. The eyes of society will be upon you, even more so than Harry. He has already pinned his colours to the mast, and of course you've noticed that nothing befell his social status. He is as he was and his peers consider him as he was. He has lost nothing. You have yet to show your colours; your choices, and your change of direction. Your contemporaries will be watching and waiting for you to make a mistake…a misstep, an indiscretion. And trust me when I say, it will be reported. Harry will know about it before you have even said goodnight and closed your front door.'

She sat again, crossing her elegant legs, then removed the cigarette from the black holder, and stubbed the cigarette out in the crystal ashtray.

'You and Harry have come to an agreement which is more amenable to you than you could have ever wished for. You'll have money and property…and access to your daughter. I advise you to wait until the ink is dry on your divorce papers, then wait even longer before you go out into society as a woman with a new man on her arm. A new future to scandalize the gossips.

'Accompany a male friend to dine when asked, yes, why not? Even agree to be escorted to a ball, it is only what society expects. But do not flaunt him. Do not kiss him in public, not even in a fashion which one would consider chaste. Harry will rip up those papers and present you with a new set which will tie you to him forever. Your reputation will be in tatters and your life will never be your own.'

Camille had listened to her Mama with growing apprehension. She'd suddenly realised she had a long way to go before she could consider herself free from her marriage to Harry, that her independent life would not be as simple to come by as she had first imagined. Oh, she knew she must be careful, but her Mama's words were a caution to her.

Being part of the aristocracy in England was almost as dangerous as the Tudor court. There were rules…one must play the game or lose. Camille had determined she would play the game to win.

Chapter 5

Dinner was served at eight o'clock. Richard and Camille had enjoyed several aperitifs and both were pleasantly mellow.

'I know it's not a ladylike thing to say,' chuckled Camille, 'but I'm starving. I've barely eaten a thing all day.'

Richard nodded and Camille frowned. 'Still so off-colour, Richard? You will eat with me won't you? I couldn't possibly enjoy the meal if you're not eating.'

He smiled and reached for her hand. 'I think for me to enjoy what looks to be a sumptuous dinner I must broach the subject I wanted to speak with you about. Once it's been discussed, regardless of the outcome, I think it will allow me to relax.'

Camille leant forward. 'Please, Richard, tell me what's on your mind. Let's get this thing, whatever it is, out in the open. My Papa always says problems should have a good airing. Leaving them to fester only causes trouble and makes the original problem seem far worse than it was originally.'

Richard nodded. Before he could speak the starter of Moules Mariniere was served. The retrieving of the mussels from the shells caused some mirth which swept away any awkwardness.

'Delicious,' murmured Camille. 'I do love this.'

'As do I. As you say...delicious.'

She glanced at him. 'So tell me. What is it that has upset you these past weeks?'

'My father.'

Camille widened her eyes. 'I was under the impression your father had passed.'

'He has.'

She looked at Richard quizzically. 'So how can he be causing you so much upset?'

'Because of his past.'

'His past? His past is bothering you now?'

'Yes.'

'Why?'

'Because of you.'

Camille dabbed the corners of her mouth with her napkin and sat back in her chair. She took a breath, wondering what she was about to hear, knowing this was something she could not anticipate. She hoped Richard would be honest with her.

'I'm listening,' she said quietly.

Richard wiped his mouth with his napkin and rested his forearms on the table. 'My father is...was Luca Vicenzu.'

Camille gazed at him, then shook her head. 'I'm sorry, Richard, it isn't a name I recognise.'

'No, I thought not. Do you recognise the name Ludo Vincent?'

Camille gasped and covered her mouth with a hand. 'The gangster?' She frowned and shook her head, trying to remember. 'He...murdered someone...a robbery I think. Was it jewellery? It was in all the newspapers, about five years ago.' Richard nodded. 'He's, he was your father?'

'I'm afraid so.'

'But…you're a police officer. A high-ranking police officer.' She chuckled but it was without mirth. 'How did it happen?'

'Can I tell you the full story?'

Camille placed a hand over one of his. 'Of course you can. You can tell me anything, you know that.'

Richard felt himself relax, but was still concerned at how she would feel when she discovered all the terrible things his father had done in his crime-riven life.

'He came to England from Sicily in 1881. He met my mother almost immediately.'

'She's English then?'

'Oh, yes.' He nodded. 'They settled in Whitechapel, in Hanbury Street, which was where he met most of his gang. There were many Sicilians living in London at that time. They weren't all criminal families of course. Most were law-abiding, but like meets with like. My father had always lived his life on the wrong side of the law, as had his father before him. He was raised amongst it, so simply continued the same life when he reached London. And he made a lot of money. My father died an extremely rich man, but of course none of his wealth was come by honestly. Most of it was from the selling of stolen goods, mostly high-end accoutrements, jewellery and such like. And protection rackets of course.'

'Do you have brothers or sisters?'

'One sister. Katerina. She lives in London.'

Camille raised her eyebrows. 'Is she…? Does she…?'

'You want to know if she's a criminal like our father?' Camille nodded. 'I'm happy to say Katerina lives quietly with her husband in Bayswater. Her husband is wealthy and thankfully an honest man. I don't see them often, but we are in contact occasionally.'

'And the money your father left? He must have left it to you and Katerina?'

'He did.'

She stared at him. 'So...where is it?'

'Where he left it. In his bank account. It's money he obtained by his criminal dealings. I can't touch it. I'm a police officer and I must live with the values I've always had. If I claim it, it makes me no better than he was, and I'm not sure my bosses would look kindly on my becoming rich because I'd inherited his fortune. I would have to leave the force. Katerina isn't interested either. She doesn't need it.'

Camille pressed her lips together and shook her head, astonished at what Richard had just told her. Her mind was in turmoil. Now she knew why he had been so out of sorts. He had been concerned about the effect his news would have on her.

'I'm shocked, Richard.' His heart fell to his boots and he was sure she must have heard it as it dropped. 'You must be an incredibly strong man to have fought your way out of your criminal family. Was there not pressure put upon you to join your father?'

He nodded. 'Every day. When my father made real money he bought a house; splendid, opulent, very expensive...in Holland Park. It cost an absolute fortune. I was about twelve I think. I remember wondering how we could have left our tiny, terraced house in Hanbury Street and moved to a house, which, to me as a boy, seemed like a palace. There were huge chandeliers in every room. The one in the hall was so long it nearly touched my head as I walked by. The kitchen alone was almost as big as our house in Hanbury Street,' Camille nodded, 'so you can imagine the effect it had on me...and Katerina.

'My mother wanted to send me to boarding school, primarily to get me away from my father's influence, but he wouldn't hear of it. He wanted me there so he could train me to follow in his footsteps.'

'But he didn't achieve it. Why? What made you decide to follow a different life?'

'My mother was desperately unhappy. She hadn't known when she met my father that he was part of a criminal gang. We used to talk, often, and she would tell me his criminal dealings may have bought her jewellery and furs, and a home she could only dream of, but she didn't approve of what he did. Her family had all but disowned her.

'My father would say, who cares?' Who cares if the little people didn't like how he made his money? They weren't important. He was the one with a brand new motor vehicle, when *they* were still using horse and carts. His wife was the one who wore diamonds every day of her life. I learnt to drive as soon as I could, and had my own vehicle, one of the first vehicles to be driven, apart from my father's vehicle of course, in 1910. He had acquired his even earlier. He was determined to have everything.'

'And then?'

He closed his eyes and leant back in his chair, the memories crowding out the songstress's crooning. Even the spotlight which highlighted part of their table seemed to dim. This was the part he had always kept hidden, even from himself. It had been difficult for him to face up to the fact that in his genes were the genes of a hardened criminal, not just a man who stole, a petty thief or pickpocket, but a gangster, an instigator of unthinkable criminal dealings. A man who was prepared to murder to get what he wanted. If someone got in his way, no matter who he was, he would simply remove them. He opened his eyes to find Camille gazing at him.

'I discovered I hated him.'

'But you loved him before?'

'No. No, not love. How could one love a man who killed for a living. I realised long ago that what I saw when I looked at him was a monster.'

'An assassin?'

To Camille's utter shock Richard nodded. 'If someone was prepared to pay him enough...yes. He didn't amass all his wealth by stealing and selling fripperies. He was an art dealer too, stole paintings to order, which made him wealthy. But there are people in this world who are willing to pay anything if they desire to be rid of someone in their way.'

'But for you to become a police officer,' she said with wonder in her voice. 'It's...it's like the opposite of what he wanted for you. The very opposite. He on one side of the line, you on the other.' She reached for his hand again. 'It couldn't have been easy to go against him. You must have been frightened of what he might do.'

Richard chuckled in spite of himself. 'He threw me out.'

'Because you wanted to uphold the law? Because you are a good person?'

'Because he knew he could not continue with his business dealings with me living under the same roof. He really didn't care what happened to me.' Richard's expression became lined and he bit his lip. 'He didn't care about anyone. Only money.'

'You could have informed on him.'

'I *would* have informed on him. I couldn't bear what he did. It made me sick to my stomach every day.'

'What did he say when you told him you had joined the police?'

'He accused me of being a traitor. He was incandescent with rage. It caused unholy rows. My poor mother...' He swallowed at the memory of his mother wringing her hands as she begged them to stop arguing, to stop shouting at each other. 'She suffered terribly. She loved us both. She still loved my father even though she didn't agree with what he did. Things were different then as you know. People didn't divorce, and he would never have allowed her to divorce him or leave him. She was there for the duration. She had no say in anything. It broke my heart.'

'His money...your inheritance...could it not go to charity? It could do some good?'

Richard frowned then shrugged. 'A conundrum don't you think? If the charities knew where the money had come from, how it had been obtained. Do you think they would want it?'

'Would they need to know? How would they find out?'

'Apollinaire knew. He knew about my past.'

Camille's mouth dropped open. 'How on earth...?'

'You see, Camille. There are no secrets. One might keep information hidden for a time, but it will always find a way out. There is always someone willing to spill their guts. I'm sorry to be so candid. There is no secret that can remain a secret, which is why I knew I must inform you of my past. If I hadn't told you someone else would have. I didn't want it to be Lord Divine. Do you think he doesn't know about my father? I'm sure he would have made it his business to know. I also knew if he thought you and I were becoming too close he would have told you himself, with embellishment no doubt. You would have been within your rights to have wondered why I hadn't told you myself. I would have lost your trust, and with it your friendship.

'You speak so eloquently of reputation, of the damage the loss of reputation within your society can do to your prospects, of Ottilie's prospects for when she's older.' He stopped speaking as their second course was served, venison with a red wine sauce which would have usually tempted him. He wanted to push his plate away, to tell the waiter to take it back to the kitchen. He felt full. Full of remorse, and grief over what he was sure he was about to lose.

He looked at Camille. She was staring at her plate, although he believed she wasn't seeing it. She was somewhere in her thoughts. He knew what he had told her could very well change everything between them. I should say it now, he thought. I couldn't possibly make things any worse.

'You know how I feel about you,' he said quietly.

Camille was startled out of her reverie. She looked up at him as if realising where she was and who she was with. She smiled at him, a beautiful, warm smile that reached her eyes, eyes bathed in sadness.

Richard held his breath. This is it, he thought. This is where she says goodbye.

Chapter 6

It sounded like firecrackers. Both Richard and Camille stared across the room to where the sound had come from, Camille leaning up on her chair.

'What was that?' she asked, turning towards him.

'I'm not sure.' He frowned then got up from his seat. 'It sounded like gunfire...but surely not...not here? Could be firecrackers, a private party perhaps.'

As he finished speaking screaming could be heard, muffled at first, but then louder, with more desperation.

When she heard it, the exotic songstress tried to ignore the high-pitched wailing emanating from the far end of the club. She raised her voice, took it to another pitch to drown out the screaming, then began to look around her, uncertain what to do. She trailed off as the band stopped playing, the ragged notes from the piano, trumpet and saxophone almost skidding to a halt.

Camille rose from her chair. 'Richard?'

'Wait here,' he said. 'It could be nothing.' He rose from his chair and made his way across the nightclub, weaving in and out of the tables as he went. Camille watched him intently. He stopped as he got to the desk just inside the door, showed his identity card to the vendeuse, Yvette, Camille thought, then left the nightclub to go into the foyer.

Camille gathered up her bag and followed, pushing her way through some of the guests who had left their seats and were craning their necks to find out what was happening. They were as curious as Camille. Some guests were hardly ruffled by all the commotion, determined to finish their meal before the inevitable happened and they were asked to leave.

She stepped up to the desk which was now without Yvette who had followed Richard into the foyer, and went through the double wrought-iron doors. The girl who had been swinging in the crescent moon stood by the entrance. She looked so much younger than she had when she and Richard had arrived. Her eyes were large and full of tears. She shivered, clutching what clothing she was wearing close to her. Camille called over to the hat-check girl.

'Could someone please get this young woman a blanket or a coat. I think she's in shock...oh and a cup of tea laced with whisky please.'

The hat-check girl ran out from behind her desk with a tartan blanket and gathered her colleague up in her arms.

'I'm Sadie, Madam,' she said as she wrapped the blanket tightly around the girl. 'This is Millie, our moon girl.'

'Do you know what happened?' Camille asked her. 'We heard screaming.'

'That was Millie,' said Sadie. 'She found 'er.'

Camille frowned and stepped closer to the two girls. 'Found who?'

'Emma,' Sadie whispered. 'She found Emma, the cigarette girl.'

'Found her where?'

Sadie pointed up toward the crescent moon still hanging high above their heads. 'Dead, Madam. Up there. Millie found her...dead.'

'Dead? In the moon? But how...why?'

Camille frantically looked around for Richard and was relieved to see him as he stepped out of an office situated next to the cloakroom. She breathed a sigh of relief.

'Richard!'

'Camille.'

She went towards him and reached for his arm. 'What on earth has happened? Sadie, the hat-check girl said her colleague, Millie, found the cigarette girl in the moon. Dead.'

Richard nodded. 'Yes, I'm afraid she's dead. I've taken a cursory look...seems she was strangled with the strap of her cigarette tray.'

'And the shots we heard?'

'They were not shots. Someone fired off some firecrackers.' He frowned. 'Seems odd to me that the release of the firecrackers should coincide with the discovery of the girl.'

Camille gasped, her eyes filling with tears. 'That lovely girl. What a waste. Where is she?'

Richard looked up to the moon. 'She's still up there. It's how she was discovered. It seems that Millie climbed down from the moon to address a call of nature. She made her way to the bathroom,' he turned and pointed to a corridor to the left of the foyer, 'just down there. It was quiet, she said. The majority of the expected guests had already arrived and they don't usually allow people in unless they've booked and they'd had a number of cancellations. As far as she was concerned all the guests had arrived. Apparently, the hat-check girl joined her in her call of nature.' He shook his head and raised his eyebrows. 'Heaven knows why you ladies must go to the bathroom together. I've never understood it.'

Camille made a sardonic, but sad, smile. 'It's a thing, Richard.'

He sighed. 'It may well be a thing, but what it also means is when the girl was hauled up to the moon and strangled, or strangled before being left in the moon, there was no one to witness it.'

Camille was astonished. She looked through the wrought iron doors to the nightclub beyond.

'But anyone can see through those doors, surely. And what about the manager? Where was he? Isn't he usually in his office...counting the takings I would have thought?' She raised an eyebrow. 'And a pretty penny if their prices are anything to go by.'

'He was in the nightclub, speaking with some important guests. The first he knew about it was probably the same time as us, when Millie screamed on finding the body in the moon. And he isn't just the manager. He owns the place, an Ivor Clemence. '

Camille stepped back and stared up at the crescent moon which didn't look quite so spectacular now all the lights were on and the tiny sparkling lights which had given it life were now extinguished. Camille considered it all looked rather garish, like a fairground in broad daylight, a different prospect altogether from the excitement one experiences in the dark of night when all is glitter and sparkle. 'How convenient,' she said under her breath.

Richard continued. 'There's a kind of long seat within the crescent which allows Millie to lie back and dangle her limbs over the edge, which was what we witnessed when we entered the foyer this evening. You must admit it's very effective. It really looked as if the moon were supporting her.'

'I do admit it, but why wasn't Emma seen before Millie climbed up to her nest? Surely her arms and legs would have been dangling over the side.'

'Because although stouter and more stockily built, Emma seems to be...was...shorter than Millie. Her body was lying flat on the long seat, almost a rather luxurious palliasse, her head crooked to one side. The strap of the cigarette tray had been removed and used to strangle her.'

'Where's the tray?'

'Up there with her.'

'You've seen the body then?' Camille's eyes clouded over. 'Are you sure she's gone?' she whispered.

'Yes...and yes, quite sure. There were no signs of life. And to answer your other question, they have a long stepladder which Sadie drags across to the moon so that Millie can climb out. It's there.' He pointed across the foyer to where a long stepladder which had seen better days was situated next to the moon.

Camille nodded. 'It's probably why they go to the bathroom together. They've synchronised it so when they return Sadie can drag the ladder back to wherever it's stored.' She turned to Richard, her eyes narrowing. 'Where is it stored?'

'I have no idea. We'll ask Mr Clemence.'

Camille hesitated. 'What about Emma, Richard?' she said softly. 'She can't be left there. Won't her family need to be informed? And what about the guests? Will they not need to be detained?'

'I called Scotland Yard and informed them of what's happened here this evening. They will inform the hospital and get a doctor and an ambulance here. The retrieval of her body will need to be done smoothly and efficiently. I want there to be no missteps. The guests have been informed there has been an incident and their presence is required until they have all been questioned. The same goes for the staff.' He stared at Camille with desolate eyes. 'I'm sorry, Camille. This wasn't what I was anticipating at all. I'll call a car for you and have you taken home.'

She chuckled. 'I have a feeling your reason for inviting me this evening has been thwarted, Richard, but it changes nothing. A girl has been savagely murdered almost under our noses. The audacity of it is quite startling. Do you not know me at all?'

Richard drew in a breath. 'But this is a young girl, Camille. It's very....unpleasant...upsetting. Will you want to be made so closely aware of what human beings do to each other, regardless of age or sex?'

'I know what they do to each other. What I need to do is find out why?'

He managed a grin. 'So, you'll stay?'

'There was never any question. There's a reason why this young woman was murdered. It was meditated upon and carefully planned. It's not something one could do on a whim. No, someone had carefully thought out this taking of a life prior to carrying it out. And it's quite likely they're still here.'

Chapter 7

At length the police arrived, followed by a doctor and an ambulance to take Emma's body to the morgue. The doctor climbed up the stepladder, one that Camille surmised was a piece of equipment which would have been used in a theatre in a previous life, and carried out an examination to confirm death. When he was satisfied he climbed down to the foyer looking morose and shaking his head. Richard introduced himself, showing the doctor his identity card, asking him what he had found. Camille stood by the wall, but made sure she was in earshot of what was being said.

'Her neck is broken,' the doctor said. 'The person who did this was extremely strong. Not only did he, or she, attempt a strangulation, but broke her neck in the process.' Camille covered her mouth with her hand, a surge of grief rushing through her. She had met Emma only briefly, but she had seemed such a bright and cheerful young woman who was simply trying to earn a living. The doctor continued, frowning. 'I've seen similar situations in the past. It's almost as though the victim was hung from a height.'

Richard nodded. 'You think it's possible?'

The doctor shrugged. 'That's for you to discover Chief Inspector Owen. My guess is there are two possibilities; she was either manhandled up the ladder and into the structure above and killed in situ,' he pulled a face, 'which I'm sure you'll agree would have taken some doing, bearing in mind the ladder is tall and almost reaches the ceiling. I would imagine there would need to be some inducement to encourage the girl to go up the ladder, a gun, or a knife...a threat of some kind. Or, she was killed beforehand, strung up which broke her neck, or at least was left incapacitated, then strangled before she was put in said structure.'

Richard nodded thoughtfully. 'And your thoughts?'

The doctor eyed him with a dry look. 'Are you asking me what I would have done, Chief Inspector?' He shook his head and laughed. 'You'd be surprised how many policemen ask the same question.'

'And what *would* you have done?'

The doctor took a step back and opened his arms as if to say, look at me. 'Bearing in mind I am of a small physique, and what my ex-wife would call a man of a weasel-like build, the first. I would have used a threat, a weapon perhaps, to encourage her to climb into the moon. The second possibility would be out of my league, I would not have the strength.' He lowered his arms and stepped forward. 'Of course it doesn't mean the person who did this did not use the second method. If he was strong, and he would need to be quite strong to do it,' he nodded and turned his mouth into an upside down crescent, 'yes, it could be done I would imagine.'

Richard and the doctor shook hands and the doctor left.

'There are two things that you and the good doctor haven't thought of,' said Camille, joining Richard as he watched the police trying to find a way to retrieve Emma's body from the structure. They'd worked out that only one man could be on the step ladder at a time as it wasn't the steadiest of structures, and they would only add to the weight on the stepladder when they had retrieved the body. It was a conundrum. 'Perhaps you should tell your men to stop.'

He turned to her looking quizzical. 'Tell them to stop?'

'Why yes.'

'Why?'

'How did the structure get up there in the first place?'

His eyes widened and he shook his head. 'I don't know, but I'm sure we can find out. Men!,' he cried. 'Wait, please. I think there is an easier way to retrieve her.' The policemen stopped what they were doing and Richard and Camille went into the office where Ivor Clemence sat behind his desk, his elbows on the table and his head in his hands.

'Mr Clemence,' cried Richard. Ivor Clemence looked up; his eyes troubled. 'Mr Clemence, how was the moon structure put into place in the foyer originally when the club was opened?'

Ivor Clemence rose from his seat and scratched his head. 'I think it was with some sort of pulley which was hidden out of sight. I'm guessing it would have been concealed in the ceiling.'

'I'm sorry, Mr Clemence, but we'll have to find it. We need to retrieve the young woman's body and there is no easy way to do it. Using the stepladder is not feasible. We need to be able to lower the structure so we can retrieve her. Do you have a man of works? A caretaker of some sort.'

'Yes, but he's never in attendance when guests are here. I'll have to call him out.'

'Then do so. He is needed here.'

'I'll need to get a message to him. He doesn't have a telephone. I'll send one of the waiters.'

'How far away is he?'

'Just a couple of streets away. It'll take ten minutes.'

Richard nodded. 'Right away, please. It's urgent.'

Ivor Clemence left the office and went into the nightclub where the waiters were offering free tea and coffee to the guests who had been asked to stay. The bar had been closed. No one was allowed to leave until they had been questioned. Richard had called for two more inspectors to join him so they could get through the questioning quickly, although Richard would have been happier if he could have administered the questions himself. Some of the guests had become difficult, particularly those who had imbibed a good deal of alcohol, and the police officers had left the foyer and entered the nightclub to ensure the recalcitrant guests were kept on their best behaviour.

Clemence joined Richard and Camille in the foyer.

'I've sent one of the waiters,' he said, seemingly out of puff. 'I need a drink. Will you join me, Chief Inspector?'

'I would have half an hour ago, but it seems I'm back on duty.' He gestured to Camille. 'Lady Divine may wish for a brandy.'

Camille shook her head. 'No, thank you. What I would like to know is where the stepladder is stored when not in use.'

'I can show you, Lady Divine,' he said, pushing past them rather rudely, going back out into the foyer. Camille raised her eyebrows thinking that Ivor Clemence had seemingly already partaken of too much alcohol than was good for him, and perhaps, bearing in mind there was to be a police investigation, should abstain from drinking any more. His breath reeked of whisky and his person of tobacco and perspiration. He was sweating as though he had exerted himself, wiping the perspiration from his brow with a grubby handkerchief. Camille winced. Clemence looked behind to make sure Camille and Richard were following. He stumbled his way towards a curtain which he pulled aside with a flourish.

'Here, Lady Divine. This is where we keep the stepladder.'

'And had the stepladder been returned to behind this curtain when Millie and Sadie went to the lady's room?'

He shrugged. 'I'm afraid I can't tell you,' he said. 'I don't know. They are instructed to always return it to behind the curtain in case any of our guest who may have enjoyed themselves just a little too much take it into their heads to climb up to the moon, but you know how it is?'

Camille shook her head. 'I'm afraid not. How is it?'

'Well, sometimes they forget...or can't be bothered. It means that when Sadie drags the stepladder over to the moon for Millie to climb down, they must put it back behind this curtain so they can go to the ladies room.'

'They always go together?'

Clemence dipped his head once. 'I gave them permission, as long as the show was under way and no more guests were expected, they could go together.'

'But you didn't give them permission to leave the stepladder where it was until they came back?'

'No, of course not. Apart from it being dangerous to our guests, it looks unsightly. No, they were to return it to behind the curtain.'

'Bit of a faff I expect,' said Camille. 'Dragging the stepladder over to the moon so Millie could climb down, then drag it back behind the curtain, only then to have to drag it back to the moon so Millie could climb back up.'

'It is, Madam, but they knew the rule on it. If they left it unattended they did so without my permission, I assure you, and may I suggest the only way for you to get a definitive answer is to ask them.'

'You didn't see anything from your office? No one coming in or going out? No sounds that were unusual?'

He pursed his lips in thought. 'Nothing like that no.' He shook his head. 'Please remember the sound of the band travels the length and breadth of the club. We have speakers in each corner of the room. I wouldn't have heard anything.'

'And saw nothing?'

'I saw nothing out of the ordinary. The first I knew there was anything amiss was when Millie climbed up the ladder to the moon and began to scream.'

'Are the doors locked when you believe the last guest has arrived?' asked Richard who had taken a keen interest in Camille's line of questioning.

'They are Chief Inspector.'

Richard narrowed his eyes. 'Which would prevent someone coming in, but not necessarily anyone leaving the club. You were in your office. You said you heard nothing other than the band and saw no one go into the foyer.'

Clemence raised his hand, still holding the sodden handkerchief, and tilted his head. 'I didn't say that, Chief Inspector.'

Richard lifted his eyebrows in surprise. 'You said you saw no one.'

'I saw no one because the office door was closed. It doesn't mean no one entered the foyer. Any of the guests could have left without my seeing them, particularly as the girls weren't on duty for those few minutes. We don't use the main lock on the door during a performance...we're not allowed to; fire safety and all that kind of thing. We use a simple locking device a child could operate, but it means no one can get in without paying, or who are unwelcome.'

'How many minutes is a few minutes, Mr Clemence?' asked Camille.

Shrugging, he answered, 'Again, Madam, you should ask Millie and Sadie.'

'Have Millie and Sadie worked here long?' asked Richard.

'The club has only been open a few months, so none of the staff have worked here long. I know they room together.' He shook his head. 'I can check for you to get the exact date, but off the top of my head I'd say about two months.'

Richard nodded and turned away, then turned back when he thought of something. 'Who joined the club first, Sadie or Millie?'

'Sadie was here first, maybe a week longer than Millie. She recommended Millie to me saying she thought she would be ideal for the Moon Girl because she was so slight, yet reasonably tall with long limbs. And good-looking of course. It helps if the staff are good-looking. Millie was in fact perfect for the job so I was happy to employ her.'

Camille looked at Ivor Clemence thinking that his own looks and dishevelled appearance did nothing to recommend him, and hiring someone on looks alone would always be a dangerous risk if one did not know the character of the person they were employing.

Just as Camille and Richard finished speaking with Ivor Clemence the doorbell rang. One of the policemen admitted a waiter and an older man whose arms were covered in tattoos and who entered the club behind him.

'That's our maintenance man, Gregory Northcutt,' said Clemence. 'He'll know how to lower the moon. He tests it at least once a month to make sure everything is in order.'

Richard turned to Camille and widened his eyes and gasped under his breath. Gregory Northcutt was known to Richard, but he could in no way be described a friend.

Chapter 8

Camille heard Richard gasp and she reached for his upper arm. He looked anxious and the muscles in his arms had tensed.

'Who is it, Richard?' She tried to make light of it. 'One of your regular villains who has put in an appearance.'

'You could say that, Camille. Unfortunately, I know the man very well, too well. I only wish I didn't.'

'Yes?'

Camille glanced at Richard then averted her eyes to the rather grizzly-looking man who had dragged the stepladder to the edge of the foyer. His face was swarthy with pockmarks; she thought perhaps a victim of the smallpox, which had riddled his skin with pits and cracks. His hair was cut close to his head, almost shaved. She wondered if he had recently been in prison, his almost shorn head a result.

He wore a thick belt on his hips on which were suspended various tools; a hammer, a pair of pliers, a screwdriver...and a Swiss army knife.

'You look nervous, Richard. Who is it?'

'A man from my past. Oh, I know him, but not as Gregory Northcutt. He must have been given a different name in prison to protect him. His real name is Miceli Tiseu. He was one of my father's right-hand men; a criminal of course, a thief, a ringer, embezzler, defrauder...and yes, a murderer.' Richard's brow was creased and he looked almost astonished that this man should be in his presence once again. Richard turned his head to her shoulder and lowered his voice when speaking to Camille. The last thing he wanted was to have Gregory Northcutt recognise him during an investigation.

'Why isn't he in prison?' she whispered.

'He has been, you can tell by his appearance. If his hair is anything to go by he has only recently been released. He had very long hair; curly, thick and to his shoulders with a centre parting. Obviously, he's much older now, his hair is grey, but those tattoos...they are unmistakable. Look at them. They're very distinctive, not the sort of thing one would forget. I was an impressionable young man don't forget. He certainly made an impression on me. My father may have been the head of the gang, the one who gave the orders, but this man, this Gregory Northcutt as he calls himself, he was the most dangerous.'

'Do you think he still is?'

Richard shrugged. 'Prison time is expected to rehabilitate as well as to punish.'

'You think he has been rehabilitated?'

'Who knows. He clearly has a job. It's quite unbelievable he is responsible for some of the security here. I wonder if Ivor Clemence is aware of his past?'

Camille raised her eyes to the top of the stepladder and watched as Northcutt took the screwdriver from his belt and removed the screws from a panel in the corner of the ceiling. She couldn't help noticing his arms were almost laced in a pattern of scars crisscrossing his skin, which were in stark relief to the rest of the skin on his forearms.

The most outstanding image, however, was the tattoo of three legs in a circle with a picture of a woman's face in the centre. It was a strange image and Camille wasn't sure what it could mean.

'The tattoo on his left forearm,' she said to Richard sotto voce, 'the one with the three legs. What does it mean?'

'It's the triskelion. It is one of the oldest and most distinctive symbols of Sicily. It's been used as a symbol of Sicilian identity and independence.'

'And the woman in the centre?' Richard looked away and closed his eyes. Camille was distraught. 'I've offended you. I'm so sorry, Richard. If this is something you'd rather not speak about then of course we must not.'

He turned and looked at her, his eyes troubled. He appeared to be apprehensive, even jittery about someone from his past coming back so unpredictably into his life. He could never have imagined the scenario. How random life could be.

'The face in the middle of the triskelion could be anyone. The image is often reproduced with myriad faces, but I know exactly whose face is in the centre of Gregory Northcutt's tattoo.'

Camille bit her lip, wondering if she should push any further. She had come this far. She had to ask him.

'Who is it, Richard? Whose is the face in the centre of Gregory Northcutt's tattoo?'

Richard sighed and rubbed his chin. 'It is my mother's face, Camille. My mother and Miceli Tiseu had an ongoing affair for many years.'

Camille's mouth dropped open. 'Your father knew?'

'Oh, yes, he knew, but he turned a blind eye. Miceli and my father were like brothers, and like brothers they shared.'

Camille gasped. 'No, Richard. And you knew about it? When you were young?'

'It was an accepted thing. My father relied on Miceli. If he had defected to one of the other gangs operating in London he knew he would have been at a disadvantage. Miceli is a skilful operator, a man who knows crime and who isn't frightened to use whatever he must to ensure he gets what he wants.'

'Could your father have been wary of him, frightened perhaps? Would that not be the only reason to allow someone to covet their wife?'

Richard laughed, but it was without mirth. He glanced at Camille. 'My father was frightened of no one.'

Camille turned her attention to Miceli Tiseu. He had opened one of the panels and released a thick rope ensconced inside. He undid the knot which secured it, then to her surprise, jumped down from the stepladder, rather nimbly for a man of his obvious age, and began to slowly lower the moon to the floor of the foyer.

They waited with bated breath while the moon slowly descended.

'Oh, Richard!' Camille clutched his arm as nausea welled in her chest. She went hot and she breathed deeply to steady her nerves. 'This is awful.'

'Don't look, Camille. Please, look away. There is no need for any more distress.'

'But I must,' she cried. 'I want to help find who did this. Her body...it will provide us with clues will it not?'

'I'm not sure this is an investigation I can allow you to become involved with, Camille. The death of a young woman...this is not in your sphere surely.'

'The murder of a woman, young or otherwise, is very much in my sphere. It happens too often in this city. No, no, I must be involved.' Camille felt her stomach roll the closer to the foyer floor the moon was lowered. When it reached eye height, Camille could see the young woman inside.

She was lying flat along the soft mattress at the bottom of the structure. Across her body lay the shallow cigarette tray, the cigarette pockets surprisingly undisturbed, all in their rows of different colours, like soldiers in uniform, Camille thought.

Her head, however, was bent at an angle, as though she were considering something before answering a question, which of course, she never would again. Her hair was a bedraggled mess covering half her face. Her eyes stared unseeing at the space in front of her.

'We'll need positive identification,' said Richard. 'Although I'm pretty sure there's no doubt. She's wearing the cigarette girl's uniform and has the tray with her.' Camille nodded and swallowed hard, closing her eyes momentarily at the sight of the poor girl in front of her.

Richard requested the presence of Ivor Clemence, Millie and Sadie, and asked them to ensure that the person lying in the moon was the correct person for legal reasons. Millie and Sadie were reluctant, both in floods of tears. They held back, begging not to be included in the identification. Ivor Clemence agreed to identify the body first.

He stepped forward, keeping a respectable distance from the body lying in the moon.

'Er, er, I think it's her. She worked part-time see. We've got two or three girls what do the cigs of an evenin'. And her hair...it's across her face...I can't see her face properly.'

Richard stood next to him. 'Are you saying you cannot positively identify this young woman as the girl known as Emma, Mr Clemence?'

'Well, it's her hair, y'see. It's across her face. I can't see her face properly.'

Richard nodded to one of the constables, who with a gloved hand, moved the girl's hair away from her face. Richard looked at Ivor Clemence waiting for an answer.

'I'm still not sure,' he said, rubbing his chin. 'Like I said we 'ave a few girls doing the cigarettes.'

Richard inhaled a breath of frustration. 'So what you're saying, Mr Clemence, is that you cannot positively identify this young woman. Can you please confirm that.'

Clemence was still rubbing his chin, eyeing the body with curiosity. 'I'm sorry, Chief Inspector. I'm afraid I cannot say for definite. I know Emma, course I do, but, well, girls these days...all look the same don't they, what with cosmetics an' all.'

Richard nodded, wondering at the man and how he could run a business such as the Café Bonbon without knowing who his staff were.

'Do you hire the staff, Mr Clemence?'

Clemence shook his head. 'My wife, she hires all the staff. She has a better understanding of what's needed in a place like this. Her father was Ron Bruce?' He looked at Richard as though Richard should understand who he meant.

'I don't know the name, Mr Clemence.'

'Ron Bruce owned all the nightclubs in New York and a couple in London until the war. Obviously, the war finished all that. There weren't no one to go to the clubs, and he couldn't get the staff anyway, so he closed them all. He *was* a very rich man.'

Richard nodded. 'We'll speak at length about it at a later time, Mr Clemence. For now I must get this poor girl identified.'

He beckoned Millie and Sadie across to him. They reluctantly joined him, clinging on to each other and trying their best not to look inside the moon at the recumbent body. Camille stepped forward and put a comforting arm around Millie's shoulders, the younger of the two girls.

'I would like each of you to step forward and identify the body. If you know her as the cigarette girl, just give a nod. Do you understand?' Both girls nodded, their eyes wide with fear.

'I'll go first,' said Sadie. 'I'm the eldest.' She stepped forward and peered at the girl in the moon. Richard and Camille waited for her confirmation. Sadie stood in front of the moon, squinting at the body, then stepped back.

'Are you all right, my dear,' Camille asked her.

'It's not her,' said Sadie, her Irish accent accentuated by her nervousness.

Richard frowned. 'Not who?'

'It's not Emma.' She turned to Millie. 'Millie, just go and look. You'll see. It's not Emma.'

Millie swallowed then stepped toward the moon, then stepped back. Camille took her hand. 'Is it your friend, Millie?'

Millie shook her head. 'No it's not. It ain't Emma.'

Chapter 9

Richard indicated for the structure to be left where it was in the foyer so the men from forensics could examine it. He was aware it might need to be removed and taken to Scotland Yard, but it would not happen before the next day.

Two men had arrived from Scotland Yard, each with an identical case of instruments. Richard expected them to be painstaking and thorough in their examination. He wanted answers to three questions. Who was the girl in the moon? Why was she murdered? And where was Emma, the cigarette girl?

The victim's body had been removed and taken to the mortuary in an ambulance. Millie, Sadie, and Mr. Clemence were seated in his office, quiet, no one saying a word, yet each wondering who the girl was who had lost her life. The waiting staff and kitchen staff were seated in the nightclub near the bar, flocking together for safety; wary, sad, and questioning.

The guests were seated at their individual tables waiting to be questioned by the police. The music had stopped and all the lights had been switched on, making the club look dingy and nothing like it had been when the guests had arrived; a place for pleasure and fun. The sparkle and shine was no longer present. The Café Bonbon had lost its glittering allure.

Richard went into the nightclub followed by Camille. She sat at the desk with Yvette who was in floods of tears.

'I want to go home,' she wailed to Camille.

'I'm sorry, Yvette. No one's going home until everyone has been questioned. Have the police spoken to you yet?' The girl shook her head. 'I'm afraid you'll have to wait until they have. You're staff, Yvette. It's likely the police will want to question the guests first so they can be released to go home.'

'But there's so many of them?' she sniffed. 'It could take hours.'

'Yes, it will, but someone has lost their life this evening, and we need to find out why.'

'Wasn't Emma, was it?'

Camille shook her head. 'No, it wasn't. You may be asked to identify the body. If no one knows who she was, all the staff will be expected to in the hope someone can identify her.'

Yvette wiped her eyes, then blew her nose loudly into her handkerchief.

'Who would do such a thing. I was so excited about coming to work here. We all were. The Café Bonbon was to have become famous all over the world. We have celebrities visit here, bringing their entourages with them. Mary Pickford opened the club. She was invited to cut the ribbon and was given free life membership.'

Camille smiled, remembering the photographs in the newspapers. 'Did you meet her?'

'Hardly. She weren't interested in the likes of me. She smelt nice though. I got near enough to smell her perfume. Expensive. *She* was expensive.' Yvette looked at Camille with red eyes. 'Why do they give things for free to them what can easily afford it?'

Camille sighed. 'Good question.'

Richard joined Camille at the desk and indicated for Yvette to make her way to a table where a detective waited to question her. He sat next to Camille in the seat Yvette had vacated.

'What a mess.'

'You didn't recognise her then? The girl? When you looked in the moon?'

He shook his head and tutted. 'I made a supposition, Camille...a dangerous thing to do in my job. One should never suppose anything. I saw the uniform and the tray of cigarettes and assumed it was the same girl who had served us. She had the same hair colour, a similar build to Emma, and she was pinioned to the bottom of the moon with her tray of cigarettes. She had also been strangled with the cigarette tray strap. I made an assumption.'

'An easy mistake to make, particularly as her hair was covering most of her face.' He nodded but made no answer. 'I wonder who she is.'

'Unless any of the staff identify her we'll have to use the newspapers. One of our artists will draw her likeness and we'll ask the newspapers to run the story and include the impression.'

'And Emma. Where on earth could she be?'

'Mm, very strange. It's almost as though the dead girl was chosen for her similarities to Emma, because I think you'll admit, from a distance there were similarities.'

'Certainly. From where I was standing I would probably have sworn it was the same girl.' Camille looked thoughtful. 'You don't think Sadie and Millie made a mistake?'

Richard pulled a face. 'I can't see why they would. They all roomed together.'

'So Emma roomed with Sadie and Millie?' Richard nodded. 'They'll need to be questioned closely then. They will probably know more about her than anyone.'

'Well, her employer certainly seems to know nothing about her. For him not to recognise her or be able to identify a member of his own staff. Pretty awful, wouldn't you say?'

'Yes, I agree. And what of his wife? Should she not be here as she is the main hirer...the actual boss and owner if my own supposition is correct.'

'Yes, I thought it too. She's on her way. Mr Clemence telephoned her at their home. Wasn't happy about being disturbed apparently.'

'Oh, dear.' Camille couldn't help but chuckle. 'I think you may have a feisty woman on your hands, Richard.'

He raised his eyebrows. 'In that I should be an expert.'

She glanced at him. 'I sincerely hope you don't mean me.'

'Of course not, Lady Divine. You are the epitome of calm acceptance and politesse.'

He turned his head to gaze at her. 'And you can be quite feisty, which is just one of the things I love about you.'

'Love, eh,' grinned Camille. 'What a word.'

'Yes, it's quite a word isn't it.' He looked up at the sound of voices in the foyer. 'Ah, I think the voices coming from the foyer might be the arrival of our Mrs Clemence. Now we shall see if she is also the epitome of calm acceptance and politesse. Something is telling me to doubt it.'

There was a tumble of voices in the foyer, a raised female one, murmurs from the police officers, some of which were still in attendance, and that of Mr Clemence who seemed to be trying to placate his wife.

'My dear, we had to rouse you. Something has happened of the utmost importance.'

'Yes, I know, Ivor. A girl has gotten herself killed on our premises. You said. But look how many of you there are here already. Why the hell do you need me.'

Camille widened her eyes at Richard. 'An American no less.'

Richard and Camille joined the throng in the foyer. Richard introduced himself to Mrs Clemence, showing his identity card for what seemed like the umpteenth time, and then introduced Camille. Mrs Clemence eyed Camille warily.

'Why would a Lady of the Realm be concerning herself in our little club?'

'I was a guest here, Mrs Clemence, when the girl's body was found. Chief Inspector Owen and I are friends, so naturally I wanted to be of help, particularly to the three girls who were so overwrought at the finding of the girl in the moon. I seemed to be the only choice at the time.'

'And where are those girls?'

'We're here, Madam,' said Sadie. She had left the office, and was followed by Millie, and Yvette who had been questioned by one of the investigating team and was getting ready to go home.

'Where's Emma?' Mrs Clemence asked them. The girls shook their heads, not knowing how to answer her. Mrs Clemence's tone was less than approachable. 'Oh, come now,' she said, offloading a rather fine fur coat on to a chair in the office, even though it was late summer. Camille couldn't help noticing the label, recognising it from one of the finest couturiers in London. Her suit was also of the finest cloth, a Chanel, Camille thought.

Mrs Clemence rummaged around in a gargantuan bag and produced a packet of cigarettes and a box of matches.

'You girls are as thick as thieves. You work together and you socialise together, then when it gets important you say you don't know where she is.'

'That's because we don't,' said Sadie, who seemed to be getting riled by the rather harsh questioning from her boss. 'She was 'ere, selling cigs, then she wasn't. Millie and I went to the ladies. When we got back and Millie climbed back up into the moon she saw someone else lying in it. She thought it was Emma.'

'It looked like Emma,' Millie said in a timid voice. 'I was so frightened I didn't 'ave a proper look cause 'er 'ead was all crooked, but 'er hair was the same colour,' she shook her head, 'and she just looked like 'er.'

Camille stepped forward and asked a question she'd been wanting to ask all evening.

'When you went to the bathroom did you slide the ladder back to behind the curtain. Mr Clemence told us you're meant to, even though you have to drag it out again so Millie can climb back into the moon.'

Sadie looked at Millie and Millie returned her look. 'We're meant to,' said Millie quietly, 'but sometimes we forget.'

'And did you forget this evening?'

'I can't remember. Did we leave it in the foyer, Sadie?' she asked, looking at her friend.

Sadie shook her head. 'I dunno. Can't remember.'

'Did you have to drag it out from behind the curtain to get back up to the moon, Millie?' Camille pressed on.

Millie put her finger in her mouth in deep thought, then gasped. 'Yeah, yeah, we did, 'cause I caught me toe on it, look.' She proffered her left foot and her big toe which had recently bled. The toenail had been misplaced and it looked extremely sore.

'So, you must have dragged it back to behind the curtain before you left to go to the bathroom, and then pulled it out again, so you could climb up to get back into the moon.'

Millie nodded and glanced at Sadie. 'S'pose so.'

Camille nodded and murmured her understanding. Richard squeezed her arm.

'What does that prove?'

'That whoever did this knew where the stepladder was hidden. If the girls replaced it behind the heavy curtain no one who wasn't familiar with it would have known where it was kept. It would have taken time for them to discover how to get to the moon to leave the body there, and they certainly wouldn't have removed the panel in the ceiling to get to the rope. It would have taken far too long. Also, they would have need tools to do it. No, we're looking for someone who is familiar with the workings of the club. It's likely whoever did this thought Millie had left for the evening and the body wouldn't have been discovered until next evening when the club opened again, by which time the perpetrator would have been long gone.'

'Which means they aren't.'

'Exactly.'

Richard squeezed her arm and gazed at her with admiration.

'You're a genius.'

'I know.'

Chapter 10

The following morning Camille slept late. The initial investigation at the Café Bonbon hadn't finished until early that morning and Camille was exhausted. Cecily brought in a tray for her, on which there was a late breakfast of orange juice, boiled eggs, and French toast.

'Madam,' said Cecily softly. 'Madam, it's eleven o'clock. Knolly says you've to have something to eat.'

Camille leant up on her elbow and sighed. 'I'm not used to late nights anymore, Cecily.' She shook her head. 'Must be my age.'

Cecily chuckled. 'Your age, Madam? You're not yet thirty.'

'Nearly thirty. Next birthday. And I'm feeling it.' She flopped back down onto the many pillows she had on her bed. 'What an evening.'

'Ooh, Madam, did it go well. I must admit when I saw you weren't in at midnight I thought it all must have gone very well. I feel quite excited.'

'Please don't.'

Cecily blinked. 'What, Madam?'

'Don't get excited. There was a murder...at the Café Bonbon. The cigarette girl that wasn't.'

Cecily frowned. 'I'm sorry, Madam...I'm confused. How can the cigarette girl be someone she wasn't?'

Camille patted the bed after Cecily had put the breakfast tray in front of her. 'Sit...and I'll tell you what happened.'

As she ate, Camille regaled Cecily with the happenings at the Café Bonbon the previous evening. Cecily sat transfixed at what Camille told her.

'So, who was she, Madam?' Cecily asked, her eyes wide.

'That we don't know. We asked everyone who was in the nightclub last night. No one knew her.'

'They looked at the body?'

'Oh no, a quick sketch was done with coloured pencils to give an outline of what she looked like. To a man…and a woman, they all said they thought it was Emma, the real cigarette girl, but of course, it wasn't. The murdered girl just looked very much like her, her doppelganger if you will.'

"Er what?'

'Doppelganger. It means a striking likeness, a twin almost.'

'Was it 'er twin?'

Camille's hand was stayed as she was about to take a bite of toast. 'You know…I never thought of it. I suppose she could have been. I never thought to ask. If it was they were certainly not identical, more of a remarkable similarity.'

Cecily nodded. 'So what will happen now?'

'The statements taken last evening from the staff and guests will be examined. They might throw some light on things.'

'Are you going to help Chief Inspector Owen? With the investigation I mean?'

Camille nodded. 'I feel duty bound to help. We investigate circumstances, you and I, and this is certainly a circumstance that has piqued my interest.' She wiped her mouth with her napkin and looked deep in thought. 'It was unsettling to see a young woman in such a condition. Someone had gone to a lot of trouble to hide her body, quite ingenious in fact, but they clearly thought Millie, the moon girl had left, and would not be climbing up to the moon again until the next evening when the Café Bonbon opened, when in fact, she and her friend, Sadie, had simply gone to the ladies room.'

'They must 'ave bin gone a while.'

Camille nodded, then pulled a face before swinging her legs out of the other side of the bed and putting on her robe. 'Yes. It would have taken a while to move the stepladder over to the moon to carry the body up to it. Quite a feat really. The person must have been extremely strong, and familiar with the comings and goings of the club.'

'Someone who worked there, then?'

'I'm guessing it would have been, unless it was a regular customer who had made a study of how things work there. Criminals do all kinds of things to smooth the way to their endeavours,' she glanced at Cecily, 'as you and I well know.' Camille went across to the bathroom, then stopped before going inside. 'Unless they knew someone who worked there who had told them how things worked, who was on duty when, and that kind of thing.'

Camille went into the bathroom and Cecily pulled Camille's bed together, then opened a window a little wider to allow the summer air and the perfume from the flowers in the small garden at Duke Street to waft into the bedroom. Phillips had done an exceptionally good job that summer, planting all of Lady Divine's favourites.

'We'll talk later, Cecily,' Camille called from the bathroom. 'Perhaps you could think about what I've told you and come up with some thoughts, or questions we could put to Chief Inspector Owen.'

Cecily nodded then realised Camille couldn't see her. 'Of course, Madam. I'll put me thinkin' cap on. It takes a while for things to start occurrin' don't it?'

'It does. I'll be going to the club later today. You can join me if you will, get the feel of the place. Hopefully it will give you some food for thought.'

Cecily grinned. She had been hoping she would be included in their latest investigation, although this one seemed to have more loose ends than a piece of frayed fabric.

'Right you are, Madam.'

Later on Camille joined Cecily and Knolly in the kitchen. It was past lunch, and Knolly was sitting at the table writing dinner menus for the following week. She looked up when Camille appeared in the doorway.

'Sounds like you 'ad an eventful evenin', Madam. Last night.'

'Yes, I did rather. Did Cecily tell you everything?'

'Indeed she did. What a carry on. And that poor girl what was murdered. Terrible things 'appen don't they?'

'I'm afraid they do.'

Camille sat at the table in the middle of the kitchen and poured herself a cup of tea from the big teapot that had belonged to Knolly's grandmother; white china with blue flowers painted on the outside. It was rather chipped and had seen better days, but Knolly said it was a lovely link to her family, and would cherish it until the day she died.

'We live in a world where criminals seem to think they can do what they like...and expect to get away with it.' She took a sip from her cup. The tea was hot and very comforting. 'If the murderer's plan had worked it was quite ingenious, but they had not bargained for the moon girl's return.'

'Moon girl? Whatever's that?' asked Knolly, scratching her head under her bonnet.

'She lays in a crescent moon, languidly,' she grinned at Knolly, 'sort of lazily, trailing her hands in the air and sipping from a cocktail glass. It made quite the spectacle I can assure you, particularly as Chief Inspector Owen and I had not visited the Café Bonbon before.' She put her cup down on the saucer with a chink. 'Although the club looked very different when all the lights were on. Rather dingy it has to be said.'

'And what did Chief Inspector Owen make of it all?'

'As perplexed as the rest of us. The owner of the club couldn't identify the girl because he couldn't remember what Emma, the real match girl looked like.'

Knolly shook her head. 'Oh, ain't that terrible, not even knowing yer own staff. Don't care about 'em much do 'e?'

Camille shook her head sadly. 'No, clearly not. They're just fodder to people like that. Money. It becomes the most important thing of all. People come a poor and distant second.'

Cecily poured herself a cup of tea after spending time folding the household linen, and sat at the table with Camille.

'So what was it all about, Madam?'

Camille frowned at Cecily. 'What do you mean, Cecily?'

'Chief Inspector Owen. It was like he needed to see you I thought you said. Like he wanted to talk to you about somethin'.'

Camille nodded. In all the commotion and the interruption to their evening together, she had forgotten what Richard had told her before the murdered girl had been found.

'It was nothing, Cecily. Nothing to worry about anyway.' She rose from the chair in the kitchen and made her way into the sitting room, leaving Cecily and Knolly staring at each other in bewilderment.

'What were that about?' whispered Knolly to an equally surprised Cecily.

'I dunno. I was sure Madam told me Chief Inspector Owen needed to speak with 'er about somethin'.'

"Ope they're still friends.'

'Oh, don't say that, Knolly. They got so close.'

'Love's a funny thing. It don't always go smoothly.'

Cecily shrugged and pulled a face. 'I wouldn't know.'

Chapter 11

Camille went to her sitting room, taking her tea with her, deep in thought. Cecily had reminded her of her conversation with Richard at Café Bonbon before they had been interrupted by what had proved to be a difficult and upsetting evening.

She rubbed her forehead, trying to think back on what he had said. What exactly was he alluding to?

He had told her about his father, a gangster by all accounts, which she had to confess had shaken her rather. Richard was certainly not a 'chip of the old block' as her Papa would have phrased it, she thought.

Richard was the epitome of...well, rightness...if there was such a word, which she doubted with a chuckle. How difficult must it have been for him to grow up in the life in which he had, knowing his father made his living by organising theft on a grand scale, and murdering to get what he wanted. What did he say his name was? Oh, yes, the gangster, Luca Vicenzu. Camille knew him from stories in the newspapers as Ludo Vincent, a man to be feared and avoided in equal measure. What a way to live. And what an admission to have to make, that one's father was a notorious gangster.

And what of Richard as a young boy, impressionable, trying to learn about the world around him, then realising his family was not like that of his friends. He went to a private school. Camille wondered which one. Whichever one it was it would have likely cost the earth; his peers probably born into families of repute, lords and ladies, aristocrats, and peers of the realm, particularly if it was in London. Did they shun him when they discovered what sort of family he came from? Was he bullied, ostracised? Surely the parents of the other children must have known about his father. It would seem he was notorious, no, famous, albeit for all the wrong reasons. Camille shook her head and leant back in her chair. Her tea had gone cold so she placed the cup on a side table. How much did Richard and his mother suffer under his father's hands?

She closed her eyes. Her early morning return to Duke Street had left her exhausted and she was reminded of what her Mama would say to her when Camille stayed out too late.

'The hours of sleep before midnight contributed far more to one's rest and beauty than the hours slept after'. Camille didn't know how true this anecdote was, but she had noticed her mirror had not been very kind to her that morning. Her eyes had been half-closed with tiredness, and the fine lines around her eyes had been slightly more noticeable. She had rubbed a gentle finger across them, then applied some face cream her Mama swore by, hoping it would stave off the damage caused by her tardy timekeeping.

'Madam! Madam. The doctor's on the telephone.'

Cecily shook Camille gently by the shoulder, waking her from a nap she hadn't intended. Camille rubbed her eyes and gazed at Emma with not a little surprise.

'I fell asleep?'

'Yes, Madam.'

'How long?'

'Just an hour or a little more.'

'And who is on the telephone did you say, Cecily?'

'The doctor, Madam. He's got Knolly's results from her tests, he says. He wouldn't give 'em to me. Said he needed to talk with you.'

Camille struggled out of her chair. 'Oh, good Lord. Quickly.' She allowed Cecily to pull her out of the chair. 'I'm apprehensive, Cecily.'

'So am I, Madam.'

'Does Knolly know he has telephoned?' Cecily shook her head. 'Right, well, at least we'll know won't we?'

Cecily looked worried, as though she was about to burst into tears. 'Yes, Madam. We will.'

Camille went into the hall and picked up the receiver from the candle telephone.

'Yes, doctor. This is Lady Divine. I understand you wish to speak with me.'

'Yes, Lady Divine. I have Mrs Laetitia Knowle's test results. Should I speak with her or would you prefer to relay them to her yourself?'

'I'm more than happy to do so, doctor, and I think Mrs Knowles would be happier if whatever the outcome is, came from me.'

'As you wish, Lady Divine. It is not serious you'll be relieved to hear.' Camille immediately felt a calmness settle over her and she inhaled a long breath, thanking the good Lord for the news. She closed her eyes momentarily and released an indiscernible breath. 'A slight arrythmia, a hiccup if you will. She is in the change of life of course. All women of her age will experience certain symptoms, a sudden rise in temperature, a flush to one's cheeks, and other female idiosyncrasies which are more personal to each patient. I would like to make a suggestion which I'm certain will help Mrs Knowles.'

'Yes, doctor?'

'A reduction in weight will help the good lady. She is a cook I understand?'

'Yes, she works for my household.'

'Mm, a difficult request perhaps, but one I would press. She informed me she is often out of breath which I think is due to the carrying of too much weight. Does she do much walking, such a simple exercise?' Camille hesitated, then decided the truth was always best. 'Almost never. She spends all her time here I'm afraid.'

'Ah, well, daily walking...a mile or more would certainly help the good lady's health, and a reduction in the consumption of pastries, sweetmeats and such like. It will be all to the good, I assure you.'

'Thank you, doctor. Of course I'm naturally relieved it's nothing serious. We'll of course take into account the symptoms she's experiencing, and I'll certainly pass on your good advice.'

'Please do, Madam.'

'And your bill?'

'Expect it in the post by the middle of the week.'

'Well I never,' said Knolly as she pummelled a ball of bread dough into submission. 'Overweight? Am I? I'm the same build as me mother. We were always a big family 'cos we was all employed in one kitchen or another. 'Ow am I goin' ter know if things taste all right?'

'The doctor wasn't suggesting you starve yourself, Knolly. We love you as you are, but it seems you are in a difficult phase of your life, and a *slight* reduction in weight would be of great help to your overall health.'

'So 'e says I've to eat less?'

'And walk.'

'Walk! Walk where? Where 'ave I got ter walk to? I don't know no-one. There ain't nowhere for me ter go. And I'm not sure I want ter go anywhere. I like it 'ere.'

Camille sighed and glanced at Cecily who was biting her lip. 'Yes, yes, I know, but it's about exercise, Knolly. You don't actually have to walk anywhere in particular, just get out into the fresh air and...walk. Somewhere.' Camille winced.

'Oh, well,' said Knolly, as she threw the bread dough into a bowl and covered it with a cloth. 'I s'pose if 'e says I'm ter walk, then I s'pose I better 'ad.'

'I'll come wiv yer, Knolly,' said Phillips who had been sitting at the table with a mug of coffee and saying nothing, as was usual in the kitchen hierarchy.

'Will yer?'

'Don't want ter go on yer own do yer?'

'No I don't. I don't like bein' by meself wiv no one ter talk to.' She frowned. 'Don't seem right, in fact it seems downright dangerous to me. What about all them murderers out there? They might think I'm good fer a few bob if they see me wanderin' down the street on me own.'

Camille smiled at them both, a surge of affection going through her. 'Thank you, Phillips. I'm glad someone will be with Knolly to protect her from the murderers lurking about our streets to pounce on Knolly.' Cecily giggled, then put her hand over her mouth.

'What about the other thing?' asked Knolly.

Camille raised her eyebrows, then remembered what the doctor had said. 'It's natural to experience a rise in temperature, and a flushed complexion...and there may be other changes you may notice.'

'What changes?'

'Er, er, well, changes of a personal nature.'

'Right you are,' said Knolly. 'I think I've 'ad those.'

Camille pressed her lips together to stop herself from laughing. Knolly was one of those people who could be amusing without knowing, or without intending it, and she was sure Knolly didn't find what was happening to her at all amusing. 'So, Knolly. I don't want you to work too hard. You look after us extremely well, but really, I think you could do with some help in the kitchen to take some of the work off your shoulders, which is why I'm sending Cecily on a course of cooking lessons.' Camille turned to look at Cecily to gauge her reaction.

Cecily looked shocked. 'Me, Madam?'

'You *are* Cecily, aren't you?'

'Yeah, but, I can just about butter toast.'

'Which is why you're going.'

'Couldn't you just get an under-cook in, someone who knows what they're about, Madam?'

'I really think it's best for you to go, Cecily. It will be another string to your bow. You learnt to drive recently, and now you'll learn to cook.' She looked up at Knolly who was watching them with interest. 'What are your thoughts, Knolly?'

'I'd rather it were you, Cecily, my love. Don't want some Gordon blue person in 'ere giving 'emselves airs and graces. We ain't that sort of family.'

'Oh, well,' said Cecily, resigned to her fate. 'S'pose I'd better go then, but I ain't promisin' anythin'.'

Camille chuckled. 'Cecily, you learnt to drive a motor car. I'm quite sure you can learn to mix up a cake batter, or make an omelette. And think what a help it will be for Knolly.'

'What about me other duties?'

'I'm thinking of hiring a cleaner, someone to do the menial tasks so that you and Knolly don't have to do them. This is quite a big house even if it doesn't appear so from the street outside. I think we could do with a person of all works, a sort of float who picks up the pieces.'

'Man or woman?' asked Knolly, frowning.'

'Oh,' said Camille. 'I hadn't thought.'

'Phillips might like a man, what do yer say, Phillips?'

Phillips shrugged. 'I dunno. Whatever Madam thinks is best.'

'I'll give it some thought,' answered Camille.

The telephone rang and Cecily scurried off to answer it.

'It's Chief Inspector Owen, Madam. He says can he speak with you? It's urgent.' Camille nodded and left the kitchen to go into the hall, but not before she heard Cecily ask Knolly, 'Who's Gordon blue?'

Chapter 12

'Chief Inspector Owen?' Camille picked up the telephone receiver and sat on the chair in the hall.

'Hello, Lady Divine. I'm going to the Café Bonbon again this afternoon. Mrs Clemence is going to be there and I want to have a word with her about the staff and perhaps have a look at the records. Someone must know who the murdered girl was. I thought you might like to come with me. And Cecily?'

'Cecily? You think she could help?'

'She usually does. She seems to have a nose for investigations. As do you.'

'How will you explain our presence?'

'Affiliated female members of staff. We don't have a plethora of female constables and sometimes they're called for, particularly when those being questioned are female.'

'I can't imagine Mrs Clemence would care. She seems to have plenty of chutzpah.'

'I can't argue with that.'

'Will she let you do that do you think? Look at the staff records, I mean?'

'It depends I suppose, on whether they have something to hide.'

'I see.'

'Will you come?'

'Of course.'

'I'll pick you up in half an hour.'

Camille and Cecily were seated in the sitting room waiting for Richard when the doorbell rang. Cecily had been like a cat on hot bricks, excited by the prospect of going into one of London's most famous clubs, but also feeling rather frightened by it all. This was a world completely alien to her and she wondered what she would see there. Knolly had of course put her straight.

'Now don't you take any notice of what any of the men there say to yer. They're likely only after one thing.'

'What thing?' asked Cecily, frowning, and wondering what on earth Knolly was talking about.

'The thing what they can only get from women. Most of 'em anyway. Some of 'em like to get it in other ways, but we won't go into that. They won't care about you. They just care for their own pleasure.'

'Knolly!,' Cecily cried. 'I ain't goin' there for anythin' like that. And Lady Divine will be there. She wants me to go an 'elp 'er.'

Knolly was whipping up a sponge cake batter with a whisk, her arm seeming to get faster the more entrenched she became in her opinions on nightclubs.

'Dens of iniquity, that's what they are. I've read about it in the papers. Nothin' good goes on in them places. The very worst of 'umans go to places like that for wickedness.'

'But Chief Inspector Owen took Lady Divine there.'

'Exactly!' Knolly cried. 'Exactly. It's what I'm talkin' about. They ain't the right places for a lady like Madam. She's got too much about 'er. And look what's 'appened. Some poor girl left in the moon with 'er neck stretched. You just be careful, my girl. Stay close to Lady Divine and don't go wanderin' off on yer own. Watching Valentino on them big screens is one thing. Runnin' into 'im when he wants 'is wicked way would be quite another. Brr...' she shivered. 'Don't bear thinking about. Fair puts the willies up me, it do.'

After the conversation she'd had with Knolly, at least, after listening to all that Knolly thought about her trip to the Café Bonbon with Camille, Cecily couldn't make up her mind if agreeing to go with Camille and Richard had been the best decision she had ever made.

'Dunno what to do now,' she'd said to herself as she'd gone up to her room for her duster coat and hat. Camille had advised her to wear her off-duty things. 'I've said I'll go and 'elp 'em. Can't back out now, can I?'

'Are you all right, Cecily?' asked Camille. 'You look a little...worried, somewhat pale. Are you ill?'

'No, Madam, I'm not ill.'

'But...'

Cecily swallowed before she spoke. 'Knolly said Café Bonbon is a place of...hini...quity. That people go there for wickedness, and that if Valentino shows up, I'm to run a mile.'

Camille began to laugh. 'Iniquity? Valentino?' She shook her head and brushed the laughter tears from her eyes. 'Cecily...was there any iniquity or wickedness in Selfridges when there was a murder there last Christmas? Or...in Brighton where families go for their holidays to enjoy the sun and sand?' Cecily stared at Camille, feeling silly. 'Night clubs are where people go to let their hair down a little. When Chief Inspector Owen took me to the Café Bonbon we danced and ate a wonderful meal...' she inclined her head a little, 'at least we would have should a poor murdered girl not have been found in the moon.' She patted Cecily's hand. 'I grant you, they do have a reputation, some deserved,' she said gently, 'but I can assure you Valentino will not be present, nor anyone like him.' The doorbell rang and Cecily got up to answer it.

'That will be Chief Inspector Owen.' said Camille. 'I think it will do you good to see what these places are really like. I think you'll be surprised.'

Chapter 13

The Café Bonbon looked dark and very ordinary from the outside. The huge lightbulbs that made the façade look so glamorous in the night hours were unlit, and the black double doors leading into the foyer were no longer guarded by security men. There were no queues with excited, chattering patrons dressed in the latest fashions waiting to get in; no plumes of smoke disappearing into the ether from the many cigarettes and cigars being smoked. Camille glanced at Cecily and saw the disappointment written across her face as they left Richard's car.

Richard had brought a young police officer with him who had said nothing the entire journey, but who had gone rather pink when his eyes had settled on Cecily.

'You were expecting something else, Cecily? A different sort of place?' Camille asked her

'I s'pose I was, Madam. P'raps somewhere a bit more glamorous...a bit more posh.'

'It looks very different at night. These places all look the same in the cruel daylight. It seems to highlight the flaws; something we women are also encouraged to attend to as we age. The Café Bonbon suffers from the same affliction. I must confess it doesn't look nearly so attractive as it did last night.' Cecily nodded and pulled a face showing her displeasure.

'Shall we go in?' asked Richard. 'I think we'll have to ring the bell.' Constable Lewis reached up and pressed a large white bell at the side of the door.

'Di'nt 'ere anythin',' said Cecily. She peered at the bell. 'Maybe it don't work.'

Richard inclined his head to the police officer. 'Give it another push, will you, Constable Lewis.' Constable Lewis stepped forward and put his thumb against the bell push.

They waited. Cecily went to the door and put her ear against it. She was suddenly startled by the sound of a key being turned in the lock and took a step back. Ivor Clemence opened one of the doors and was standing in the doorway. He nodded to them.

'Ladies. Chief Inspector Owen. Officer. I apologise for keeping you waiting. Please come in.'

They stepped through the double doors into the foyer. Camille couldn't stop herself from looking up at the ceiling, her eyes squinting into the darkness. The crescent moon had been hauled back up as though nothing of any note had happened the previous evening.

'Is Mrs Clemence here?' Richard asked Ivor Clemence.

'She is, Chief Inspector. We'd assumed you would probably want to speak to both of us.'

'Yes, I do, and your staff again. I'm guessing many of them aren't here. Will they arrive later? Are you opening this evening?'

Ivor Clemence looked uncomfortable. 'We're opening as usual. The wife, Louise...Mrs Clemence, says all publicity is good publicity, even if on the surface it would seem to be bad. Of course we're very sorry about what happened here last night, and we know you will want to find out who did the dreadful deed, but we've got a living to make. If the club closes we'll lose customers, and to be frank Chief Inspector, we can't afford it.' Richard nodded and glanced at Camille who looked less than impressed.

'Surely a few days of closure would be respectful,' she said.

'Mrs Clemence thinks not. And she's the boss.' It seemed the conversation was closed.

He led them to the office where his wife sat behind the desk. An attractive blonde woman of some bearing barely glanced up as they entered. She had a large glass of whisky by her side, and a cheroot in the ashtray which sent a plume of smoke up to the ceiling. She scarcely looked up to acknowledge them.

'You're back,' she said, her American accent broader than Camille had remembered.

'Yes, Madam,' said Richard. 'We would very much like to speak with you about what happened last night.' Ivor Clemence moved two chairs from the side of the room and placed them in front of the desk, indicating for Camille and Richard to sit. They sat in the chairs proffered, but turned down the offer of a drink. Cecily and Officer Lewis stood behind them.

'Is that your maid?' Mrs Clemence indicated Cecily.'

Camille felt her stomach roll with annoyance. 'She is an associate.'

'To the police?'

'Yes. She would like to observe if you have no objection. She is cognisant of police procedure.'

'Why would I have an objection?' She looked up and observed Camille. 'There's nothing to see here. The girl is unknown to us...we have asked the staff.'

'Surely there's plenty to see, and Chief Inspector Owen will want to question the staff. You had a dead body on your premises last night. Don't you want to know what happened?'

'Of course, but that's your job, the police inspector's anyhow, not mine.'

Louise Clemence picked up her whisky and her cheroot and came around the desk, perching herself on the edge of it in front of them, crossing her legs at the ankles. She wore a grey suit which was edged in black velvet along the collar and cuffs, and a white blouse with a pussycat bow at the neck. The suit jacket was completed with gold buttons down the front and on the cuffs. The skirt was tight to her body and ended mid-calf, the new fashionable look.

'Schiaparelli if I'm not mistaken,' Camille said with admiration.

Louise Clemence laughed, then drew on her cheroot, blowing a plume of smoke to the side. 'You know your designers, Lady Divine. But then you would. Your reputation is well known.'

Camille raised her eyebrows, determined not to be rattled. '*My* reputation? I rather think we're here to discuss yours, at least the reputation of your business.'

'I was taught by the best,' she purred. 'My husband, bless him, has a lot to learn about the nightclub and entertainments business.' Camille glanced at Ivor Clemence who had gone an unattractive shade of puce with embarrassment. 'My father, Ron Bruce, had a string of clubs like this one…merely a starting point for where Ivor and I wish to be in a few years' time. We would like a string of Café Bonbons across London. I would very much like us to emulate him.' She took a breath. 'Unfortunately we haven't had the best of starts.'

Richard crossed one leg over the other looking interested. Up to that point he had let Camille take the lead.

'How so, Mrs Clemence?'

'I had a Café Bonbon in Manhattan, back home. It closed because it was being targeted by protection gangs. There isn't just one, there are many.

We were paying out as much as we were taking for their so-called protection. My plan had been to open another club with the profits from the one in Manhattan, but when I closed it down we were at an all-time low moneywise. Ivor and I took the decision to come over here and open a new club.' She shook her head looking sad. 'I didn't want to leave my home, but I knew whatever I did in Manhattan I was a marked woman. There was no way they would allow a woman like me to succeed in what is a male dominated business. Nightclubs are a prime target for protection rackets. My father knew how to handle them, and of course he was a man. It makes a difference. I think they even had a kind of respect for him.'

It went quiet for a moment. 'How did you and Mr Clemence meet?' Camille asked her. Ivor Clemence answered.

'My first wife was killed in a road accident, knocked down by a car whose driver was going too fast. We'd both been working hard on our business in Hertfordshire where we lived. I wanted to treat her to some time off, somewhere different. We were on holiday in New York, a month-long trip for our tenth wedding anniversary. I was distraught. I'd let go of her hand,' he shook his head and grimaced, 'just for a moment. She hesitated and was hit. It happened right outside Café Bonbon in Manhattan.'

Louise Clemence continued the story.

'The commotion outside the club was something else. We had only just opened the doors so there was still a queue waiting to get inside. They saw everything... the motor vehicle which came around the corner too fast, Ivor's wife being flung into the air and landing on the tarmac. It was...dreadful. And Ivor was inconsolable. We took him into the club so he didn't have to see the ambulance take her away. We took care of him...'

'We?' asked Richard.

'My brother and I. The club was my responsibility. We weren't exactly partners but he had an interest.'

Richard took a notepad from his inside jacket pocket. 'Could I have his name please, Mrs Clemence?'

'Sure, Ronnie Bruce. He was named for my father, Ron Bruce.'

'And where is Mr Bruce now?'

She shrugged. 'New York I guess.'

'When was the last time you spoke to him?'

Louise Clemence sighed. 'About a year ago. He came to England for our wedding, just a small affair, but he's the only family I've got left.'

'You haven't kept in contact with him?'

She raised her hands still holding the whisky and the cheroot. 'I tried. Beats me why he doesn't return my calls or answer my letters.'

'Was there an argument?'

She shook her head. 'Nope. We always got along just great.'

'Older or younger than you?'

'Younger.' She frowned. 'Now wait a minute. He has nothing to do with this. Ronnie wasn't a natural businessman it's true, but we worked well together. He wanted the club to be a success as much as I did.'

'Have you noticed anything else untoward since you opened the club?'

'Like what?'

Richard pursed his lips. 'Staff walking out at a moment's notice, money going missing. That kind of thing.'

Louise glanced at her husband and he shrugged then nodded. 'We had a break in,' she answered. 'About a month ago. We've only been open a couple of months.'

'What did they take?'

'Well, that's the thing. They took nothing of any value. Usually it's the money out of the tills, or the booze or cigarettes that go, but all that was taken was a green jade Buddha I had sitting on my desk. It had no real value whatsoever and wouldn't have meant anything to anyone else.'

'Was it a gift?' asked Camille.

'No.' Louise Clemence shook her head. 'I bought it for myself as a kind of congratulations present that I'd gotten Ivor and I out of what was going on in Manhattan. I got it in Selfridges when we first came over here. We decided to go sight-seeing before we started looking for premises for the club. It wasn't that expensive,' she screwed her face up in thought, 'a few pounds.'

'Is that all,' Camille heard Cecily say under her breath.

'And it held no intrinsic value?' asked Richard.

'No, none.'

'We must ask you about your staff.'

Louise nodded. 'Sure. Go right ahead.'

'You have quite a lot of people working here, chefs, waiters, waitresses, the hat-check girl, Sadie, and Millie, the girl in the moon.'

Louise shrugged. 'Yeah, we do, what of it?' She went round to her chair on the other side of the desk, stubbed out her cheroot and finished off the last of the whisky in her glass.

'You also have a maintenance man, er,' Richard looked at his notes, 'Northcutt.' Louise nodded once. 'Have you known him long?'

'He came to us about six weeks ago. He's an offender, been in jail. We decided to give him a chance.'

Richard nodded and narrowed his eyes. 'You know that's not his real name.'

'I guessed it,' said Louise. 'You know him, don't you?'

'I do.'

'How well?'

'Very well. He's a hardened criminal. I'm just wondering how much he told you.'

Louise glanced at Ivor who was leaning against the wall. 'He spoke to Ivor more than me. 'What did he tell you, Ivor?'

'That he'd spent some time in prison and was determined to go straight. He said he would appreciate it if I gave him a chance.'

'You had no reservations?'

'Yes, we had reservations, but everyone deserves a second chance, Chief Inspector. And he does a good job. Did a maintenance course in prison. Came out with papers.'

'Which jail was he in?'

'Pentonville I think.'

Richard nodded. 'Ever had any suspicions about any of the other staff?'

'No...none that I can think of.'

Ivor Clemence pushed himself away from the wall and perched on the desk in front of Richard and Camille.

'Look, Chief Inspector. I don't think the murder of the girl was anything to do with the staff. They were all busy, it was a busy night. You were here. You saw how it was. None of them would have had the time to drag some woman off into the shadows, murder her, then climb up to the moon and dump her body. Frankly, it's ludicrous.'

'Someone did, Mr Clemence,' said Camille. 'And you didn't even know if the dead girl was on your staff or not when you inspected her body. You said you weren't sure.'

'I said she looked like Emma, which she did. I think anyone would have said the same. I didn't want to identify her as Emma if I wasn't sure. I didn't want to make a mistake. It would have been wrong wouldn't it?'

Richard snapped his notebook shut and made a tight-lipped smile.

'Could we have a tour of the premises, Mr Clemence? And some information where everyone was at the time of finding the girl could be helpful.'

'I can show you around, Chief Inspector, of course,' said Clemence, 'and I know where everyone was supposed to be, but clearly I can't vouch for it.'

Richard nodded. 'Of course. I understand. Shall we?'

He allowed Camille and Cecily to leave the office before him, then turned to Louise Clemence. 'Thank you for your help, Mrs Clemence. Should anything occur to you which might help in this case I would be grateful if you would contact me.' He pushed a calling card across the desk towards her.

'Of course, Chief Inspector. We'll help in whatever way we can, but short of seeing whoever it was did the deed, I'm not sure how much help we can be.'

Richard made a smile which didn't reach his eyes. 'I understand, Mrs Clemence. However, something might come to mind and it could be helpful, no matter how small a detail.' Louise Clemence nodded and put the card in the desk drawer, then went back to the papers on her desk as though she had no intention of using it.

Richard waited with Camille and Cecily in the foyer as they waited for Ivor Clemence.

'What are your thoughts, Richard?' Camille asked him sotto voce.

'On the face of it everything seems above board. They're not saying anything untoward that has made me suspicious.

'So you think they're not involved?'

Richard made a quiet chuckle and raised his eyebrows. He glanced at her. 'Well, I wouldn't say that. Everyone is under suspicion. I'm curious about the staff. My men are sifting through the statements back at Scotland Yard as we speak. Something will come to light. It usually does.'

'And what about the man you know, er, Northcutt? Do you think he's involved?'

'The problem is, Camille, it would be too easy to suspect him. Of course, he is under suspicion as is everyone who was here that night, and the taking of a life would not be of any consequence at all for him, but of course there must be a motive.'

'And there isn't one?'

'He's been in prison for the last ten years. I checked. He's out on licence. If he does anything he shouldn't, he'll be back inside. Having said that, nothing surprises me these days.'

'Nor me.'

'There is more to life than criminality, Camille.'

'Yes, I know, but sometimes I have to remind myself of that.'

Chapter 14

Clemence led them out of the foyer into the nightclub which was devoid of guests and only a few staff who were cleaning tables and rearranging chairs. Behind the bar were two bartenders who were polishing glasses and restocking bottles. No one spoke, the only sound to be heard was the clink of the bottles as they were placed on the mirrored shelves at the back of the bar.

'Big, innit, Madam?' said Cecily, her voice breathy with wonder. 'Never been in a nightclub before. Wonder what it's like at night.'

'Nothing like this,' answered Camille. 'A nightclub in the daytime is a very different place from the one at night when the staff are bustling in between tables and there's wonderful cooking smells coming from the kitchen. The bar will be lit in myriad colours, flashing on and off, like a rainbow interspersed with lightning, and the chandeliers will be lit, the facets from the crystals sending prisms of light into the corners and onto everyone's faces. There will be a band, and dancers, and the singer here is a dream. Yes, Cecily. It's an entirely different place.'

'I'd like to see the kitchens and the storerooms,' Richard said to Clemence who looked at him with surprise.

'Really, Chief Inspector? What on earth do you think you'll find there?'

Richard shrugged. 'I have no idea, but no stone should be left unturned. I need to see everywhere.'

'As you wish,' answered Clemence, but the expression on his face showed precisely what he felt; that neither the kitchen or the storeroom would throw up any evidence with regard to the young girl's death. He shrugged impassively, letting Richard know in no uncertain terms he thought it would be a waste of time.

He led them through the nightclub and into the kitchen. Richard and Camille went first, with Cecily and Officer Lewis behind. When Clemence stopped suddenly in front of the bar to speak to one of the barmen, the young police officer went into the back of Cecily, nearly knocking her over.

'Ooh, miss, I'm sorry,' he said, his face turning bright pink.

Camille turned as she heard Cecily's 'oohff', and gave a smile as the police officer tried to put Cecily to rights.

'I can do it meself,' said Cecily, brushing herself down, and the officers hands away from her. 'I'm all right. No need to get yer knickers in a knot.'

'I thought I'd hurt you.'

'Well, yer didn't.'

'Sorry.'

'Like I said, there's no need to be sorry. Just don't walk so close be'ind me next time.'

Officer Lewis nodded and took a step back. 'All right.'

Clemence introduced Richard to the two barmen behind the bar and Richard began to question them.

'We've already been questioned,' said one. The other nodded.

'I'm aware of that, but I wondered if anything had occurred to you in the meantime. Little things often spring to mind, for example, did anyone look particularly suspicious?'

The first barman laughed. 'They all look suspicious. Most of 'em have got their eyes on the absinthe although we try to limit the sale of it. Mrs Clemence thinks it causes too much trouble.'

'So why sell it?'

The barman shrugged. 'Gets people in I s'pose. We're a nightclub. We 'ave to offer everything to keep up with the others.'

Richard's eyebrows rose. 'Everything?'

'Within reason,' interjected Ivor Clemence. 'We stay within the confines of the law at all times.' Richard nodded and glanced at Camille who narrowed her eyes.

'Would you care to go into the kitchens now, Chief Inspector?' Ivor Clemence asked. 'Not all our staff are here but chef is. He takes sole charge of the kitchens.'

'Certainly,' said Richard. 'It's what we're here for.' Clemence pushed through a pair of swing doors with a small window in each. Richard, Camille, Cecily, and Officer Lewis followed Clemence into the kitchen.

The kitchen was stark white, the walls, floors and cabinets. The ovens and the many utensils hanging from the ceiling were stainless steel and caught the beam from an overhead light making them glint. It was impeccably clean and well-maintained. Camille was impressed. Cecily wasn't.

'Knolly wouldn't like this,' whispered Cecily.

'You don't think so?' asked Camille. 'Why ever not? It's spotless.'

'Too clinical,' shuddered Cecily. 'I know it's clean, Madam, but it looks like it's never used. Knolly always says a kitchen should be the cleanest part of a home. It should also be warm and inviting, and should be the centre of everything. Don't feel like that about this place. Something about it feels...odd.'

Camille sighed. 'I've eaten here...well, I nearly did. The food looked scrumptious. I would imagine the chef is quite masterful.'

'I think we're about to find out,' murmured Richard.

Ivor Clemence went across to a door in the kitchen and knocked. He turned as he waited, and made a small smile at them, which Camille thought was more like a grimace. No one answered. Clemence knocked again and waited. Nothing. He leant toward the door, placing his cheek close to it.

'Monsieur Gaultier. Are you inside?'

The door opened with some speed. In the frame stood a tall, swarthy man wearing a white coat and a chef's toque. The dark stubble on his face showed he hadn't shaved for some time. He smoked a pungent cigarette, and after opening the door he proceeded to pick pieces of tobacco from his lips. Cecily frowned. Camille winced.

'Oui, Monsieur? What is it that you want?'

'The police, Monsieur. They wish to speak with you.'

'I have already been questioned. I don't have time to speak with them.'

'Monsieur,' Clemence said in a low voice. 'They are here. In the kitchen.'

Richard stepped forward and held out his hand. 'Monsieur Gaultiere. I apologise for the intrusion. We won't take up much of your time. There are a few questions I must ask, then you can get back to work.'

Gaultiere drew on his cigarette, then nodded. 'I have menus to plan,' he said. 'This place will only survive because of the quality of its food.' He threw Clemence a look which was none too friendly, and which both Camille and Cecily noted.

'You can come into my office but you'll have to stand. I have no chairs for visitors. I don't encourage people to visit and the staff always stand in my presence. Of course the management always want their guests to come in here to inspect what we're doing as if we are insects in a jar. It would not 'appen in France. In France the chef is king. 'E is not 'ere to be inspected.'

Cecily gasped. 'What an 'orrible man,' she whispered to Camille. 'What's 'e got ter be so nasty about?'

'Heaven knows,' answered Camille. 'And he wasn't respectful to Ivor Clemence bearing in mind he owns the club.' She frowned. 'Very odd.'

Richard and the others stood in front of Gaultiere's desk like school children waiting to be admonished by the head teacher. He kept sniffing and clearing his throat which was very unpleasant, and Camille decided at that moment she would not want to eat at the club again.

'So, Chief Inspector. What is it you want to ask me? I cannot imagine what more you need from me. Your detectives were very thorough.'

'Your staff, Monsieur. How many were here last evening?'

'Er, two.'

Camille frowned. 'Just two? For a club this size?'

'Just two,' Gaultiere replied, sullenly, narrowing his eyes at Camille.

'And who were they?' continued Richard, taking out his notebook and pen.

'Robert Waites and Peter Cornish. They are sous chefs.'

'Did they leave the kitchen at any moment last night?'

Gaultiere began to move pieces of paper around his desk, faltering, as though looking for the answer. 'I, er, I don't know.'

Richard blinked. 'You don't know? Do you not have overall charge of the kitchen?'

'I do.'

'But...?'

'I wasn't here last night, at least, not until the late hours. I 'ad somewhere to be?'

'Which was where?'

Gaultiere glanced up at Richard, his face darkened. 'It is private, Chief Inspector. It has no bearing on what happened here.'

'Even so, Monsieur...I would ask you where you were.'

'And I would not tell you.'

Richard pursed his lips as he nodded. Camille couldn't help but watch him closely. He was every inch the detective. She could see the cogs and wheels in his mind working and knew that if Monsieur Gaultiere thought he would not tell Richard where he was last evening, he was very much mistaken.

'I'd like to know a little about you, Monsieur Gaultiere,' Richard continued. 'When you came to London. What you were doing before you came here? Your background if you will.'

Gaultiere looked less than pleased. 'Is it important?' He frowned. 'I had nothing to do with what happened last night.'

'It will simply give me a detailed picture of everyone, Monsieur Gaultiere. Mr and Mrs Clemence have already provided me with their answers.'

'Must I speak in front of these people?' Gaultiere waved his hand towards Camille and Cecily. 'Why do they need to be present?'

Richard turned to Camille and pulled a face Camille interpreted as a request for her and Cecily to leave. She took Cecily's arm and they left the office, closing the door behind them. They stood in the starkly clean kitchen, waiting for Richard and Officer Lewis.

'Wonder what that's about, Madam? 'E's a strange one ain't 'e?'

'He is rather. Clearly there's something he's perhaps not proud of...an affaire de coeur perhaps.'

'A what?'

'An assignation, an affair. Perhaps he's seeing someone he shouldn't.'

'Like who?'

Camille shook her head. 'A married woman? It's usually a married woman.'

'A married woman like Mrs Clemence?'

Camille gaped at Cecily. 'Surely not. I wasn't thinking of her.'

Cecily shrugged. 'You said she didn't turn up until much later, and it sounds like Monsieur Gaultiere turned up about the same time, although 'ow 'e can run a kitchen when 'e ain't there beats me. Maybe they were together when Mr Clemence telephoned her. Bit of a coincidence, ain't it? Chief Inspector Owen don't believe in coincidences.'

'No, Cecily. He doesn't. And neither do I.' Camille narrowed her eyes. 'Should we go for an explore do you think?'

Cecily grinned and nodded. 'Yes, Madam. I do think.'

Chapter 15

They left the kitchen and went back into the nightclub where the tables had been set for that evening's guests. There were no members of staff present. The club seemed quiet, too quiet, and almost eerie...and there was a pungent smell; dirty ashtrays and stale alcohol.

'You would 'ave thought the chef would 'ave been preparin' stuff for the diners,' said Cecily. 'Ain't that what they 'ave to do, prepare stuff? And what about the other people what work there? Where are they?'

'Dinner is usually served around seven-thirty,' answered Camille. 'Perhaps they'll be in later.'

'And 'ow did 'e get away with 'avin' only two members of staff in last night?' she asked, frowning. 'It don't make sense. You said the food was lovely.'

'It *looked* lovely. We had the starter, which was very nice, Moules Mariniere, but didn't get a chance to eat the main course. We had to leave it on the table which I must admit I was sorry about. I was ravenous. Hadn't eaten all day to make the most of it, which ended up to be the wrong thing to do. There was so much commotion in the foyer I completely forgot about the food.'

'D'yer think 'e's a bit dodgy, Madam? The chef I mean.'

'I'm not sure he's completely above board, although I'm sure Chief Inspector Owen will find out what he needs from him. He's certainly not the type to let him get away with not answering his questions. If Gaultiere doesn't answer them to Richard's satisfaction now I'm sure he will find a way to make him answer them later on.'

'Where should we go first, Madam?'

'Through that door,' said Camille, pointing to a door on the other side of the club. 'I've been wondering about it, and as there's no one around to stop us I think we should have a look, don't you?' She smiled at Cecily.

'I do, Madam. We can always say we got lost if we get caught.' They stepped down from the platform on which the bar was situated and walked towards the door on the other side of the club.

'I'm not sure they would believe us if we said we were lost, Cecily, but I don't really care. We're here to investigate, and investigate we will. I just hope the door isn't locked.'

Cecily put her hand on the door handle and pushed it down. The door opened with a click. Cecily glanced up at Camille and grinned.

'It's unlocked,' she whispered. 'We can go inside.'

'I'll go first, Cecily,' said Camille. 'There might be something down there you shouldn't see.'

Cecily frowned. 'Like what?'

Camille shook her head. 'Er, things.'

She rubbed her gloved hand up and down the wall on each side of the door, looking for a light switch. On the right-hand side she found one.

'Ah, just what I was looking for.' She pressed the switch down and the small landing was flooded with light.

They were standing in a vestibule decorated with photographs of movie stars, black and white images in black frames. In front of them was a flight of steps, concrete and spiral, with a metal handrail that swirled down into the dark.

'I wonder how far down it goes, Madam,' said Cecily as she peered down into the dark. 'Looks like it's a fair way. I can 'ardly see to the bottom.'

'And where does it lead, I wonder,' said Camille. She took a deep breath in. 'Well, Cecily, there's only one way to find out.'

Cecily grinned again. 'And that's to go down there.'

'Exactly.' Camille braced herself, then put her foot on the first step.

"Ope there ain't any spiders down 'ere,' said Cecily as she followed Camille down the flight of steps. 'I 'ate spiders. Can't abide 'em, ugly, 'airy things what look like they'd pounce on yer as good as look at yer.'

'Yes, thank you, Cecily,' Camille said with a sigh. 'Please don't say any more about spiders.'

'Sorry, Madam. D'int realise you d'int like spiders neiver.'

'Cecily, please!'

Cecily bit her lip. 'Sorry, Madam.'

Camille falteringly made her way down the steps until her foot hit a smooth landing at the bottom.

'I think this is the end,' she said with a relieved sigh. 'There must be a light switch down here somewhere otherwise one wouldn't see anything.' She went towards the wall at the bottom of the steps and felt for one. 'Ah, here we are.' She flicked it on and a dim, sickly yellow light surrounded them.

'It looks like the entrance to storerooms, Madam,' said Cecily, peering down a corridor which led away from the landing. She straightened up, frowning. 'Are we going down there?'

'I think we must,' answered Camille. 'There could be something hidden down here that the Clemences would rather we didn't see.'

'Like what, Madam?'

'Contraband, perhaps. Remember Brighton? The inhabitants were hiding all sorts of things in their basements and privies so the customs men and the police wouldn't find them. Cigarettes, cigars, brandy, lace. There's seemingly money to be made when storing such things.'

Cecily peered down the corridor again. 'It's a bit dark, Madam. Wish we 'ad a torch.'

'Yes, I agree. I rather think we need to put together an investigating pack for when we're on one of our investigations...a torch, some string, hairpins for picking locks, hand cream...oh, and a lipstick.'

Cecily looked perplexed. 'A lipstick, Madam?'

'For writing messages on mirrors.'

Cecily nodded. 'Of course, Madam. I understand.'

She followed Camille down the corridor, her hands steadying herself against the walls. Beneath her palms she could feel old paintwork flaking, and the plaster crumbling, making a smattering, gritty sound as it fell to the floor.

The further they got down the corridor the smell of spilt alcohol and cigarette ash became more prevalent. The temperature had dropped by a good many degrees, and Camille could feel the chill of a draft on the back of her neck, coming from she knew not where. There were no windows as far as she could ascertain. She wondered if it was an air vent, but it was so dark she could barely see a hand's length in front of her. Suddenly, the corridor was flooded with light. She drew in a gasp, startled, and turned to see Cecily with her hand on a light pull.

'Sorry, Madam. It hit my face as I went by and I just gave it a yank. At least we can see now.'

'Indeed,' said Camille, taking a deep breath and steadying herself. She looked about her. 'Definitely a storeroom,' she said, pulling a face, ' but not much down here. I had imagined the Clemences would have stored alcohol and cigarettes down here, but there's nothing. Seems a bit odd.' She spotted something in the corner. 'What on earth's that?' she said, sotto voce. 'It looks like a bed of sorts. And isn't that a little stove? Is someone living down here?'

'Yes, Madam,' said a gruff male voice. '*I* live down here.'

They had been joined by an elderly man whose grey hair was down to his shoulders. He had appeared from the other side of the corridor and was wiping oily hands on an old towel. He was dressed in an old brown duster coat which seemed to be serving as overalls. His trousers were too long and puddled on his boots which were scuffed, the shoelaces replaced with lengths of string.

'There was a bit of trouble with one of the valves in the plumbing system,' he said, 'but I've managed to fix it. The other chap does the big jobs, the real emergencies. I just keep things ticking over.' He glanced at them and made a small smile. 'I might ask what two lovely ladies are doing down in these rather insalubrious storerooms.' He looked around at the empty shelves. 'Not that there's anything much being stored down here. Don't think they can afford to keep a stock of anything much.'

'Do you actually live down here?' Camille asked him. 'I should apologise for the intrusion. It looks as though we've stumbled into your bedroom.'

He laughed and sat on the bed. 'Bedroom, dining room, drawing room...and today it would seem it is also my receiving room. I'm sorry I don't have chairs to offer you. People don't usually come down here. You're the first visitors I've ever had, apart from Louise...and sometimes Monsieur Gaultiere.'

Camille glanced at Cecily, wondering if she should ask the man questions. 'So...you do live down here?'

He inclined his head once. 'Certainly.'

'How long have you lived here?'

He scratched his head with a yellow fingernail. 'About three or four years I'd say. It was a clothes shop before it was a nightclub. The owner had been here for nigh on thirty years. When she died her daughters did not want to continue selling apparel so they closed it. Then the Clemences took it over.' He grinned. 'There's certainly more going on these days…and it's a good deal noisier of course.' He shrugged. 'It keeps me connected with the land of the living. Nightclubs aren't the easiest places to run.'

'You know what's happened I assume?' asked Camille.

'The poor young lady who was found in the moon?'

'Yes.'

He shook his head. 'Mm. Well, someone is responsible. She didn't get there by herself.'

'Who do you think it was?'

He narrowed his eyes and stared at her. 'No idea. I don't venture upstairs much. They would really rather I didn't go up there at all, but sometimes it's necessary when they forget to pay me.'

'Do they do that often?'

He chuckled. 'Too often. They forget I'm down here I'm sure because they're never aware of the things that go wrong, like this morning when the plumbing went awry. I doubt they even noticed.'

'The police will want to know about you I'm afraid,' said Camille. 'Everyone who was present last night will need to be questioned.'

He shrugged again. 'I've nothing to hide, my dear. My name is Aaron Kaplan. And I live here. That's all there is to know about me.' He glanced at Camille with a smile. 'Now you know my name, am I permitted to know yours?' He looked from her to Cecily.

'Of course. I'm Lady Camille Divine, and this is Cecily Nugent, my assistant.'

His eyes widened. 'Lady Camille Divine? Of Kenilworth House?'

Camille pulled a small smile. 'Once of Kenilworth House, but no longer. I reside in Duke Street with my staff.'

He nodded. 'I see. And does your cook, Mrs Knowles still serve you?'

Camille look surprised. 'She does. Do you know her?'

He inhaled deeply and smiled to himself. 'Once upon a time...a long time ago. Sounds like a fairytale doesn't it? I suppose it is exactly what it was in those days. A fairytale, with an unhappy ending. I was fond of her, followed her career. She did well, working at Kenilworth House. Lord Divine is of the old school. We were together at Eton College, although he is quite a bit younger than I, of course.' Camille frowned.

'What're you doing down here, Lady Divine?'

A garrulous female voice interrupted them. Louise Clemence was approaching them from the end of the corridor they had come from. Camille turned and pulled her shoulders up to give her some height.

'We got lost I'm afraid.'

Louise Clemence looked unconvinced. 'You got lost? Through a closed door? That takes some doing.'

'Your chef, Monsieur Gaultiere, did not want us present while Chief Inspector Owen questioned him about the activities of his staff last night. Understandable I suppose. We...decided to explore a little. I apologise if we overstepped the mark.'

Louise Clemence shrugged. 'No harm done, but this is a rather unpleasant part of the building. No one ever cleans down here. Perhaps you would like to come back upstairs and have some coffee. I've just made some. And I think we have some pastries too.' She peered around Camille and Cecily to address Aaron Kaplan. 'Have you had breakfast, Mr Kaplan?'

'Not yet, my dear.'

'I've told you before, you must eat.' She shook her head with frustration. 'If you come upstairs in about fifteen minutes I'll have something ready for you. Coffee or tea?'

'Coffee, please,' he answered in a low voice. 'And one of those pastries if there is one going spare.'

'Coffee it is. Ladies,' she said ushering Camille and Cecily out of the storeroom.

'Goodbye, Mr Kaplan,' said Camille. 'I'll remember you to Knolly...Mrs Knowles. I'm sure she'd love to hear about you.' Kaplan nodded but made no answer.

Chapter 16

Back at Duke Street, Camille hung her coat on the hall stand and Cecily continued into the kitchen.

'Do you need anything, Madam?' she called over her shoulder.

'A chat I think, Cecily,' said Camille, joining Cecily and Knolly in the kitchen.

'Yes, of course, Madam.'

Knolly picked up the kettle and filled it from the tap. 'Reckon you'll be needing a cuppa the pair of yer. What 'appened? Did you 'ave to fight yer way out? Was there kidnappers around every corner?'

Cecily giggled. 'It weren't like that, Knolly. Nothing like that at all. I think you'd be surprised.'

Knolly folded her arms under her bosom. 'Hmm, is that right. Well, I don't like surprises, 'specially with my constitution the way it is at the moment. I like things nice and calm.'

'But that's just the point, Knolly, it was calm. And a bit...well, disappointing to be honest.' Cecily took the cups and saucers from the dresser and set them on the table. 'And there was no sign of Valentino.'

'Good job,' answered Knolly. "E spends most of 'is time trying to get women into...situations, and usually ones what benefit only 'im.' She glanced up at Camille, smiling. 'Would you like a lemon fancy, Madam? I know how much you love 'em.'

'Ooh, Knolly, that would be wonderful, but there is something I'd like to ask you about. Could you take a break now and we can have tea together.'

Knolly frowned. 'I've done everything I need to do for lunch, so yes, I can take a break.'

'And are you taking regular breaks? I hope you are. I asked Phillips to keep an eye on you.'

Knolly tutted and shook her head. 'The day I need a man to keep an eye on me, Madam, will be the day I give up. Keep an eye on me indeed. 'E needs to keep an eye on 'iself, never mind keeping one on me. I think 'e's getting' a bit old for work, Madam. 'Ope you don't mind me sayin' it. 'Bout time 'e retired.' Cecily glanced at Camille. It sounded as though Knolly had taken exception to someone keeping an eye on her. Camille smiled, thinking that Knolly's quick tongue meant she was getting back to her old self.

They settled at the table with Cecily pouring the tea, and each of them with a lemon fancy on a tea plate in front of them.

'So what is it, Madam, what you wanted to ask me about?'

Camille took a sip of tea and nibbled her lemon fancy.

'Do you know a man called Aaron Kaplan?' Knolly drew in a breath, so deep Camille thought she would never release it. Her face took on a strange colour and she pushed her tea plate and cup and saucer away from her. Camille rose quickly from her chair and went around to the other side of the table, placing her arms around Knolly's wide shoulders.

'Knolly,' cried Cecily, frightened by Knolly's pallor. 'Knolly, what is it?'

Camille knelt in front of Knolly who was still seated, her breath coming in short gasps. 'Knolly. My dear. I'm so sorry. What is it? What have I said?'

Knolly held up a trembling hand and shook her head. 'Give me a minute,' she said through rasping breaths. 'Just give me a minute.' Camille sat back on her haunches, holding Knolly's hands in her lap. Cecily left her chair and put her arm around Knolly's shoulders, tears running down her cheeks. She was biting her lip so hard she almost drew blood.

After a few minutes Knolly recovered. Her pallor returned to normal, and she began to breathe easier.

'Was it a funny turn, Knolly?' asked Cecily, her voice shaking. 'Is it what happened before, when me and Madam was in Paris?'

Knolly shook her head. 'No, ducks. No, it weren't that. It was the name, that's all. Nearly knocked me off me feet, that it did. I 'aven't 'eard that name in a very long time.'

'What name? You mean Aaron Kaplan? Who is it, Knolly?'

Camille and Cecily sat in their respective seats, each holding one of Knolly's hands. Camille's heart fluttered with fear at the thought she had brought Knolly even more distress, no matter how unwittingly. She was shocked at Knolly's change of countenance. Knolly gently pulled her hands away and took a long gulp of tea and a bite of her lemon fancy which seemed to steady her a little. She sighed.

'I'm sorry, Lady Divine. That weren't no way to behave in front of my employer.' She looked downcast.

'I think you're a bit more than that, Knolly. Well, an awful lot more. We care about you; you must know that. Please, tell us, if you can, and of course, if you want to. Who is this man to you and why did hearing his name shock you so terribly?'

Knolly sniffed, gave herself a few moments, then began her story.

'I knew 'im when I was young. He came from a prominent family, a Jewish family what lived in Highgate. 'Course, I was just a lowly maid working for a family in one of the 'ouses down there. It were a good job and I was 'appy there. All the maids were 'appy.

'One day I was walking in the park on me day off, 'ampstead 'eath it were. We only got 'arf a day and I used to like getting out into the fresh air. The 'ouse I worked in was a bit of a fusty old place, although the people was nice, Mr and Mrs Goldblum. They were quite elderly, treated us well. Always grateful for what we did for 'em. Please and thank yous from 'em as well. Not all employers do that,' she glanced at Camille and smiled, 'unlike my lady what I work for now.' Camille returned her smile affectionately.

'Anyway, one afternoon, when I was on the 'eath, a young gentleman came running up be'ind me. I heard 'is footsteps and I could tell 'e was comin' for me. I was bit scared to tell the truth, but when I turned round, I saw 'e'd picked up me 'andkerchief what I'd dropped and he was just returning it, that was all. I remember I breathed a sigh of relief. A woman walkin' alone is a bit vulnerable to my mind. I know the fashion is different now. It's why I'm always tellin' you two to be careful. Any'ow, we got talkin' and 'e told me 'e lived in 'ighgate. I said I was a maid there and 'e offered to walk me 'ome. I 'ad a room at the 'ouse, yer see. Me Ma and Pa 'ad passed by then so I didn't 'ave an 'ome to go to.

'The next time I was on the 'eath,' Knolly proceeded to flush quite pink, 'I looked for 'im, 'oped 'e'd be there I suppose, and 'e was. From that moment on we was inseparable on me afternoons off. I told the other maids about 'im and it got back to Cook who wasn't 'appy. She said she knew the family and told me to steer well clear. He weren't for the likes of me,' she said. 'E came from money, and I was a maid and not of 'is class, and I shouldn't agree to see 'im no more. 'What the 'ell does 'e want with you?' she said. 'A maid for Gawd's sake. 'E'll be married off to the aristocracy you mark my words.' It was then I realised 'ow much 'e meant to me. I was only seventeen, but I reckoned I'd fallen in love.'

Knolly sighed again. "E were very 'andsome...dark 'air that curled on his collar which was the whitest collar I'd ever seen, starched to within an inch of its life. 'Is clothes were the best, anyone could see that. He wore lovely cravats with precious stones in 'is cravat pins. I knew Cook was right, course I did. I knew before she even said anything about it, but I didn't want to know it. I didn't want to hear that I wasn't good enough for 'im. I wanted the dream to carry on.'

'And what was your dream, Knolly?' asked Cecily, whose eyes glistened with tears.

'I 'ad this dream that we'd be married and 'ave a family, and live 'appily ever after. I s'pose it was cos I'd lost me own parents when I was so young. All I wanted was a family.' She raised her face and looked at them both. 'You can laugh if yer like.'

'We're not going to laugh, Knolly,' said Camille. 'It's important to you so it's important to us.'

Knolly nodded. 'Well, Cook was right weren't she. 'E stopped coming to the 'eath, and then one day he turned up, looking a bit bashful-like. I asked 'im if anything was wrong, and that's when 'e told me 'e was getting' married to a girl from 'is synagogue. It was the day he kissed me. My very first kiss, and it was with a man who was betrothed to another.' She shook her head sadly. 'I've never forgotten it, that kiss. 'E was the sort of man any girl would 'ave been proud to 'ave bin with, but that was the problem, weren't it. I *was* just any old girl, a maid who would spend 'er life doin' for others, doin' for people like 'im and 'is new wife. I was the sort of girl they would employ. I was no one special, but I think he liked me, p'raps even loved me a little.' She inhaled, then sighed.

'The next time I saw 'im was on 'is wedding day. 'E came down the steps of 'is 'ouse to get into a beautiful carriage with four white 'orses, his groomsman by 'is side, one of 'is brothers I think. They looked very much alike. Me and the other maids were allowed to watch as the family got into their carriages. Really posh it was.' She drew in another deep breath and smiled. ''E saw me.'

'Did he?' asked Camille. 'Oh, Knolly, it must have been so heartbreaking for you.'

'Funnily enough it weren't. I knew yer see, deep down. I knew it would never 'ave 'appened. I 'ad me dream and I 'ad me memory of that kiss. When 'e saw me 'e smiled and 'eld his hand up in a wave. I just nodded. I didn't want 'is parents to single me out or think something 'ad been goin' on. I might 'ave lost me place with the Goldblums and it would 'ave been terrible. I'd made a life there, and they, and the girls I worked with, was me family of sorts. I just watched the carriage go off, and that was that.'

'Did the cook say anything to yer, Knolly?' asked Cecily.

Knolly nodded. 'She put an arm around my shoulders and sat me at the kitchen table, made me a cup of tea and gave me an 'andkerchief so I could blow me nose. 'We've all been there,' she said. 'You're not the first and you won't be the last. 'E shouldn't 'ave befriended yer like that. It ain't fair.' Then she lowered 'er voice and said, ''E didn't do anythin' did 'e, yer know, what 'e shouldn't?' I shook me 'ead. I didn't mention the kiss, cause it was just a kiss, nothin' more. She patted my 'and said, 'Good girl. You're more sensible than some others what 'ave been taken in and been left with a load a trouble.''

Knolly sniffed again. 'Thing is, I'm not sure I deserved her sayin' that. I'm not sure I would 'ave resisted 'im should it 'ave come to it, and that's the truth. I s'pose I 'ad a lucky escape. Then I met Mr Knowles and I fell truly in love. He was perfect for me. We was very 'appy together until the day he passed.'

Camille nodded, then reached forward for the teapot and poured Knolly another cup of tea. Knolly frowned, then took a sip from her cup.

'D'yer mind me asking why we're talking about 'im, Madam? It's just that...I 'aven't 'eard that name in such a long time it sort of shook me a bit.'

Camille took a breath. 'You remember we went to the Café Bonbon this morning with Chief Inspector Owen.' Knolly nodded, then placed her cup down on the saucer and folded her arms over her bosom. 'Cecily and I did some exploring while Chief Inspector Owen was interviewing the chef. I'd seen a doorway in the nightclub, so while Chief Inspector Owen was in the kitchen, Cecily and I opened it. It led down to the storerooms which were in the basements.'

'Ooh, dear,' said Knolly. 'Them buildings there are ever so old, Madam. Must 'ave been 'orrible.'

'It was rather. Anyway...we didn't find anything, that is until we got to the very end of the corridor which was deep inside the basement. ' Knolly nodded again wondering why Camille just didn't get on with it. 'Someone had been making a den in the storeroom. There was a bed, a little cupboard with food inside, newspapers strewn across the bed, and a cup of cold tea on a bedside cabinet.'

'A den,' cried Knolly. 'Why on earth would anyone want to live in a storeroom?'

'That's what we were wondering. It wasn't very salubrious I can tell you. Not a good way for someone to live. Just as we were wondering who was making their home down there, a man came from out of the corridor. He'd been working on the plumbing. It transpired that he had lived under the buildings for two or three years. I asked his name, and he asked for mine. Unfortunately we couldn't speak with him for any longer. We were discovered in the basement by the owner, a Louise Clemence. She was none too pleased I can tell you.'

'About the den?'

'No, Knolly. She obviously would have preferred it if we had stayed in the nightclub and not gone exploring. Apparently, the gentleman who lives there is the caretaker of the building, not just of the Café Bonbon, but also of the hairdressing salon and beauty parlour to the left of the nightclub, and the restaurant to the right.'

Knolly shrugged. 'So what 'as this got to do with me and Aaron Kaplan?'

Camille bit her lip, then glanced at Cecily, willing her to continue with the story. Camille just couldn't do it. Cecily reached for Knolly's hand again.

'Mr Kaplan is the caretaker, Knolly,' said Cecily softly. Knolly gasped, her hand flying to her mouth in shock. 'When he found out who Lady Divine was he asked after yer, said he'd followed your career and 'eard you'd been working at Kenilworth 'ouse, but then moved to be with Lady Divine. 'E said he'd always bin fond of yer and often wondered 'ow you were.'

Knolly rose from her seat, her legs wobbling. She held onto the table then went across to the sink and stared out of the kitchen window.

'I 'ave thought about 'im,' she said softly. 'Yer know, in passing like. Just wondered if 'e was still in London and whether 'e was 'appy.' She shook her head. 'My last memory of 'im was when he turned and waved before 'e got into the carriage to take 'im to 'is weddin'. Such an 'andsome face, such beautiful 'air an' all. Lovely 'e was. And 'is eyes so bright, yet when 'e turned that day 'e looked sort of, well...sorrowful, like he 'ad regrets.' She smiled to herself as she pictured a handsome groom going off to a supposedly better life. 'I never told Cook mind. She wouldn't 'ave been 'appy.'

Knolly returned to her chair at the table, her hands in her lap, a frown crossing her face.

'What I don't understand is...what's he doin' there? He's a man of wealth, of family, of connections. 'Ow the 'ell did 'e end up being a caretaker and living in a basement.' She looked imploringly at Camille and Cecily. ''Ow is 'e, in 'imself?'

Camille wasn't sure what to say after what Knolly had told her. She sighed and reached for one of Knolly's hands. 'Not in a terribly good way, Knolly. If he began life such as you say, he certainly hasn't continued like it. Something catastrophic must have happened. He is older now, of course, everyone gets older, but he looks in poor health.'

'Why is 'e there, Madam? Aaron Kaplan came from one of the richest families on the street where I worked. They 'ad everything, a beautiful 'ome, carriages, 'orses...and the clothes. 'Ow could 'e 'ave ended up in such a way? A caretaker of all things. And living in squalor by the sound of it.' Can it be the same man?' She stared at Camille as though hoping she would refute that it could be.

'He knew you, Knolly,' answered Camille. 'It must be the same man.'

Knolly's hands covered her face. 'What's 'appened to 'im?' she cried. 'Why is he there?'

'I'm afraid there's something else,' said Camille, wishing she did not have to be the one to break the news to her.

'Somethin' else, Madam? 'Somethin' else. Ow can it get any worse?'

'It is worse I'm afraid. Because he was on the premises at the time of the girl's murder, to which he freely admitted, Chief Inspector Owen will want to speak with him. He is a suspect.'

Knolly pulled her hands away from her face, her features contorted with horror. 'In a murder?' she cried.

Camille sighed and nodded. 'I'm sorry, Knolly. There's nothing I can do. Perhaps you could speak with Chief Inspector Owen. You could tell him you know Mr Kaplan, give him a sort of... character reference.'

'But I don't know him anymore, Madam. I 'aven't laid eyes on 'im for, well, it must be over thirty years. I thought he'd just get married and 'ave 'is family and that would be that. This 'as come as a bolt out the blue this 'as.'

'Do yer want ter see 'im, Knolly?' asked Cecily. 'You might feel better if you see 'im.'

Knolly inhaled and glanced away. 'I don't know, ducky' she answered softy, as though miles away. "E might not want to see me. And what could I do to 'elp 'im? I s'pose I could talk to 'im, make sure 'e 'ad nothing to do with it, which I'm sure 'e didn't. 'E always seemed kind ter me, not the sort to get involved in anything not right.'

The telephone in the hall rang shrilly. Cecily reluctantly left her seat to answer it. When she came back she look flustered. 'It's Lord Divine, Madam. 'E says it's urgent.'

Camille nodded, and releasing Knolly's hand left the kitchen and went out into the hall. Cecily began to load the sink with crockery, and not very carefully.

'Don't know why 'e 'as ter be so bloody rude,' she said crossly. 'I 'ate answering the telephone to 'im. 'E speaks to me like I'm somethin' mucky on the bottom of 'is shoe.'

Knolly pushed herself up from the table. 'Well, yer can bet your bottom dollar that he 'asn't rung for anything good.' She thumbed into the hall. 'Poor Madam can't seem to get away from 'im can she?' she whispered. 'I dunno what's wrong with the man. It was 'im who told 'er to go after all.'

'Yeah, well,' said Cecily, slamming a bowl down onto the draining board. 'I don't blame 'er for leavin' like she did. Best thing that could 'ave 'appened to 'er. She's worth an 'undred of 'im.' She looked through her eyelashes at Knolly who had proceeded to get the plates from the plate rack to serve lunch. 'You all right, Knolly? Cecily asked her quietly.

'I don't know, Cecily. I don't know if I'm all right,' she said, her voice almost a whisper. 'I'm a bit wobbly after what I just 'eard and that's the truth.' She stopped what she was doing and shook her head. 'I just don't understand it. Bugger me if it can 'appen to a man like that it can 'appen to any of us. 'E 'ad 'is life mapped out for 'im, that 'e did. 'E married a girl who came from as wealthy a family as 'is own and yet 'e's livin' in a filthy basement underneath a nightclub.' She shook her head. 'It don't bear thinkin' about.'

Chapter 17

Richard lit a cigarette and took a deep draw on it. He shook his head at what he'd heard during his conversation with Monsieur Gaultiere, wondering at the lives of other people.

'So what did you make of that, Lewis?' he asked the police constable who sat next to him in the driver's seat of the police vehicle.

'I don't know what to say, sir, if the truth be told. 'Ow can someone be a chef if they don't cook?'

'He *is* a chef, Lewis, a renowned one if what he says is true, and I don't think we have reason to disbelieve him.'

'He doesn't cook, sir.'

'No, he doesn't.'

'And the owners of the nightclub are pretending he does. His name is on the menus and on the advertising board outside the club.'

'That seems to be the size of it.'

'Why don't they just get a chef who does the cooking?'

'Because Monsieur Gaultiere is Mrs Clemence's first husband, and she is trying to help him rebuild his career. Mrs Clemence confirmed it.'

'Because when they were in New York he killed someone and he lost his nerve?' Richard nodded. Lewis turned to him. 'He said it was an accident, that the oysters had come from a different supplier and had been tainted with something.'

'So it would seem.'

'And they killed one of the diners in the restaurant he worked in?'

'A young woman apparently. Many of the diners were taken ill at the same time, some almost immediately, but the young woman lingered for days then passed away after being poisoned.'

'So where does all the food come from they give the guests at Café Bonbon?'

Richard nodded toward the restaurant next door to Café Bonbon. 'They have it brought in from there. They make their order every evening, just like any other customers, then send in a couple of members of staff to pick it up. It's taken into the kitchens and served on Café Bonbon plates as though it was cooked in their own kitchen.'

Lewis frowned. 'What happens if someone wants to compliment the chef? Do they 'ave to go next door?'

Richard rolled his eyes. 'Don't be ridiculous, Lewis. Of course not. Monsieur Gaultiere takes the credit.'

But ain't that,' Lewis shook his head, 'fraud...or something like it?'

Richard shrugged. 'I don't think he could be prosecuted for it.'

Lewis pursed his lips and blew out a breath. 'Beats me 'ow these people get away with it. I understand he's trying to save his name, but he was bit up 'imself, sir,' he went red, thinking he'd overstepped the mark, 'yer know, a bit...'

'I think you mean arrogant, Lewis.'

'Yeah, that.'

'He is an arrogant man, but when you left the room to question Mrs Clemence about what was happening in the kitchen, or rather what wasn't happening, the man broke down in tears, saying his life had been ruined by an oyster.'

'Was he prosecuted?'

'The restaurant where he was head chef was closed down and there was an inquest into what had happened and the girl's death. He wasn't directly prosecuted because he hadn't supplied the oysters. It was the other company who did that.'

'So if he wasn't prosecuted why is he frightened to cook?'

'Reputation, Lewis. It's everything. He lost his nerve when he lost his reputation. He told me every time he tries to cook his hands shake.' Richard's thoughts went immediately to Camille.

'Who owned the restaurant what was closed down?'

Richard stubbed out his cigarette in the ashtray and flipped open his notebook. 'The restaurant was called, Le Petit Champignon, and was owned by a Monsieur Claude Abreo. The restaurant had been in Manhattan for many years and had an extremely famous client list until the fateful day when a company they hadn't used before, and who was unknown to both Gaultiere and Abreo, supplied the restaurant with tainted oysters.'

'Do you think what he told you is significant, sir?'

Richard pulled a face. 'It depends.'

'What does it depend on, sir?'

'Connections, Lewis. There are connections to be made and we must find them. It is how we solve crime, by looking at the stories surrounding all those involved. If the stories connect in any way we investigate. Someone will say something out of turn, or allude to something they either shouldn't know or wouldn't have known unless they were involved.

'This investigation has only just begun. The girl's body was discovered last evening and already we know a great deal about the people who have significant roles in the running of Café Bonbon. Somewhere there is something which will point us in the right direction and we will discover who murdered the young woman...and why.'

'Could I be involved in the investigation, Chief Inspector Owen? I'd like to work my way up to be an inspector or detective one day.'

Richard grinned. 'I'm not sure, Constable Lewis. It's usually Sargent Fellowes who accompanies me when I'm called upon. We need young constables on the streets. It's an important role to play in the fighting of crime.'

Richard turned and gazed out of the vehicle window towards Café Bonbon. 'The streets are where most crime occurs, Lewis. I admit, pounding the beat can be a tedious exercise, but we catch many criminals that way.'

'Does Lady Divine's maid accompany her on all her...investigations, or...interests?'

Richard grinned to himself. 'Cecily Nugent is not simply a maid, Lewis. She is very astute and has a nose for solving crimes. I've no doubt her skills will be helpful in this investigation, as will Lady Divine's. They have been extremely helpful in the past.' He turned towards Constable Lewis whose cheeks had turned pink. 'I think we should get back to the station, Lewis. Our work at Café Bonbon is done for today. I'm hoping there will be information waiting for me regarding the murdered girl from our forensics chaps.'

'Yes, sir,' said Lewis, who started the engine.

'And Lewis.'

'Yes, sir?' Lewis said with a sigh.

'Cecily Nugent does not have a beau.'

Constable Lewis stared at Richard for a few seconds, then his face broke into a smile. 'Thank you, sir.'

'You're welcome, Constable Lewis.'

It was lunchtime by the time Richard arrived back in his office at Scotland Yard. He flung his hat on to the coat stand and gave a satisfied, 'Mm,' and a grin when the hat landed successfully on one of the hooks. He loosened his tie and sat at his desk. There was a stack of files he knew he should attend to and he rolled his eyes at them until he spotted a sheet of paper that someone had left on the top. He reached out and grabbed it. It was from the forensics team in the basement of the offices in Scotland Yard. They had made a preliminary examination. The murdered girl was not blonde like her counterpart, Emma, the cigarette girl. The unknown girl was a brunette. She had worn a wig.

Chapter 18

Camille placed the receiver back on the stand and blew out a frustrated breath. As soon as she knew Harry was on the telephone she surmised it wouldn't be good news, and of course, it wasn't. He wanted to see her, and urgently.

'Can't you tell me why, Harry, or even speak with me over the telephone? Why must I come to Kenilworth House?'

He'd drawn in an impatient sigh which he hadn't tried to hide. 'Because it's safer for us to speak here. Your staff... you're too close to them, and this is a private matter. It grieves me that they know everything about us.'

'You didn't seem to mind when you were inviting your 'friend' to Kenilworth House, did you? They've got ears and they're not blind. Of course they knew what was going on.' She gave herself a moment to think. 'Are you going to shout at me? Is that why you want me to come to Kenilworth House, because you know you can't raise your voice to me in my own home?'

A tut this time, and she could imagine him shaking his head. 'It's not yours yet, Camille. The ink is not yet dry on the divorce papers and they're still with the legal people. Things can change, can be rescinded. You would do well to remember it.'

She'd sighed and agreed to visit him that afternoon. 'As if I don't have enough to think about,' she said under her breath. 'Well at least it'll give me an excuse to take the car out for a spin. He won't like me turning up in it of course, but it's just too bad. I might need a quick getaway and I don't want to rely on a cab...or to give Harry gratitude for finding me one.'

After lunch she asked Cecily to help her dress, and also because she wanted to discuss with her what had happened that morning at the Café Bonbon.

'Have you spoken to Chief Inspector Owen, Madam?' Cecily asked Camille. 'I wonder what was said when we were exploring?'

Camille shook her head. 'I don't know. I haven't had time to speak with him yet. And of course there's the rather unexpected thing with Knolly and Aaron Kaplan. I must admit I hadn't expected anything like it. Poor Knolly. She looked rather heartbroken.'

'It broke *my* heart to see her like that, Madam.' She helped Camille out of her shift and into a smart, calf-length suit with a nipped in waist in blue linen. 'She's been on 'er own for such a long time and I know she still misses Mr Knowles. She often talks about 'im.'

'We don't think of Knolly being young and in love do we. We only think of her as how she is now, and of course, it's completely wrong. She had a life before she knew us; before she came to Kenilworth House and then to Duke Street with us. She's done things and seen things we don't even know about.' Camille sat at her dresser so Cecily could arrange her hair. 'I'm just wondering now what she'll do. Whether she'll agree to see him. It's quite clear he's fallen on hard times. It makes one wonder how on earth he could have been born into a wealthy, well-connected family, and end up as a caretaker in an old building and living in the basement. He had nothing; no possessions. His clothes were ragged, his appearance clearly deteriorated, and it seemed he relies on Mrs Clemence for food. I wonder what happened to him?'

'I hope Knolly does speak with 'im, Madam. It was a friendship once. Mrs Knowles has done all right, ain't she, bearing in mind she started out as a scullery maid. It don't seem like 'e's 'ad the same sort of life. Something's gone 'orribly wrong for 'im.'

'And what about the Café Bonbon, Cecily? What are your thoughts?'

Cecily met Camille's eyes in the dresser mirror. 'First of all, I di'nt like the feeling what I got when I was there.'

Camille frowned. 'The feeling? What kind of feeling did you get?'

Cecily pulled a face, flattening her lips together as though trying to find the right explanation. 'It felt wrong, like...not quite right.'

'Do you mean the atmosphere?'

Cecily nodded and smiled. 'That's right, Madam. The atmosphere. There's somethin' goin' on there, I'd put me wages on it...there's somethin' what someone's tryin' to 'ide.'

'Did you get the feeling for what, apart from the fact that a young girl's body was found in the hanging moon?'

'Did you not feel that everyone there seems very closed up, Madam? I know it's early days, and I think Mr and Mrs Clemence are probably all right, but, they didn't seem to be that 'elpful, did they, bearing in mind someone was found dead on their premises...a girl an' all. It sort of, didn't cause any ripples. She was still at 'er desk working, 'e seemed less then bovvered about it.' Cecily shook her head as she pushed the last hairpins into Camille's hair. 'That's what it was I think. They didn't seem to care that a young girl 'ad lost her life. They're even opening Café Bonbon this evenin' an' all, which I think is very disrespectful. 'Ard as nails, that's what

I thought. Business comes first an' it don't matter about the staff...alive or dead they're not worth worrying about.'

Camille drove the car through the wide, double, wrought-iron gates at Kenilworth House, the tyres making a rather satisfying, crunching sound on the gravel. She pulled up in front of the narrow steps which led up to the front door, and turned off the engine.

The afternoon sun was casting shadows across the crenelations at the top of the house, and dappling the trees and flower beds lining the drive. It was beautiful, she couldn't deny it. The perfume from the rose garden had wafted through her window and she breathed in deeply. The smell of roses usually relaxed her, but not today. Today she felt nervous, more so because Harry had refused to tell her what he wanted to see her about. She swallowed and closed her eyes momentarily, then opened them to see Harry waiting at the double front door.

'Why does he always look so grim these days?' she said under her breath as she got out of the car. 'I feel like I'm about to be told off.'

She locked the car then ran around the front and went up the steps, determined not to be cowed by Harry's stern appearance. He held the front door open for her which she frowned at. Harry had a butler, and footmen, and many more staff besides. They answered the door when there were visitors. He was obviously keen to see her, but she was sure it wasn't because he looked forward to her visit. Certainly it was a visit she had not wanted to make. Returning to Kenilworth House brought back too many unpleasant memories which unfortunately overshadowed the good ones. She felt it was rather sad that coming back to a house she once loved had become such a trial for her. The day she left was a day branded on her memory. She was the cuckolded wife of a lord of the realm, and everyone knew it. It had caused her great anxiety and sorrow, and if it hadn't been for the loyalty of Cecily, Knolly, and Phillips, and of course her beloved daughter, Ottilie, she wasn't sure she would have survived it.

'Harry,' she said firmly as she passed him and went into the hall which was now bereft of the flowers she had always made sure graced it to welcome visitors. 'What can possibly be so urgent you need me to visit Kenilworth House? Surely, a discussion on the telephone would have been more convenient for both of us?'

He took her arm and led her into his study, shutting the door behind them. He indicated for her to sit in the chair opposite his desk with a flick of his hand. It sent a frisson of worry through Camille as she took the seat, sitting with her back ramrod straight. She was sure there would not be a moment of comfort during her visit.

Harry sat in the chair behind his desk, then poured a post-prandial brandy. He offered her one and she refused. She felt she probably needed to keep a clear head for what was about to follow.

'I heard some rather unsettling news yesterday,' Harry said after taking a slug from his brandy glass, 'at the House. It concerns your...policeman.'

She widened her eyes. 'My policeman. I do not have a policeman, Harry. To whom do you refer?'

He lit a cigar and leant back in his chair, observing her. 'Let's not play games, Camille. We're both adults, and I'm sure you are fully aware of who I mean.'

If that's the way you want to play it, she thought. 'I assume you're referring to Chief Inspector Owen, who has become a friend.'

Harry chuckled and took another mouthful of brandy. 'A friend? Is that what it's called these days?'

'I'm sorry, Harry, I have absolutely no idea what you're talking about.'

'You are seeing this man.'

She nodded. 'As a friend. That is all.'

'I'm not sure I believe you.'

Camille felt anger boiling up inside her chest. 'And I'm not sure I like your interference in my life, or, as it happens, whether I care if you believe me.' She stood up and began to stroll around the study. Sitting in the chair in front of Harry's desk made her feel like a naughty schoolgirl who had been caught with her hand in the biscuit jar, and set her at a disadvantage which she was sure was entirely the atmosphere he wanted. 'Let's not forget how this started, Harry. You grew tired of me and did your best to replace me with someone else.' She raised her hand to stop him from interjecting. 'It's old news. You and I are separated and we go our separate ways. It suits me as I'm sure it suits you.' Harry inclined his head. 'So, why are you questioning me about my friendships? I do not question yours, in fact I have no idea what you get up to these days simply because I have no interest. Your private life is your own. I would like to be given the same respect.'

'But our daughter is not our private life. She is very much our public life, simply because she is our daughter, the daughter of a lord and lady of the realm. Anything we do affects her.'

Camille threw her head back and laughed. 'And were you thinking of her when you were bedding…what was her name…Delphinium, the one-time whore and vaudeville princess?' She turned to face him; her face lowered to almost a growl. 'Were you thinking of her then, Harry?'

Harry looked uncomfortable. 'Everyone makes mistakes.'

'Indeed, and you made the mistake of choosing the wrong person and making yourself, and I, and our daughter a subject of derision.' She shook her head at him, wondering at his arrogance. 'And what exactly have you heard?'

'Your policeman is not as squeaky clean as he would probably have you believe.'

So here we are, Camille thought. This is why Richard told me about his father and the people with whom he consorted. Someone has told Harry about Richard and he will use the information to wrest any happiness I may have had away from me. 'I'll ask again, what have you heard and why should it have any bearing on my life?'

'His father. Do you have any idea who his father is?'

'Of course.'

'Luca Vincenzu...commonly known as Ludo Vincent.'

'Yes, what of it?'

Harry looked incredulous. 'What of it? Is that a joke, Camille? You are Lady Camille Divine and you are consorting with a man who comes from a family of criminals.'

'But who himself is not a criminal. He is a member of the constabulary, a chief inspector no less, with honours to his name. He arrests criminals, Harry, he does not consort with them. He lifted himself out of his father's grip many years ago, so what you think you know now is old news.'

'And what of Ottilie?'

'What of her?'

'She knows him?'

'She has met him, yes.'

'And you think it is acceptable?'

Camille frowned. 'Why would it not be? He isn't a gangster?' She tutted and shook her head, wondering just how Harry would use this information. She wanted to bring the conversation down a notch, so wandered around the study, perusing the artwork on the walls. 'He's a friend, Harry. That is all. We've had dinner together, taken tea. I hardly think you could describe it as the love affair of the century, which is precisely what you are trying to intimate.'

'He may have connections.'

'Of course he has connections. He's a police officer of the highest calibre, and quite honestly, Harry, I think you're making rather too much of this. His father is deceased, he has one sister who lives in Bayswater and who is married to a perfectly respectable businessman with no criminal connections whatsoever.' She tutted. 'They are not their parents. It was all a very long time ago and I believe Chief Inspector Owen lifted himself out of the life his father led to embark on a different life completely. He lived on a farm for a while I understand, then went into the police force, rather to mitigate the behaviour of his father.'

'Who was a murderer.'

'Yes, but please do not visit the sins of the father on the children. He does not have a criminal bone in his body, regardless of who his father was.'

'And you're sure of it?'

'Utterly sure.'

'And when we divorce?'

She turned and glared at him. 'I shall remain a divorcee, with a daughter who has a father who happens to be a lord of the realm. I will uphold my reputation and that of my daughter. She comes first...in all things.'

Harry took another long swig from his glass. Camille frowned. He had refilled his glass twice since she had been in his company.

'And you will not remarry?'

Camille sighed. 'I don't know, Harry. Will you?'

'Yes.'

Taking her seat again she narrowed her eyes at him. Was this the real reason why he had demanded she visit? Perhaps his concerns about Richard weren't so real after all.

'You seem very definite about it.'

'I am. I need a wife...someone to take on the title of Lady Divine.'

'You have a wife...and the title is mine.'

'I'm sorry, Camille. I failed to mention in the divorce papers that if I remarry you will lose the title. The person I marry will have to take on the title, which is only fitting. As my wife the title will belong to her and she should be allowed to use it. There cannot be two Lady Divines.'

'So you can marry whom you please, yet you think you have the right to tell me whom to marry. Is this not why I'm here.'

'Most women who are no longer married to a Lord refrain from remarrying.'

Camille chuckled but it was without humour. Inside she boiled. 'And so, in your own, rather unsubtle way, you're telling me I should not remarry. That's right isn't it?'

Harry shrugged arrogantly. 'I'm just informing you of the etiquette. Of course if you decided to ignore the accepted etiquette of a divorced member of the aristocracy, one would expect you to choose wisely.'

'And does this perceived etiquette apply to you...to men?'

'My choice would always be wise.'

'Oh,' cried Camille, her eyes wide with astonishment. 'You mean like Lady Delphinium, or wasn't she really Mabel Crocket? You felt she was a wise choice, Harry? I think perhaps your judgement may have been impaired on that particular occasion.'

Harry emptied his brandy glass and rose from his chair. 'As I said, we all make mistakes. That particular event turned out as well as it could have.'

She gasped. 'With a young woman murdered?'

'It was unfortunate, I grant you.'

Camille rose from her seat. 'Am I being dismissed?'

'I...wanted you to be aware that I know about Chief Inspector Owen. I'm relieved your relationship has gone no further than friendship. Of course, whom you decide to marry is your affair, but we have a daughter who will go out into society. I want nothing to mar her appearance into society as she makes her debut.'

Camille gritted her teeth. 'If any young man decides to pursue Ottilie, I hope it will be because of her beautiful nature, her kindness, and her brain, not because she has a title.' She bit her lip. 'I would not wish that on her.'

Camille turned to leave, then turned back when something occurred to her.

'You clearly have someone in your sights for yourself, Harry. Am I to know who this paragon of virtue is, or must I wait until it is announced in The Times.'

Harry shoved his hands into his pockets and had the grace to turn slightly pink. 'Lady Petronella Grayson, Lord Percival Grayson's daughter. We have met socially and at dinner. She is perfect for the position.'

'You make it sound like a job vacancy, Harry, but then, I suppose it is exactly what it is. She is so young, a girl who has no knowledge of how life really is. She's pretty, I grant you, and will no doubt try her best to give you the son you crave even though you know it's likely impossible. It seems you still haven't accepted the medical professions view of things. A lamb to the slaughter. I pity her.'

Camille left the study and went out into the hall where the butler waited for her to leave. He opened the door and she thanked him, then went down the steps towards her car. Harry followed her at a slower pace, a look of regret crossing his face.

'I wish it could have been different, Camille.'

Camille opened the motor car door, then stood for a moment and glared at him. 'No you don't, Harry. You'll get your way, you always do, but there's one thing you must understand. Whilst I agree to give up my title when you remarry, presumably I don't have a choice, I will not give up my right to choose.

'Divorce me, Harry. For goodness sake get on with it. Hurry the men of letters so that we can be free of one another. Let us put this so-called marriage out of its misery so we can be free of each other. It's over. It's done. And if I am to be known as plain old Camille Divine, or even to retake my family name, so be it. But please, let's prolong this no further. Let us be done with it.' She looked up at the house with not a little sadness. 'And I make a promise to you with certainty. I will never return to this house of misery.'

Chapter 19

Camille drove through the streets of London, tears of frustration rolling down her cheeks. She put up a hand to brush them away so they didn't impede her view of the road, thinking how dismissive Harry was of her, even though they had been married for over ten years.

She hadn't given him a moment's concern. She had done her best to be a good wife, no, the perfect wife for a lord of the realm, an important man, one who had status and a name to maintain. Not that any of it had meant anything to her. She came from a wealthy and revered family herself, an old family with connections across Europe, yet the damage had been done when Harry had decided to take a lover, Lady Delphinium, a vaudeville actress and one-time prostitute, whose real name was Mabel Crocket, who had put her carnal knowledge to good use and had hooked herself a Lord, namely Harry Divine, who had fallen for her questionable charms.

By the time she reached Duke Street and had parked the car in the wooden building at the back of the house which protected the car from the weather, she had regained her composure. She didn't want Cecily, Knolly, and Phillips to see her indisposed. They would worry, because unlike her former husband, they cared about her and wanted the best for her.

As she entered the front door, Cecily came out into the hall.

'Chief Inspector Owen telephoned, Madam. He asked if you would telephone him back.' Camille nodded and Cecily frowned. 'Are you all right, Madam? 'As 'e upset you again?'

'No, no, I'm fine, Cecily. I would love a cup of tea if you have time.'

'Right away, Madam. You look like you could do with one.' Camille smiled to herself. She couldn't keep anything from Cecily, who was rather like her conscience in human form.

She took off her duster coat and hung it on the stand, then removed her hat before sitting at the telephone table. She dialled for the operator and asked to be put through to Scotland Yard where she was answered by the operator.

'I'll put your call through, Madam. Wait a moment please.'

Richard answered immediately. 'Chief Inspector Owen.'

Chief Inspector, it's Lady Divine. I'm sorry I wasn't here to take your call.' Camille knew better than to address Richard as Richard, or to announce herself as Camille. She and Richard were all too aware that the operator at Scotland Yard listened in to conversations which should have been private.

'There are some questions I need to ask about the unfortunate demise of the girl at Café Bonbon where I understand you were present.'

'Yes, that's correct.'

'Are you available, Lady Divine?'

'I'll be here for the rest of the afternoon.'

'Would four thirty suit?'

'Yes of course.'

Camille replaced the receiver onto the candlestick and went into her sitting room. Cecily followed her inside with a cup of tea and a plate of French fancies.

'Knolly says you're to eat these if you've 'ad a shock. They'll keep your chin up.'

Camille smiled and sat in her favourite chair. 'Chief Inspector Owen is coming here at four thirty this afternoon. I'm guessing he has some information he wishes to impart.' She leant towards the little occasional table and picked up the cup of tea Cecily had placed there. 'I needed this. Thank you, Cecily.'

'He upset you didn't he? Lord Divine? We can always tell. I don't mean to be so forward, Madam, and it's none of our business, but we wish you didn't 'ave to go back there just because 'e says you 'ave to.'

Camille took a sip of tea and settled back into her chair. 'I'm not going there again, Cecily. Lord Divine is marrying as soon as our divorce is finalised. Kenilworth House will be closed to me. I will never be expected to go there for which I am eternally grateful. That once wonderful house doesn't mean anything to me anymore. It's such a shame. It's a different place. I think you would have quite the shock if you went there.'

'The only reason it was a beautiful 'ouse was because of you, Madam. The flowers, the décor, everythin' was you. I can only imagine it's a drab old place now.'

Camille sighed. 'And Ottilie will need to get used to having a stepmother.'

Cecily's hands flew to her face. 'Oh, Madam. That's awful.'

Camille shook her head. 'Not if the new Lady Divine is kind to her and befriends her.' Camille took a deep breath. 'No, I must be adult about this. Ottilie's happiness comes first. If she is comfortable and happy with her new stepmother, then so must I be.'

Cecily could not keep the sadness off her face. The doorbell rang and Camille sat up.

'That will be Chief Inspector Owen. I'd like you to stay, Cecily, and tell the Chief Inspector what you told me about your feelings when you went to the Café Bonbon. It's all relevant and together we might come up with some clues.'

'Fair enough, Madam,' said Cecily, bobbing a quick curtsey, then running to the front door to open it.

'Good afternoon, Cecily,' Camille heard Richard say as he entered the house. 'How are you today?'

'I'm very well, sir, thank you.' Cecily answered. Camille thought how different he was from Lord Divine; how friendly and respectful to everyone. She knew Harry would never greet Cecily in the same way, in fact he would hardly acknowledge her presence except to give her his hat and coat to hang up for him.

Richard joined Camille in the sitting room, removing his hat and giving her a beautiful, warm smile.

'Camille. Lady Divine. Thank you for seeing me at such short notice.'

'It's no trouble, Richard. I'm sure you have something interesting to tell us. I've asked Cecily to stay if you have no objection. This case seems to be full of twists and turns and I think her astute brain will certainly be of help.'

'Absolutely, Camille.' He smiled at Cecily, then eyed the French fancies on the coffee table. 'Ah, I see Mrs Knowles has been baking again.'

Cecily giggled. 'I'll get you a cup of tea to go with them, Chief Inspector. I won't be long.'

'Mrs Knowles up to speed again?' he asked Camille.'

'Yes, but I have to make her rest. I don't know what we'd do without her.'

'Is Cecily going to cookery classes?'

'All arranged. She begins the course next week.'

Cecily returned with a tray on which there was a teapot, a tiny jug of milk, a bowl of sugar and two cups and saucers.

'This will keep us going,' she said, smiling at them both.

Camille indicated for Cecily to pour tea for both her and Richard, then settled back to listen to what he had to tell them.

'Well, Richard? What did you discover?'

'Monsieur Gaultiere does not cook the food at the Café Bonbon.'

Camille blinked at him. 'What?'

Richard bit into a French fancy then shook his head. 'They order the food served there from the restaurant next door.'

Camille frowned. 'But, why?'

'Monsieur Gaultiere worked at a restaurant in Manhattan for many years, Le Petit Champignon.'

'The Little Mushroom.'

'Exactly. They ordered some oysters from their usual supplier but he could not deliver, so they used one they had never used before. The oysters were tainted. A girl died from food poisoning.'

Camille gasped. 'Oh, how dreadful.'

'The restaurant was forced to close, and Gaultiere has not cooked since.' Camille shook her head, astonished at the turn of events. 'There's something else.'

'Oh?'

'He and Louise Clemence were married before she married Ivor Clemence.'

'Yet he works at the Café Bonbon.'

'She's trying to give him back his confidence. He could not find it in himself to cook again. His hands shook and his nerve was completely gone. He was frightened of it happening again.'

'Do you know this for the truth.'

'Louise Clemence confirmed it.'

'You think there's a connection?'

'It's possible. Anything is possible of course. And...the murdered girl was not a blonde like Emma. She was a brunette. She was wearing a wig.'

Camille shook her head. 'But why, Richard?'

'Cos, she wanted to look like Emma,' said Cecily, then quickly covered her mouth with her hand. 'Sorry, Madam, sir. P'raps I shouldn't 'ave said nothin', but it seems to me that Emma wanted to get away from the club without being found out, so she asked this girl to stand in for 'er. The wig was to make her look like 'er. Obviously I didn't see 'er so I can't vouch for the likeness.'

'Oh, they definitely looked alike, do you not agree, Chief Inspector?'

'I do, apart from the hair of course, but it throws up another question. Where is Emma?'

'Perhaps she was meeting someone...a man...a boyfriend. It could be she asked this other girl to take her place so she could leave her post as the cigarette girl at the nightclub so she wouldn't lose her wages, or her job.'

'Don't it mean whoever murdered the girl, thought he, or she, was murdering Emma?' said Cecily.

'I rather think it does,' answered Richard. '

'Which means Emma is in danger, wherever she is,' said Camille.

'And why 'asn't she come forward? Why 'asn't she returned to her job.'

'She might tonight. The murder only took place last night don't forget. She might not even know about it. We must go to the club this evening. If she's there we must question her. She could have all the answers. You must come too, Cecily.'

'And if she isn't,' said Richard, lighting a cigarette with Camille's permission.

'Then I can only imagine she's either too frightened to show herself to come back to the club, or, she's being held somewhere. I think she is the key to all this.'

'We need to find out more about her, where she lives, who her friends are,' said Richard. 'It's the only way to conduct an investigation, to be thorough and follow every lead.'

'I think she is the most important one.'

'Indeed. If we find Emma and talk to her, I'm certain she will point us in the right direction.'

Chapter 20

'Mrs West is here, Madam,' said Cecily as she joined Camille and Knolly in the kitchen.

Camille frowned. 'Elsie? I wonder what she's doing here?'

'I've put her in the sitting room. She's asked for a whiskey, but I said I'd leave that to you as I wasn't allowed to touch the drinks cabinet.' She glanced at Camille. 'Fink she's already been on the sauce if yer don't mind me sayin'.'

Camille chuckled. 'Well, it is the usual state of affairs. I don't know how she does it.'

'I do,' said Knolly with a low voice. 'She's used to it. It's like drinking tea ter people like that.'

Camille smiled and left the kitchen to join Elsie in the sitting room, wondering why she'd visited. Elsie usually only visited when she thought she was missing out on something. The murder was in the morning papers, she thought. And she'll have seen Richard's name. She chuckled again. Of course. She wants to know what's happening.

Elsie was sitting in Camille's chair when Camille joined her.

'Elsie. How lovely to see you. How are you? I haven't seen you for, ooh, it must be at least a week.'

Elsie laughed. 'You're me friend, ain't yer? I should always be welcome.'

'And so you are,' said Camille, smiling. She sat in the chair opposite Elsie who had fished a small packet out of her bag.

'I've started smoking these,' she said, waving the box of cheroots in the air. 'Think they give me a bit more sophistication. D'yer mind?' Camille shook her head. 'D'yer want one?' Camille shook her head again.

'So...is there a reason for your visit?' Camille asked her.

'It's in the papers, innit, 'bout the murder at Café Bonbon. Old Clemence owns it don't 'e? That's what 'e tells everyone anyway.'

Camille's eyes widened. ' You know him?'

'Course I do. 'E's a regular at my place.'

'What?'

'Oh, yeah, come wiv a French bloke, Goolish, Goulash, oh I dunno. They don't always give their real names. I'm surprised any of 'em do, but I don't reckon Clemence is quite wiv it. Gave 'is name right away. Asked for credit an' all, cheeky git. Like we give credit for what we do. I pay my girls every week an' I can't do that when it's chalked up on a board, can I? And my girls can't eat credit. Some people.'

'Do you mean, Gaultiere? The man who visits your establishment with Clemence. His name is Gaultiere.'

'Yeah, that's it. 'And that Clemence. Nah, don't like 'im. 'Ard faced geezer. Bit rough wiv the girls an' all. I 'ad ter tell 'im. Try that again and you'll be barred. We don't need that type wiv what we do. Don't deserve it.' She looked pointedly at the drinks cabinet. 'Got any whiskey goin'. I'm as parched as a bear's bum.'

'Wouldn't you rather have coffee, or tea. So much more refreshing.'

'No, I wouldn't.'

Camille got up and went across to the drinks cabinet where she poured Elsie a whiskey.

'Is it a double?' Camille raised her eyebrows, continued to pour, then handed Elsie the glass. She took a big gulp then wiped her mouth on the back of her hand. 'That's better. Been looking forward to that. I don't drink in the mornin's no more. Just the afternoon and the evening.' When you make up for what you didn't have in the morning, thought Camille.

'Any'ow,' continued Elsie. 'I thought you and Cecily would be investigatin' this one, seein' as it's a young girl what got 'erself killed and Chief Inspector Owen is on the case. 'An' I thought you might want my 'elp, like yer usually do.'

'We're going to the club tonight. You can join us if you like.' Camille was aware that if Elsie found out they visited the Café Bonbon that evening and hadn't invited her there would be hell to pay.

'Oh, yes, yes, I'd very much like ter join yer. I might pick up some new punters.'

'Elsie!' cried Camille as she sat opposite Elsie again. 'That isn't why we're going there. You said you wanted to help.'

'And I do, but I got ter keep me eye on me business ain't I? These clothes what I'm wearing don't come for free yer know.' She smoothed down her skirt and tilted her hat slightly. 'Madame Lanvin only designs the best.'

'I'm aware of that,' said Camille, her lips twitching into a smile.

'So what time are yer goin'.'

'Chief Inspector Owen is picking me up at seven o'clock. Perhaps you could get a cab here and we could go together.'

'Oh, that would be fine, that would. Pity I don't 'ave a beau. We could 'ave made up a foursome.'

'We will be a foursome. Cecily will be joining us.'

'Oh, yes, well, she's the one with the detectorist skills, ain't she?'

'I rather like to think I have some input, Elsie.'

'Course yer do. An' I've done me bit 'aven't I. We're a proper little team.' Camille smiled inwardly, thinking that Elsie's presence lightened every load, in her own, very unique, way. 'I best get back 'ome and start to get ready,' said Elsie, handing her empty glass to Camille who stared at it with astonishment, wondering how Elsie could drink strong whiskey so fast. 'Got a nice new little number I'll be wearing. Anything goes in them places don't it, and I might be able to use me feminine wiles to find things out…for the investigation I mean.'

'Yes, and I'd best tell Chief Inspector Owen we have an extra guest.'

'See yer at arf six then,' said Elsie. 'We can 'ave a few before we go. The prices in them clubs are as high as a kite. Don't see why we should pay 'em when we can get it cheaper at 'ome.'

Mm, as long as it's my home, thought Camille.

Chapter 21

They arrived at the Café Bonbon just as the club was about to close its doors. Elsie had turned up late to Duke Street, three sheets to the wind, as Knolly would put it, and seemingly ready for a good night out, dressed in a most outrageous style, leaving very little to the imagination.

'It's 'ow they dress in these places, ain't it?' she cried. 'And this dress cost a week's takin's. Worth every penny I think you'll agree.'

Cecily had raised her eyebrows and giggled. 'Bloody 'ell,' she'd said under her breath, to which Camille had given a sardonic smile. Camille, Richard, Cecily, and surprisingly, Constable Lewis, who had accompanied Richard, to which Cecily had frowned, had averted their eyes from Elsie's decolletage which seemed to be in danger of putting in a surprise appearance. Camille glanced at Richard who said nothing, which he decided was the seemly, and gentlemanly, thing to do.

The club was busy. The discovery of a girl's body the previous evening had done nothing to dent the intentions of determined club goers, and the revellers were in high spirits. Richard and the others were shown to their table in the middle of the floor and were immediately offered drinks.

'On the house,' said the waitress. 'Mr and Mrs Clemence are aware you were unable to enjoy your evening here last night, and want to ensure you have a good time.

'That's very kind,' said Richard. 'I'd like to buy some cigarettes. Is Emma here?'

'Er, no, sir. She didn't turn up for work this evening. We've got Millicent on cigarettes and cigars. I'll send her over.'

'Yes, please do. Thank you.' Richard turned immediately to Camille. 'She's not here.'

'Do you think she's in danger?' They were interrupted by Millicent who had taken on Emma's role of cigarette girl. Richard purchased his favourite brand. 'I don't know. She's either being held somewhere, or she's in on it.'

Camille gasped. 'In on the murder?'

'Yes.'

Camille shook her head. 'That lovely girl.'

'Don't be fooled by appearances, Camille,' Richard said under his breath. 'You and I both know it means nothing.'

'I almost rather hope she's being held. She had such a demure countenance. One could not imagine her deliberately taking a girl's life without some sort of conscience.' She shook her head feeling sad until Cecily leant forward to say something. She had been very quiet, and seemingly none too pleased when she had seen Constable Lewis.

'Wos 'e doin' 'ere?' she'd said under her breath when she'd seen him in the cab. Of course Elsie had been all over him, pinching his cheek and telling him he was a lovely boy, which had made the poor young chap completely red in the face, and Cecily bristle. He was certainly not familiar with the likes of Elsie West.

'I've brought Constable Lewis along because he has shown an interest in the investigation,' Richard said, with a small smile on his lips. He had given Camille a look which had made her chuckle. Constable Lewis had clearly fallen for Cecily, although she was being off hand with him and not the slightest bit encouraging.

'What did the statements say, Chief Inspector Owen?' Cecily asked him. 'Didn't any of them come across as off, or a bit odd? Did any of 'em sound like they was lying, or obviously made up. I mean, the kitchen staff don't 'ave much ter do, do they, bearing in mind they don't actually do anything in the kitchen. They certainly ain't doin' preparations, or plannin' menu's no matter what that French chef says, when all they're doin' is what anyone could do, what we did when Knolly weren't 'erself; go into a restaurant and order food. It ain't 'ard.'

'It seems the kitchen staff, of which there are only two apart from Monsieur Gaultiere, help with serving the food at tables.'

'Spect they do,' answered Cecily. 'What else would they be doin', unless they was murderin' some poor girl.' She tutted. 'The point I'm makin' is, from what I've seen tonight, everyone else who works 'ere is obvious, they're out in the mix of everythin', but not the kitchen staff. They can do anythin' they like, cos they're out of the way, in the kitchen. I've been watching the waiting staff. When they put a plate of something on the tables no one pays 'em no never mind. The guests 'ave all got their eyes on their plates and take almost no notice of the staff. It's the food what they're interested in.'

Camille frowned. 'So what you're saying is that whatever the guests say in their statements they probably wouldn't have known who served them.'

Cecily nodded. 'Exactly, Madam. I mean, do you remember who brought you your food?'

Camille glanced at Richard. 'No, in all honesty I couldn't tell you who it was. I remember Emma, the cigarette girl, Yvette who runs the book, the girl in the moon, and the young woman who runs the cloakroom. I could probably pick them out from others, but not the waiting staff, although after a period of time I would probably forget the faces.' Camille glanced at Richard. 'Cecily has a point don't you think?'

He nodded. 'I do indeed, but my detectives questioned the kitchen staff last night, and I have read the reports, admittedly briefly, and I could discern nothing of any interest.'

'What about Mr Kaplan?' asked Camille reluctantly. 'I take it he hasn't been questioned yet?'

'Not yet. One of my men will come here first thing tomorrow and speak with him.'

'Knolly is acquainted with him.'

'The caretaker?'

'She knew him when she was young. Apparently he was once a wealthy man who came from a notable family.'

Richard raised his eyebrows. 'How did he end up as a caretaker in a place like this?'

'I think it's something which needs to be ascertained, Richard. I'm hoping fervently he has nothing to do with what happened here last night. I'm quite sure it would break Knolly's heart, and she has had enough to deal with lately.'

'They were close?'

Camille inclined her head to once side. 'Their circumstances did not coincide. There was an attraction there, but...nothing could have come of it.'

Richard shook his head. 'Circumstances, eh?' He stared at Camille. 'Life can be so hard sometimes.'

Camille looked away, tears pricking under her eyelids. If she could have, she would have thrown herself in to Richard's arms and asked him to be part of her life, to be her soulmate, her forever love. And she did love him. She had realised it on her drive back from Kenilworth House after her meeting with Harry. The thought of not seeing Richard, of he not being part of her life was unthinkable. She had wept on the way back to Duke Street, not just because of her frustration with Harry for assuming he could control her life, but because she knew, if he wanted to, he could destroy everything that made her happy; her relationship with Ottilie, her life as an independent woman...and the love she had for Richard, a kind, respectful, wonderful man.

She cared for him, cared about him, wanted to be with him when she wasn't...worried for him and celebrated with him when his investigations went well. He had become incredibly important to her, and the thought that Harry would try to come between them had filled her with anxiety.

She knew if Harry was determined he could easily make life difficult for her as far as a relationship with Richard was concerned. Harry was a bitter man; why she was yet to fathom. He seemingly had everything any man could possibly require or want, yet still he wasn't satisfied.

He could choose whomever he wanted to be his wife; he had already chosen it would appear; a girl young enough to be his daughter, the daughter of an aristocratic friend, a girl who had seen nothing of life, had not travelled or learnt the ways of the world. She had been schooled to look pretty, to speak a smattering of French with which to get by, and to keep her mouth shut on anything of importance. A doll, someone to be used to simply look the part. It sickened Camille and in truth she was glad not to be part of the world she once occupied. She could only hope she could protect Ottilie from the same fate.

'Camille?' Richard was looking at her with some concern.

She smiled and made a small laugh. 'It's nothing. Sometimes a thought goes through one's mind and changes one's expression. I was thinking about Knolly and the circumstance she found herself in when she was young. I can only pray Aaron Kaplan is not involved in any of this.'

'And if he is? Presumably Mrs Knowles has not seen him since those early days?'

'She has not. And I think she will have quite a shock when she sees him.' She leant forward and placed a hand on Richard's arm. 'Please question him soon and take him out of the equation, Richard. Then I will help Mr Kaplan, a shave perhaps, and a haircut. A new suit of clothes. I don't want Knolly to be upset.'

Richard put a hand over hers. 'Of course.' His eyes softened, exuding warmth and an unmistakable attraction to the beautiful, caring and loving woman who sat before him. 'I understand. You want to help him for the sake of your beloved Knolly.'

'Yes, Richard. For Knolly.'

Suddenly, the table was rocked by someone sitting next to Constable Lewis, who yet again flushed red and swallowed so hard his Adam's Apple went into overdrive.

'So when does the dancing start,' cried Elsie. 'We've bin 'ere nearly arf an hour and I ain't 'eard no music yet.'

'They like to get the starters over with before the songbird comes on,' answered Richard, chortling into his hand as Elsie leant on Constable Lewis's shoulder making him visibly embarrassed. Camille glanced at Cecily who looked somewhat cross.

'Oh right. What did we 'ave? Must 'ave missed it. I was talkin' to someone on the door, Jeffrey Blundell, one of Len's old muckers. Nice man.'

Camille doubted Jeffrey Blundell was a 'nice man' if he had had anything to do with Len West. 'We haven't eaten yet, Elsie. Seems you're just in time.'

'Oh, that's good. I'm bloody starving. Only 'ad soup for lunch. Not enough to keep a fly alive.'

'You're always starving, Elsie,' said Camille, smiling. 'God knows how you maintain that wonderful figure of yours.'

'Oh, there's ways and means,' she said, smiling slyly and chucking Constable Lewis under the chin who looked like he wanted to sink into a hole. Anything to get away from this woman who insisted on paying him unwanted attention. 'I exercise, don't I? Wiv paddles.'

Camille frowned. 'Paddles?'

'Yeah. Wooden fings shaped like paddles what people use in boats. You swing 'em around. keeps your arms firm and your waist tight. Bin doin' it for ages. You should try it, Camille. Means I can eat what I want when I want. I swear by them paddles.'

Camille shook her head then smiled. Elsie was always surprising her, keeping her entertained. The pair of them were like chalk and cheese, but for a reason Camille couldn't fathom, the friendship worked.

'You know the doorman, Mrs West?' Richard asked her, wondering if he would get a straightforward answer bearing in mind the amount of alcohol she had obviously imbibed.

'Yeah, I know 'im. 'E was one of the good'uns. Weren't many of them around when Len was about, but I always thought 'e was the best of the lot. Quiet like, not mouffy like some of 'em.' Camille noticed how Elsie's language disintegrated into that of the estuary when she'd had a lot to drink. 'Nah, he were one of the good'uns.' She turned to Richard frowning. 'Why? D'yer want me to 'ave a word wiv 'im.' She nudged Constable Lewis in the ribs, who sat ramrod straight, looking directly ahead. Even Richard was amused. 'E'd do anythin' for me. Fancies me I reckon,' she sighed dramatically, 'but then who can blame 'im. Specially wiv me dressed like this.' She pulled the front of her dress down even further, exposing even more of her bosom. Camille thought Constable Lewis might faint. He was clearly doing his best to keep his eyes firmly on the other side of the room.

'It would be extremely helpful if you would, Mrs West. We rely on you and your superior knowledge to assist us at these times,' said Richard, using honey where vinegar would never do, particularly with someone like Elsie. 'Doormen often have inside knowledge of what's going on in a premises, even though they spend the majority of their working life outside.' Camille looked down to her hands, a wry smile on her face.

'Oh, yes, course I can 'elp, Chief Inspector. It's why I'm 'ere innit. To 'elp. But I'd like to eat somethin' first if it's all right with you. Need to line me stomach. Feeling slightly faint, prob'ly cos I ain't 'ad much to eat today.' Camille grinned and glanced at Richard thinking it was more likely Elsie was feeling faint because she'd drunk so much on an empty stomach. He returned her grin, shaking his head with amusement.

After the starters had been served and eaten, a melange of tender vegetable and herbs mixed with seafood, the singer approached the stage and began to croon. It was the same singer as the previous night, this time dressed in a sophisticated silver sheath dress accessorised with a white feather boa.

'She looks like you, Camille,' Elsie said as she shovelled the last forkful of starter in her mouth. 'Got that same striking look. You...an' her could earn a fortune at my place. My clientele favour the exotic.'

'Thank you for the invitation, Elsie, but I'm quite sure I wouldn't be right for your establishment.'

Elsie shrugged. 'Suit yerself.' She looked around. 'Is anyone goin' ter dance?'

Suddenly, Constable Lewis leant across the table and grabbed Cecily's hand.

'Miss Nugent. I would be honoured if you would favour me with this dance.'

Cecily's eyes widened with astonishment, and not a little embarrassment. 'Er...well, I...'

'Go on, Cecily,' said Camille. 'Go and dance with poor Constable Lewis before he's swept up into Elsie's arms.' Cecily shrugged and rose from her chair, following Constable Lewis onto the dance floor.

'Aw,' cried Elsie. 'Ain't that nice. Two young people in each uvver's arms. It's what makes the world go round ain't it.'

'Will you go and speak with your friend please, Elsie?' asked Camille. 'It could point us in the right direction. Heaven knows we need some clues.'

'I'll go now,' said Elsie, pushing herself away from the table. 'If anyone can 'elp yer, I can. I pride meself on it.'

When Elsie had made her way to the foyer, Camille sighed and sat back in her chair. She leant her elbow on the arm of the chair, and her chin in her hand, and grinned.

'She's like a whirlwind. I feel as though I've been rushed at and missed when I'm in her company.'

Richard laughed. 'But she adores you. And for all her roughness and lack of etiquette, she has a heart of gold.'

Camille nodded. 'Yes, I've seen it with my own eyes. I just wish she wouldn't drink so much.'

'Perhaps it goes with the territory of what she does for a living. It can't be easy.'

Camille looked contrite, straightening up to watch Cecily and Constable Lewis on the dance floor. 'No, I'm sure it isn't. She's had a troubled life. I'm glad things have worked out for her.'

Camille and Richard joined Cecily and Constable Lewis on the dance floor.

'So Emma isn't here,' said Camille. 'Do you think it's possible we've been lied to with regard to her.'

Richard nodded, then swirled Camille around as they danced a waltz. She revelled in what a good dancer he was. Richard suddenly looked thoughtful. 'I've been thinking exactly the same thing. Do you mind if we go back to the table and talk this out. I know we're in a nightclub and ostensibly here to enjoy ourselves as well as pull this thing together, but there are things happening here which don't add up.'

'Of course,' said Camille. Richard followed her back to the table so they could talk before the entrée was served. He pulled her chair out for her before taking out a notebook from his jacket pocket.

'So, we have a murdered girl who was dressed and wearing a wig to resemble the cigarette girl, presumably so Emma the cigarette girl could get away from the club without raising suspicion and presumably not to lose her wages.'

'Yes, I've been thinking about that,' Camille answered.

'What were your thoughts?'

'Why would a young woman agree to work an evening for what was likely to be half an evening's wages? Emma would have been paid for one night. If she'd asked someone to do her a favour and stand in for her surely she would have had to share it with the murdered girl?'

'They get tips from the customers don't they?'

Camille frowned. 'Yes, but I can't imagine it would be lucrative...not enough to make it worthwhile for either of them.'

'What are you thinking?'

Camille pursed her lips. 'I'm thinking I would only do something like that for a close friend, someone I thought a lot of. Unless I was being paid over the odds. Let's face it, the girl could have been caught...she was wearing a blonde wig I understand, which would have got her into trouble and lost Emma her job.' Richard nodded. 'And also, didn't any of the girls who were working here last night not notice it wasn't Emma? They know her yet they are pleading ignorance. Emma must have ducked out not long after you had bought cigarettes from her.'

'Was it Emma though, Camille?'

Camille pressed her lips together, then frowned and gazed at him. 'I hadn't thought of that. We don't know Emma. So you think Emma did not put in an appearance at all last night.'

'It would be my strongest guess.'

'You think the girl who served you was in fact the girl who ended up in the moon. Dead.'

Richard nodded. 'I'm afraid I do. What did Cecily say...we rarely take notice of staff. I wouldn't be able to tell you who brought our food to us last night. Could you? With certainty?'

Camille swallowed hard and thought, then shook her head in dismay. 'No, no I wouldn't be able to describe them, not with any certainty. I know what they were wearing, but only because they all wear the same thing. They're wearing the same uniform this evening. It could have been anyone.'

Richard shrugged. 'We have to rely on the statements of the staff and the guests.'

'And what about the guests? You've hardly mentioned them. Was there anyone on the guestlist who would have caused concern?'

'No one who stands out. Most of the guests were in couples; husbands and wives generally, or business partners. My men have been checking them out all day, following up what they claimed when they were questioned. Most of them had eaten the first course on the menu, as had we, which meant they must have been in the actual nightclub when the murder was taking place, or at least when the poor girl was left in the moon, because every table had the starter at virtually the same time. There wouldn't have been enough time for anyone to commit the crime then come back to the table without someone else noticing.'

'What about the Clemences? What are your thoughts about them?'

'I can't help feeling they're not telling us everything. They seem…reluctant to help. I've been wondering why. And, I also consider it's unfeeling of them to open the club this evening after what happened less than twenty four hours ago. They give the impression of not caring, yet Mrs Clemence seemingly cares a great deal for her ex-husband. And she is kind to Aaron Kaplan. Monsieur Gaultiere must be a millstone around her neck. He won't cook the food they serve here, even though the posters outside and the advertisements they put in the newspapers laud him as one of the greatest chefs of the age. I don't doubt he was when he worked at Le Petit Champignon in Manhattan, but he's certainly not doing anything at the moment.' Richard drew in a breath. 'One could say they are defrauding their guests who think they are eating food prepared by a five star chef, when actually the food is coming from a rather non-descript restaurant next door.'

'It proves the point that one can get someone to believe anything if one is convincing enough.'

A silence settled on them while the singer crooned a rather melancholy song, the opposite of the songs she had sung the previous evening. Perhaps she alone held some respect for the demise of the dead girl.

'So who do we have, Richard?'

'Main suspects?'

'Yes.'

'The Clemences, of course. Monsieur Gaultiere. Misceli Tiseu, also known as Gregory Northcutt, the kitchen staff, and of course until we can clear him, Aaron Kaplan.'

'What about the hat check girl and the moon girl. They room with Emma. Would they not know her comings and goings...who she was friends with? Perhaps she shared her thoughts with them. Maybe there was a man on the scene. It would need to be someone important to her to go to all the trouble of finding someone to replace her. I am in agreement with you. I think there is a lot going on here we haven't been given access to. Cecily said exactly the same thing.'

'Cecily?'

'Oh yes. She said the atmosphere wasn't right, and honestly, I know what she refers to. There's an undercurrent. It's almost as though a cloud or a cloak is being drawn over everything and everyone here, and the staff are being not just evasive, but actually obstructive.'

'Richard!' Camille suddenly grabbed Richard's arm. 'There were shots, remember? We weren't sure if they were shots or firecrackers, yet the murdered girl was strangled, was she not? Her neck broken. So...what were the shots we heard? Were they firecrackers, and if so, where did they come from?'

Richard nodded. 'Yes, you're right. I got so caught up in everything that was happening I'd forgotten it. Someone either fired a gun or let off firecrackers, and someone must know who did it.'

'But why would they do it? What could they possibly gain from making a sound that everyone heard just at that moment?'

'Obvious isn't it?'

'Is it?'

Cecily and Constable Lewis rejoined Camille and Richard at the table, slightly breathless, and Camille noticed, holding hands.

'To take everyone's attention from what was really happenin', Madam,' said Cecily who had heard the tail end of the discussion. 'The girl was found in the moon just after the crackers went off. You'd only do that if you were trying to make people think a shot had been fired. Whoever set them off knew everyone would go running into the foyer, and the girl would have been found by then or at least soon after.

'So...if everyone was runnin' towards the foyer because of the firecrackers, or if their attention had been taken by the moon girl screamin', it would have given someone else time to get away. Me and Russell think they could have been a diversion. We've been talking about it, and Russell mentioned the firecrackers.'

Camille raised her eyebrows. 'Russell?'

Cecily's gaze wandered to Constable Lewis, and his gaze wandered to the other side of the room. 'Er, Constable Lewis, Madam. His name is Russell.' Camille saw Cecily surreptitiously release Constable Lewis's hand.

'So you think there was a deliberate diversion away from what had happened in the foyer so the killer could get away without anyone seeing him.'

'Or her,' said Russell Lewis. 'Or...they simply wanted to draw attention to the girl in the moon to ensure she was found at that particular time.'

Richard shrugged. 'It could very well have been a 'her' so to speak, but I'm rather leaning towards a 'him'.' He threw his hands up. 'Don't ask me why. Just a policeman's hunch.'

'I suppose we must work out what the motive was. What do you say, Richard?' Camille said turning to Richard. 'Love or money...or a combination of the two.'

Richard nodded. 'Certainly. And usually we must look at who had the most to gain from the girl's death.'

'But we can't do that until we know who she is.'

'True.'

'Who was the closest to Emma?' asked Cecily.

'Her friends,' said Russell. 'In the absence of knowing who her family are we must look toward her friends.'

'And her friends are...?'

Russell glanced at Richard. 'It's not the Clemences is it, sir?'

'No, indeed...at least that is what we're being led to believe. The first ports of call must be Millie, the moon girl, and Sadie, the hat-check girl.'

'She ain't no girl,' a voice said, interrupting them. Elsie sat at the table, a glass of champagne in her hand.

'What do you mean, Elsie, she ain't...she isn't a girl? Why do you say that?' asked Camille

'I've just been speakin' to Jeffrey. They've been steppin' out together and 'e reckons she's older than she looks. She's got a kiddie.'

'Where does the child go when she's working, Elsie? How old is the child?'

'He's two...an' 'e goes to some woman what lives in the same 'ouse what Sadie lives in. She takes care of 'im at night so Sadie can work, sleeps there by all accounts. Sadie picks 'im up in the mornin's.'

'Your friend knows Emma?'

'Yeah, he does, and Millie too. They're all rooming together. If one of 'em ain't workin' they 'elp Sadie out with the kiddie.'

'So...how old does Jeffrey say Sadie is, Elsie? He must have some idea.'

"E reckons she's in 'er mid-thirties.'

'She doesn't look it,' answered Camille. 'She doesn't look much older than Millie the moon girl.'

Camille turned to Richard. 'Does it have a bearing on the investigation, Richard?'

'Indeed it does. The relationship between all the women will have a bearing on what happened. I cannot believe they did not know who Emma was seeing or who the other girl was, or even where she came from. They're coming in for questioning tomorrow. It has already been arranged. Millie first, then Sadie. As harsh as it seems they will be thoroughly questioned simply because as we've said they're the closest to Emma, in age too. Then Mr Kaplan who I'm hoping we can eliminate from our enquiries.'

'I hope so too,' said Camille with a sigh. She glanced at Cecily who pulled a face.

'And what if he isn't eli-im-inated, Madam? Who will tell Knolly? I reckon it will break her heart, because I 'ave to say, I fink she still 'olds a candle for 'im.'

'Yes, Cecily. I think she does too. And I do believe her heart is in grave danger of being broken again.'

Chapter 22

The following day, Richard arrived at Scotland Yard almost before the sun came up. He'd had a restless night and wasn't in the best of moods. It was the day of the interviews and he knew it would be exhausting. They were short of staff; police officers had taken holiday owing to them to make the most of the remaining good weather. He sighed as he sat at his desk, longing for a cup of strong coffee to keep him alert.

'Lewis,' he called out of his office door.

Constable Lewis came bursting in through the door, his cheeks red as though he'd been running.

'I suppose you'd like to join me on the interviews today?'

Russell Lewis smiled then tried not to look too eager. 'I think it would be very helpful for me, sir...I'm sure I would learn something.'

'I'm sure you would. And I'm sure I would love a cup of strong coffee to take with me. Make one for yourself. You're going to need it I'm almost sure of it. Today you will hear all kinds of stories, some truthful, some not truthful. The problem is Lewis, we have to sort the wheat from the chaff. And then we have to look at those we think were lying and try to discover why they were lying. You've picked a good day. We're so short of staff my sergeants aren't available, apart from Keen, who between you and me, *isn't*, so it's your lucky day. 'Today we're interviewing Millie the moon girl, Sadie, the hat-check girl, and Aaron Kaplan.'

'D'yer think he's involved, Chief Inspector?'

'My instinct says not, but, as doubtful to you as it may seem, I've been wrong before.' Constable Lewis looked glum. 'So...' said Richard rising from his chair and gathering his notes from his desk, 'go get that coffee, make them large ones, and we'll start.'

The interview room was small and windowless. Richard always thought it had been constructed deliberately stark to intimidate the interviewees, but he couldn't be sure. He knew he didn't like having to interview in this particular room. It made him feel claustrophobic, so he reckoned the crims, the maybe crims, the prostitutes, murderers, petty thieves, vagabonds and anyone else who was suspected of doing something they shouldn't have, would very likely have felt much worse.

Sitting at the table was Millie Spencer, the moon girl. She looked very different from the girl who had been wrapped in gauzy, diaphanous material on the night of the murder, her face painted with silver paint and glitter, her hand clasping a champagne glass as her other hand trailed out of the moon, just above the heads of the guests. Instead, she looked what she was; a young girl of nineteen, skinny, dressed in a plain brown shift, unadorned, with a matching jacket. Her shoes were plain brown pumps. Richard was shocked at the word that sprang to mind when he walked into the interview room...which was, 'dowdy'.

'Miss Spencer,' he said as he sat down, indicating for Constable Lewis to take the chair next to him. 'I see you have no representation.'

She stared at him. 'What's that?'

'A solicitor...a man of letters to speak for you and make sure justice is done on your behalf.'

'Do I need one?'

'That's your decision, Miss Spencer. You may want to take some advice, perhaps from the Clemences.' She nodded and lowered her eyes.

Richard shuffled his papers on the desk in front of him. He looked at the girl from under his eyebrows feeling slightly sorry for her. She looked terrified.

'Right, Miss Spencer. Can you please state your name for the record, and your address.'

'Millie Spencer of No.7 Battersea Court, Whitechapel Road, London.'

Richard inclined his head in thanks. 'You and I are both aware of what happened on the night of the 5th September, just two days ago. A girl who had been strangled and had had her neck broken was found at the Café Bonbon in the structure called The Moon which hangs above the foyer to the premises, the structure in which you yourself usually occupy as an employee of Mr and Mrs Clemence at the Café Bonbon. Is that correct?' Millie Spencer nodded. 'Miss Spencer will you confirm verbally please?' She looked up, frowning, as if she didn't understand.

'You need to say it to confirm what Chief Inspector Owen just said is right,' said Constable Lewis. Richard gave him a sideways look but said nothing.

'Yes, that's right,' Millie Spencer said in a small voice. 'I know what happened, and I am the moon girl who works for Mr and Mrs Clemence at the Café Bonbon.'

Richard nodded and smiled. 'Thank you, Miss Spencer.'

'What can you tell me about the girl who was found?'

Millie looked askance. 'Nothin'.' She shook her head, her gaze going from Richard to Constable Lewis then back again.

'You didn't know her?'

Millie shrugged. 'I thought I did, but then it turned out I didn't. I thought it was Emma...it looked like Emma with 'er blonde 'air and everythin', but it weren't 'er was it?'

'And you have no idea at all of who the girl was, or how she came to be in the club in the role of the cigarette girl, or why Emma would have not been present.' Millie bit her lip. 'Miss Spencer, it is in your best interests to tell me the truth. You are a suspect,' she looked up and gasped, 'and as a suspect you could be charged with murder, aiding and abetting, or obstruction, the list is endless.'

'I want to tell the truth,' she said, as a large tear ran down her cheek.

'Then I advise you to do so.'

Millie nodded and swallowed hard. 'Emma was seeing someone, but we don't know who it was. She wouldn't tell anyone. She said it had to be a secret because it would cause all kinds of trouble if it got out.'

'Trouble with whom?'

'I dunno, she never said.'

'Do you think the girl who was found in the moon was a friend of hers?'

'She did 'ave other friends besides us. She was that kind of girl, popular like. Not like me.' She looked down at her hands which were clasped tightly in her lap. 'I don't 'ave any friends outside of Emma and Sadie. I'm too busy trying to earn money to give to me Ma. She's got four kids younger than me. Our Pa went out one day and never came back. Left 'er properly in the lurch he did. We've not 'eard from 'im since. Me Ma di'nt have no work so she 'ad to take in washing and mending. She works every hour God sends, so I give 'er what I can from me wages.' Millie shook her head as more tears ran down her cheeks. 'And now this. I never thought it would end up like this. For two pins I'd leave, but there ain't anyone willing to give me even two pins so I 'ave to stay there, that's until the Clemences get rid of me.'

'Why do you think they'll get rid of you?'

She shrugged. 'They can do what they like, can't they. There ain't no rules. The longer they keep us the more we owe them. They don't want to get to know us or get close to us. It's why Mr Clemence didn't know who the girl was. She could a been anyone. And they like new faces. If someone else comes along what's prettier, with more, yer know,' she indicated her body with not a little embarrassment, 'less skinny prob'ly, they'll get rid of me in the blink of an eye.'

'What about Mrs Clemence?'

'She's all right, more caring than 'im.' Millie nodded to confirm what she was saying. 'Yeah, I like 'er. She's straight talking all right, but, she's an American ain't she. She says what she finks. Some of the fings she says makes us laugh, but no one can get away wiv anythin', sure as eggs is eggs. She's on the ball. That's what Sadie says.'

'And what about Sadie?'

She glanced up at Richard. 'What d'yer mean?'

'Tell me about her.'

She pulled a face. 'Not much to tell. We room together, wiv Emma.'

'Doesn't she have a child?'

Millie nodded. 'Yeah, a little boy, Sean.' She smiled, for the first time, Richard thought. It transformed her face, but he couldn't help wondering if she had much to smile about. 'He's a lovely little boy, just two. Does as 'e's told an' all, not like my brothers and sisters. Little hooligans they are. When I'm not working I take care of 'im so Sadie can work. I don't charge 'er or nothin'. 'E's no trouble, no trouble at all.'

'Does Emma take care of him too.'

Millie chuckled. 'Don't be daft. Emma don't do fings like that. She says she ain't got a maternal bone in 'er body. She don't even pay 'er own rent.'

Richard raised his eyebrows. 'She doesn't?'

'Nah.'

'So who does pay her rent?'

'I ain't got a clue. I never ask questions like that, not anymore. Sadie asked her once and she proper bit Sadie's 'ead off, so we know better now.'

Richard turned to look at Constable Lewis, his eyebrows raised. 'Do you have any questions, Constable Lewis?'

Russell Lewis eyed the girl sitting in front of him. He couldn't help but feel sorry for her, but there was something about her that he wasn't quite sure about.

'What would you do for money, Miss Spencer?' he asked her. Richard looked away, thinking the lad had more nous than some of his sergeants.

Millie frowned. 'Wot d'yer mean, what would I do fer money?'

'Well, it sounds like you and your family haven't had an easy time of it.'

'No, we 'aven't, but I wouldn't kill a girl for it. I wouldn't kill anyone for it. I couldn't...do anything like that.'

'But if you knew who had, and they'd paid yer to keep quiet, would you?'

Millie Spencer suddenly seemed flustered. 'Nah, course I wouldn't. I wouldn't take money from someone for something like that. Against the law innit?'

'Yes, of course,' said Richard. 'But some might think it's far enough removed from the actual crime to make them think they had nothing to do with it which of course is wrong. Nothing could be further from the truth. Anyone who has any dealings with this particular crime will receive the full weight of the law.'

Millie looked down at her hands, her fingers linked together in her lap, and shrugged.

Chapter 23

'Well, Lewis? What are your thoughts?'

Richard and Constable Lewis were sitting in his office with yet another cup of coffee, discussing the interview that had just taken place with Millie Spencer.'

'I want to believe she's telling the truth, sir.'

Richard nodded. 'We always want to believe that, Lewis.'

'But I don't think she is.'

Richard nodded again. 'Why so?'

'Her need for money. When you're in a position like she is, at least, like her mother is, with four kids to feed, I've 'eard people say they would do anything for money...within reason.'

'I've heard it too, and perhaps if we ourselves were in such a position we may very well do the same thing.'

'That's what I was thinking, sir.'

'So, you think she knows more than she's letting on.'

'I'm afraid I do, sir.'

'Right, well...we'll hopefully find out more from Sadie Murphy.'

'She's the next interviewee, sir?'

'She is.'

Richard and Constable Lewis returned to the interview room where Sadie Murphy had taken the seat Millie Spencer had just vacated.

It was the same drill as before, with Richard shuffling his papers on the desk in front of him and the girl sitting opposite, except this girl didn't look nearly so intimidated as Millie Spencer. Sadie wore a bright pink shift dress with a matching pink bolero cardigan. Her shoes were in the wedge style, white on the front, with a rose decoration across the toes.

'Miss Murphy?' She nodded. 'Can you state your name and address please.'

My name is Sadie Murphy. I live at 7 Battersea Court, Whitechapel Road.

'You don't have representation, Miss Murphy.'

'I don't think I need any. I've done nothing wrong. And anyway they cost. I can't afford to hire someone like that, not when I can speak for meself.'

'I detect an Irish accent, Miss Murphy.'

She smiled. 'Oh, aye, I'm originally from Donegal. Wish I was still there an' all. Different to 'ere. Nicer, friendlier. It's still my home even though I ain't been there in years.'

Richard listened carefully, then nodded, looking down at his papers which had nothing on them except the facts of the case, but just gave him the time to think.

'What was your relationship to the deceased, Miss Murphy? The dead girl.'

Sadie stared at him, then at Constable Lewis. 'There *was* no relationship. I didn't know her.'

'You saw her face?'

'Yes. We were asked to look weren't we, to see if we knew her.'

'And you didn't?'

'No, like I said. I didn't know her.'

'Had you ever seen her before, in the Café Bonbon...perhaps she was a friend of Emma's who came around to your lodging house.'

Sadie shook her head. 'Nope.'

'And what about Emma?'

'What about 'er?'

'Have you seen her since the girl's body was found?'

'No. I wish she'd come back from wherever she's gone. She owes me five bob. That's a lot for a girl like me.'

'A girl like you? Describe a girl like you, Miss Murphy.'

She stared at Richard, her eyes narrowing. 'A woman what earns 'er own money and don't expect nothin' from nobody. I don't believe in handouts. I make my own bread.'

'And you have a child?'

'Yeah, what of it?'

'How old?'

'Two.'

'Where's the father?'

She chuckled but with sarcasm. 'Ow the 'ell should I know. Scarpered when he found out I was expecting di'nt 'e?'

'His name?'

'Sorry...ain't prepared to give you 'is name.'

Richard frowned at her. 'Why would that be?'

'Cos it's none of yer business, and cos I don't want yer lookin' for 'im. He's gone and I want 'im stayed gone. I don't want 'im sniffing 'round thinking he owns somethin' of me. My boy don't need 'im and neither do I.'

'Is the boy's father of British nationality.'

She paused to consider the question. Richard saw her eyes flicker so assumed she was about to lie. 'Irish.'

'You're sure?'

'I think I'd know.'

'How do you think the girl's body got up to the moon when you and Miss Spencer were in the ladies room?'

"Ow the 'ell should I know? What I do know is Millie screamed the place down and fair near frightened me to death. Christ, she sounded like a banshee.'

'How long have you worked at the Café Bonbon?'

'Since it opened, about two to three months.'

'And you got Millie the job as the moon girl.'

'You could say that. I introduced her.'

'How did you meet Millie?'

'She was lodging at Battersea Court when I was looking for rooms for me and my boy. It's big enough for three to share.'

'Was Emma already living there?'

'Yeah, she was.'

'How do you get on with Emma?'

Sadie shrugged. 'All right.'

'Just all right?'

'Well we ain't bosom buddies if that's what yer mean. She's too up 'erself, thinks she's better than anyone else.'

'Who's she seeing, Miss Murphy?'

'I dunno.'

'So she didn't tell you she was seeing someone?'

'Yeah, we knew, but she wouldn't say who it was. Said it might cause trouble if anyone found out so it was best we didn't know.'

'Is she seeing Mr Clemence?'

Sadie burst out laughing. 'Are you 'avin' a laugh. Come on, Chief Inspector. You've seen 'im. I don't even know what Louise sees in 'im. He's such a fusty old git.'

'Louise? You call Mrs Clemence by her first name?'

'Sometimes. If she's in a good mood.'

'Do you think the girl was murdered instead of Emma?'

Sadie crossed her arms and gazed at Richard and Constable Lewis. 'I don't think anything. It don't pay to think. I ain't paid to think neither.'

'Have you ever been a prostitute, Miss Murphy?'

She drew in a breath. 'Why you askin' me that?'

'I ask the questions, Miss Murphy. Please answer.'

'When the boy was about two we 'ad no money, and I needed it...well, I 'ad to find a way to get some. No one would give me a job when they found out I 'ad a kid.' She shrugged. 'I did what I 'ad ter do.'

'There's no judgment here, Miss Murphy. We're just trying to get to the truth.'

Sadie's face went red and she gritted her teeth. 'The truth is that Emma is no better than she should be. She uses people, borrows their clothes and their money and don't give 'em back. Dunno why cos she don't even pay her own rent. She 'as more money than I do at the end of the week that's for sure. I'd love to know what she spends it on. She ain't all that.'

'Who does pay her rent?'

"Er boyfriend I 'spect, poor bastard. She's pro'bly takin' 'im for every penny an' all.'

Chapter 24

'Your thoughts, Constable Lewis?'

'On Sadie Murphy?'

Richard bit into a sandwich, cheese, floppy at the edges, and chutney, too vinegary, that he'd bought from the canteen. He pulled a face, one which told Constable Lewis that what he was eating wasn't particularly pleasant. He eyed Constable Lewis's sausage in pastry, wishing he'd chosen something similar, even if the sausage was made from an animal from an indeterminate source.

'Yes, Sadie Murphy. What do you think?'

Lewis shook his head. 'It's not easy is it, sir...working out whether someone is lying or not.'

'No, but it's what we're paid to do. And,' he said as he wiped his hands on a paper napkin, 'it gets easier.' He took a gulp of tea to wash down the questionable repast he'd just eaten, another purchase from the canteen, and wiped his mouth on the napkin. 'I'm just interested in what you think, as an inexperienced interested party if you will.'

'Well,' said Lewis, his mouth full of sausage and pastry, crumbs sitting on his chin, ' she's a different prospect to Millie Spencer. More upfront. Willing to fight her corner. Millie seemed to be a more pliable personality, placid...if that's the right word, like she would have agreed to anything just to make it all go away.'

Richard nodded. 'My thoughts exactly, Lewis.'

Russell Lewis straightened in his seat looking pleased. He attacked his sausage in pastry with great gusto, his confidence increasing by the day. Emboldened by Richard's agreement of his observations and assessment, he decided to go further in his evaluation.

'I think she's the sort who would like to keep people at arm's length; yer know, on a bit of elastic. And, sir, I think she knows more than she's letting on.'

'People usually do, Lewis. It would be wrong to assume suspects tell us everything at the first interview. It is often the second, or even the third interview where they inadvertently let something slip, usually because they can't remember what they told us in the previous interviews. It's usually the moment when we get our man...or woman.'

'You don't think it was a woman who murdered the girl do you, sir?'

'I'm not sure a woman would have been strong enough to inflict those injuries, but it doesn't mean a woman is not involved somewhere along the line. The most important thing right now is to find Emma because I feel sure she will throw some light on the matter. She will know who the murdered girl is. The girl was obviously at Café Bonbon to take Emma's place, I suspect because Emma was doing something she perhaps shouldn't have been, or had arranged a meeting she couldn't get out of.'

Lewis frowned. 'What kind of meeting?'

Richard drew in a breath. 'One which has not yet come to an end, Lewis, otherwise Emma would have shown up by now.'

Chapter 25

Aaron Kaplan sat quietly in the interview room waiting for Chief Inspector Owen to arrive. He had been anticipating the interview with some reflection as it took him back to another time when he was questioned about another murder; that of his wife, Isabel.

Of course, he knew if the police, and the Clemences, and their employees were looking for a scapegoat for the recent murder, they would very likely point the finger at him, not so much Louise Clemence who he looked upon as a friend of sorts, but certainly her ill-fitting husband. He always thought of Ivor Clemence as ill-fitting because that's exactly what he was, not suited to the life he was currently leading as the owner of a nightclub, and certainly not suited as Louise Clemence's husband. Aaron shook his head, wondering at how things turned out.

He sat in the uncomfortable metal chair with his feet firmly on the ground, encased as they were in boots that had probably seen myriad pairs of other men's feet, his hands resting gently in his lap. From grey, lank-haired head to ill-shod foot he was the epitome of quiet dejection. Society, life, those he thought he could trust, and even the universe, had not been kind to Aaron Kaplan, and his down-at-heel, dishevelled appearance betrayed the negative experiences in his life.

His unwashed hair rested on the dusty shoulders of his jacket, a garment procured from a clothes stall on the Whitechapel Road and where one of his friends from the Jewish community had resided for many years. The shop dealt in second-hand clothes. He didn't know who had worn it before him; the price Aaron had paid, just three pennies, had led him to believe the jacket had been bought and sold many times. No one but he had seen and recognised the label on the inside of the jacket, Stein and Bertorelli. He had been lucky. The jacket had been brought in in a bundle of clothing and hadn't been sorted. He was sure, had his friend seen the label, he would have been asked to pay much more.

Aaron Kaplan knew Stein and Bertorelli well. He, and his father and brothers had been patrons of the celebrated tailors in Saville Row and had had many a suit made by them. It had amused him to think the jacket he now wore, one which had been purchased for just three pennies, could have been one of theirs.

He glanced up, interrupted in his reveries by the arrival of Chief Inspector Richard Owen and a young constable, who entered the small and rather stuffy interview room. Richard sat opposite Aaron and indicated for Constable Lewis to stand by the door. Lewis did as he was bid, standing by the door with feet slightly apart, hands clasped in front of him. The constable who had stayed with Kaplan since his arrival at Scotland Yard left the interview room.

Richard did his best not to stare at the man sitting in front of him, fascinated though he was by the person sitting on the opposite side of the table placed between them. He got his papers in order, then leant on it with his forearms.

'Thank you for attending this interview, Mr Kaplan. Is there anything you need...a cup of tea perhaps?' Kaplan shook his head. 'Could you please state your name and address for the record.'

'Aaron Gabriel Kaplan of no fixed abode, although currently residing in the basement of three commercial buildings on Chancery Lane.'

'Do you know why you've been called for interview, Mr Kaplan?'

Aaron Kaplan looked down at his hands. 'I assume it's because of the poor young woman whose life was taken at the Café Bonbon. And because I was questioned extensively twenty years ago when the police were looking into the murder of my wife, Isabel Kaplan, for which I was completely exonerated. You want to know if I could do such a terrible thing.'

Richard admired his frankness. He thought it best to be as equally frank.

'Could you?'

Aaron Kaplan shook his head slowly. 'No, Chief Inspector Owen. To take the life of another goes against everything I promised in my Bar Mitzvah when I was thirteen years old. We uphold the sanctity of life, we do not take it from others, regardless of their faith, their gender, or their station in life.' He raised his rheumy eyes and met Richard's across the table. 'I am of the Jewish faith, Chief Inspector. Nothing will change that. My circumstances do not dictate my beliefs.'

'And what are you circumstances, Mr Kaplan?'

Aaron Kaplan pulled a sardonic smile and held his gnarled, trembling hands out to the sides. 'As you see.'

Richard nodded and looked down at his papers. A surge of sorrow went through him which almost brought tears to his eyes. It shook him, this depth of feeling, the deep sympathy he held for this man who had fallen on hard times. Richard observed that even through the dishevelled and world-weary appearance, Aaron Kaplan had once been a handsome and upright man who was still broad in the shoulders and carried himself, albeit in a somewhat stooped fashion, with dignity.

'I'm interested in your thoughts, Mr Kaplan, as to what happened at the Café Bonbon.'

'Why?' Aaron Kaplan frowned. 'Is it because of what happened to my wife? You think I know about murder, about killing, the brutality of man against man?'

'No, Mr Kaplan. You have been the caretaker of three shop buildings in Chancery Lane for some time. I appreciate you live and work apart from the other members of staff, but I'm curious about your thoughts. Surely, with living on the premises, and an apparent friendship with Louise Clemence, you must hear things, see things perhaps others would not notice.'

Richard turned to Constable Lewis and indicated for him to make coffee. Lewis nodded and left the room.

'I am the caretaker of three commercial premises, Chief Inspector, and that is all I am.' He pulled his mouth into an upside down crescent. 'They tell me nothing. Why would they?' He held his hands out expansively once again. 'I'm no one.'

'But you have opinions, surely?'

Kaplan placed his hands on his knees and chuckled. 'I have a certain amount of intelligence, Chief Inspector, so yes, I have an opinion, although I am not usually requested to profess it. No one is interested in what I think.'

Richard smiled. 'Well, here's your chance, Mr Kaplan. Your opinion is as important as anyone else's. I'd like to hear it.'

Kaplan nodded slowly. 'Is everyone to be questioned?'

'Of course.'

'The new maintenance man?'

Richards stomach churned. 'Yes, why do you ask?'

'I don't trust him.'

Constable Lewis returned at precisely that moment with a tray of coffee mugs, and a report which he placed in front of Richard.

'From forensics, sir.'

Richard nodded and took a mug of coffee from the tray, pushing it towards Kaplan as he read the report. He raised his eyebrows and the information contained within, then placed the report face down on the table. He turned his attention back to Aaron Kaplan.

'May I ask why you don't trust him? Has he given you reason?'

Kaplan sniffed, then took the coffee mug from the table. He took a long gulp and made a noisy swallow. 'I imagine a lot of your decision and machinations when you are considering a suspect are made because of your gut instinct?'

Richard inclined his head. 'One gets used to the messages sent to us by our gut, so yes, I do rely on gut instinct much of the time.'

'Well, I am the same. I have instincts, and my instincts have told me that all is not well in the particular premises under which I live, partly because of that man, the new maintenance person Ivor Clemence employed in his infinite wisdom.'

'In what way is all not well?'

Kaplan shrugged. 'I feel Mrs Clemence is a good woman, a little outspoken perhaps which seems to be the fashion of the day, but with a good heart.'

'Her husband?'

'Not so much.'

Richard raised his eyebrows. 'Why?'

'He has proclivities. He pretends he has no interest in the staff, yet he insists on interviewing the young girls who come for jobs. Louise

Clemence allows him to do it because he has insisted he is responsible for the hiring of staff. It was he who hired the Italian.'

'The maintenance man?'

'Indeed. Louise Clemence is the one who actually manages the Café Bonbon, not him. She knows what she is doing, was brought up within an entrepreneurial family, a family who owned nightclubs and restaurants. He does not know what he is doing. He is swayed by a pretty face, a shapely appearance, and a sob story.' Richard nodded but said nothing, hoping Aaron Kaplan would continue. 'I am almost invisible to those who work for the Clemences, and the Clemences themselves, but I am aware of plenty, not because of gossip, because I assure you, Chief Inspector, no one gossips with the caretaker. It is my instinct, which in all honesty is not always welcome. Sometimes I don't want to know.'

'Who do you think killed the girl, Mr Kaplan?'

Kaplan shrugged his dusty shoulders. 'I have no idea, but I know it was not me. I have no motive, no reason to want to hurt a young woman I did not know.' He shook his head. 'These places, they bring out the worst in people. They feed into the basics of human nature. Anything goes. Any behaviour is acceptable.'

'Who *do* you trust?'

Kaplan inclined his head to one side and thought about it.

'Apart from myself, Louise Clemence and Monsieur Gaultiere. They have both shown me kindness, offered me a place to stay. Monsieur Gaultiere brings food down to the basement for me and we talk about our lives.' He shook his head again. 'Why Mrs Clemence did not stay with him is a mystery. He is a nice man. He tries to be arrogant and hard, but I have seen him cry, particularly over the girl who died of food poisoning in the

Manhattan restaurant where he was Head Chef. He has still not learnt to accept that what happened was an accident.'

'Who do you not trust?'

'The so-called maintenance man as I have said, and Mr Clemence who has never given me a kind word or wondered who looks after his building when there is no one else here. Underneath all that buffoonery and wide-eyed innocence, and false friendliness, I believe there to be an unpleasant man.'

'Is there anything else you can tell me that might help me in my investigation?'

Aaron Kaplan was silent for a moment. He gazed at Richard as though wondering if he should say what he wanted to say. He shrugged, to himself rather than Richard, as though his contemplations had made his mind up for him. His instinct perhaps.

'You are aware, Chief Inspector, that the girl Emma is Louise Clemence and Monsieur Gaultiere's daughter.'

Richard was stunned. He sat back in his chair and reached for the cigarette packet he had left on the table. He offered one to Kaplan who refused, then lit his own, taking a long draw on it. He shook his head with amazement.

'Well.' Richard chuckled, a mirthless sound which said everything he was thinking. 'You certainly know how to drop a bombshell, Mr Kaplan.' He narrowed his eyes. 'I was not aware of it.'

Kaplan looked surprised. 'They did not tell you? I wonder why?'

'I'm wondering the same thing myself.' Richard frowned. 'Is it common knowledge?'

Kaplan shook his head. 'No.'

'Why?'

'Louise Clemence said it wasn't necessary for others to know. That it might put her daughter at a disadvantage with their other employees.'

'In what way?'

'Financially I think. She shares rooms with young Millie, and Sadie the hat-check girl. Mrs Clemence pays her rent as well as her salary, while the other girls must live on what they earn and any tips they receive.'

'So, jealousy then?'

Kaplan nodded. 'I suppose it was in her mind.'

'It didn't work. The girls know about her having her rent paid for her. I think it has caused some consternation amongst them.'

Kaplan chuckled. 'Young girls these days. So acquisitive, so envious. It only leads to unhappiness. I wish I could tell them.'

Chapter 26

Richard walked Aaron Kaplan to the double doors which fronted the Scotland Yard building and led out onto the embankment next to the Thames. The view from the doors changed with the seasons and could make one's heart soar, or send it plummeting to the very depths of melancholy, depending on whether the sunbathed The Embankment and Thames in sunshine, or enveloped it in fog. The last days of summer had brought with it an odour from the river, of old rope, discarded oyster shells, the dung from the horses which pulled the dray carts, and worse. It caused Richard to shiver, as though someone had walked over his grave.

The greyness of the murky water and the rather grey day perfectly matched Richard's state of mind. He shook Aaron Kaplan by the hand and bade him farewell, watching as the dishevelled, down at heel man walked stutteringly from the building to the path, wishing there was something he could do to help him. Whatever had befallen Aaron Kaplan had devastated his life, had turned it on his head, and changed his future.

Richard had checked Aaron Kaplan's file for a criminal record but found nothing, apart from the fact he had been questioned extensively when his young wife had been found murdered at their Bayswater home. Richard shook his head. How the mighty fall, he thought. The descent from Bayswater to the basement of an old and dusty building in Chancery Lane would have been one which most would not have survived, yet here he was, Aaron Kaplan, clinging onto life no matter how distasteful and unpleasant it had become.

As Richard turned to go back inside the building, a motor car had turned in from The Embankment and appeared through the entrance, a long bonnet, bright yellow Lambda. He grinned to himself thinking if anyone could cheer him up it would be Camille. And only Camille. As she got out of the car she lifted her hand in a wave.

'Are you free for a few minutes, Chief Inspector Owen,' she called.

'Of course, Lady Divine,' he answered, smiling. He watched her closely as she walked towards him. She had allowed her hair to grow a little from the rather severe, fashionable bob she'd worn previously. Her hair now framed her face in soft curls, and made her velvety brown eyes look even larger in her heart-shaped face.

'I see you've just interviewed Aaron Kaplan,' she said on reaching him. He held the door open for her as she went through into Scotland Yard's foyer.

'Yes, he's an interesting man.'

She glanced up at him. 'You think so?' He nodded. 'His situation?'

Richard shrugged then led her through to his office. He requested a tray of tea and biscuits from the constable on duty at the desk.

'I didn't have the heart to ask him.'

Camille glanced at Richard askance as she sat in the chair opposite his. 'Really?'

Richard pulled a face. 'Something has clearly happened in his life, a catastrophe that changed everything. A fall from grace like the one he seems to have experienced would be difficult to accept,' he shrugged again, 'and I understand he came from a wealthy background. Did Mrs Knowles not say as much? There is no wealth there, no support of sustenance, nothing to connect him to his former life.'

'Did you not find out anything about him? I thought it might be helpful.'

Richard took a packet of cigarettes from his jacket pocket and offered it to Camille. She refused. He lit a cigarette for himself and leant back in his chair ruminating over whether he should tell Camille Aaron Kaplan's history.

'There is history there. His wife was murdered many years ago at their home in Bayswater. He was questioned over the murder but had a rock solid alibi.'

Camille gasped. 'Oh, my goodness. How awful.' Richard nodded. 'Do you think he did it?'

'No, but it may point to why he is living the way he does now.' He lent forward and put his elbows on the table, steepling his fingers, deep in thought. 'I am curious. Aren't you?'

'Certainly.' Camille frowned. 'One would have expected him to have received a certain amount of money on her death. Isn't that the way it works?'

'Usually, but it seems it has not done Aaron Kaplan any good.'

'I would like to help him, Richard, for Knolly's sake as much as anything else. I think she still cares about him, although what she would think about the way he is currently living is anyone's guess. She has a huge heart of gold, but she should know about his wife. I think it's something I should look into before offering any assistance, or even before Knolly meets him again, if it's what she chooses to do.'

The door opened and the constable from the desk brought in a tray with two rather chipped and stained mugs, and a plate of not very appetising biscuits was placed on the desk between them. Richard looked up at the constable and tutted.

'Constable Fields, have you ever heard of knocking before you enter a room?' The constable looked contrite and turned to go. 'And,' continued Richard, 'for God's sake take some money from the petty cash box and buy some decent crockery. I could use these for stubbing out my cigarettes.'

'Yes, sir,' answered the poor, beleaguered constable who closed the door quietly behind him.

Carrie pulled a "sorry for him" look. 'Poor young man,' she said with a giggle.

'He's not a poor young man. He's a police officer with Scotland Yard. At the very least he should know not to serve tea in chipped mugs to a Lady of the Realm.'

Camille pressed her lips together. 'Not for much longer,' she sighed.

Richard's eyes widened as Camille reached for one of the mugs and sipped from it. 'What do you mean?'

'Harry's getting married again after our divorce.'

Richard's mouth dropped open. 'Is that seemly? Do people marry again right after a divorce is granted?'

'The aristocracy do what they like whenever they wish, Richard. It is clear Harry has not given up on the idea of producing a son and heir for the Divine name, even though he has been told by the medical profession it's unlikely. He has chosen a girl young enough to be his daughter, a chinless wonder who will be pushed about from pillar to post and be expected to do as she is told.' Camille took another sip of coffee. 'I feel sorry for her.'

'Do you know her?'

'I know of her. She's half his age, but it isn't something the aristocracy worry about. Her parents will be crowing with delight no doubt. Poor girl. I hope she knows what she's letting herself in for. Harry is not the man I married. He has changed a great deal; not so flexible, rather embittered I would say.'

Richard shook his head, unable to understand why Lord Divine would even think of giving up a woman like Camille. 'He must be mad,' he said quietly.'

'Perhaps. I must make sure Ottilie doesn't suffer the same fate with some old Lord, Harry has decided to marry her off to. Over my dead body I think the saying goes.'

'I did discover something very interesting from Aaron Kaplan, a piece of information it would seem both the Clemences and Monsieur Gaultiere kept under wraps.'

'Oh? What was that?'

'Emma the hat-check girl is Louise Clemence and Monsieur Gaultiere's daughter.'

Camille's eyes widened in astonishment. 'They were together?'

'They were married. Gaultiere told me when I interviewed him and Louise Clemence confirmed it.'

'Why on earth didn't the Clemences tell you?'

'That will be my next question to them. It's rather an important piece of information to have forgotten I would have thought, so I can only surmise it was withheld deliberately.'

'Why do people think they can get away with withholding something so important?'

'I'm not sure they do. I think they call it chancing their arm. I think the reason they've tried to do so is more important.'

Camille nodded. 'Yes, yes you're right. It could be the key.'

'Hmm, I certainly hope so. This case gets trickier and more convoluted by the day.'

'Do you have many more of the staff to interview?'

'No, just the two members of staff who work with Monsieur Gaultiere in the kitchen. We've had no helpful revelations so far, apart from the fact that the murdered girl was not a blonde as we thought. She was wearing a wig, an extremely convincing one. I would never have guessed. She's actually a brunette.'

'Is that all? I can't imagine it helps you in the investigation.'

'What I got from it is this. Either Emma and the murdered girl organised it between them; that the girl was a stand-in so the Clemences and Monsieur Gaultiere did not realise she wasn't at the Café Bonbon...or, she was a decoy installed by the murderer for the same reason.'

'To make everyone think that Emma was still at work when she had either chosen to be elsewhere, or had been forced to be somewhere else by someone else.'

'Exactly.'

Camille nodded. 'Yes, I understand.' She bit her lip and Richard smiled, loving the look on her face. He knew something was coming. 'Cecily and I have been talking.'

Richard chuckled. 'Yes? Why do I feel frightened of the outcome?'

Camille chuckled with him. 'We've come up with a plan. I think it's a good one, although perhaps a little dangerous.'

'Go on.'

'We think someone should pose as Emma...at the Café Bonbon. Be the cigarette girl.'

Richard narrowed his eyes. 'Why?'

'We think it will shake the monkey out of the tree.'

Richard snorted with laughter. 'I beg your pardon?'

'It's what Cecily said. I don't really know what it means but she does. I assume it means it might bring the murderer out into the open so to speak. To shake their confidence.'

Richard nodded. 'Who did you have in mind for this piece of theatre?' Camille stared at him pointedly. 'Oh...oh, no. Not Mrs West? You can't be serious?'

'It can't be Cecily. One of the things I noticed about the girl who served you with cigarettes was her voluptuous figure. One couldn't help but notice, it was all rather on show. I suppose it's what the girls must do to get customers, as distasteful as it is. One would not want to think of any young girl needing to put themselves on display in such a way, but when one is relying on tips...I suppose one must do what one must do. Elsie is perfectly built for the part.'

Richard nodded. 'Yes, yes, I suppose she is,' he said absentmindedly.'

Camille raised her eyebrows. 'Oh. So you've noticed?'

'Only in a professional capacity of course. Cecily is more...well...more.' He stopped, eying Camille, worried he might say the wrong thing.

'I think you mean boyish.'

'Yes, yes, that's what I meant. A different bone structure entirely.'

Camille pulled a grin. 'So Cecily wouldn't be the best fit to take Emma's place, but Elsie could certainly pull it off.'

'Have you mentioned it to her?'

'Not yet. I thought I would speak to you first. Do you have any objection?'

'Other than the fact it could be dangerous?'

'I suppose so.' Camille frowned. 'But what could go wrong? There will be people everywhere, and we will be there, will we not? She'll be protected.'

'Mm, well on the face of it it's a good idea. If Mrs West will agree then I'll make sure there are constables placed at strategic points at the Café Bonbon. I'll need to speak with the Clemences to get their agreement. They've withheld information from me so I rather feel they owe me some co-operation, and an explanation.'

'I'll go to Elsie's first thing tomorrow. I'll have more chance of persuading her face to face rather than speaking to her on the telephone. She can be a bit cantankerous.'

'Which means you'll appeal to her softer side, her more maternal side.'

'Exactly. And the fact we are friends and friends help each other.'

Richard nodded, thinking he had as yet to come up with a better plan. 'Oh and there's something else about the murdered girl.'

'Oh?'

'Unfortunately, she was pregnant.'

Chapter 27

Camille and Richard shook hands as she left Scotland Yard. They were both aware they had been the subject of some speculation amongst the constables at Scotland Yard, not least because the switchboard operator often listened in to their conversations and likely gossiped about them, so they had come up with a kind of code, always behaving in a professional manner when at Scotland Yard and on the telephone. Richard smiled warmly at Camille as he held her hand a little longer than was necessary, and she returned it. The attraction between them was as strong as ever, and Camille thought little would be gained by telling Richard that Harry knew about his father's past and had warned her off. It was something for her to think about, but not at this moment.

She wanted to be part of the investigation into the girl's death...her murder. When she had seen the body lying in the moon, a young girl snuffed out in the prime of her life it had sent shivers down Camille's spine. The girl had been in the wrong place at the wrong time...if she had not been there one can only assume it would have been Emma whose demise they would have been investigating. Now they must find out more about Emma, about her friends, those with which she socialised, those whose society she moved in and whether they were people whom any parent would be happy to accept as friends for their children. Camille rather thought this was not the case.

And now they had discovered that the murdered girl was pregnant. Was this significant? Camille thought not, that it was just a coincidence. Then she remembered something Richard often reiterated. He did not believe in coincidences.

Richard reluctantly said his goodbyes to Camille at the entrance to Scotland Yard and watched as she returned to the Lambda, waving as she drove off. He drew in a sigh, wondering if their conversation regarding his past had changed Camille's view of him. He'd like to think not. The news that Harry Divine was to be married shortly after his divorce from Camille had not perturbed him, rather, it had had the opposite effect and led him to believe that perhaps he could hope...hope there was a future for himself and Camille. It must have shaken her, he thought, to discover she was to be so easily replaced, and by a younger woman, yet she did not seem to be moved by it. She's strong, he thought. It's one of the things I love about her.

'Sir?' Richard was startled out of his reverie by Constable Field who had come around to the other side of the foyer desk to speak to him.

'Field?'

'There are some people waiting for you, sir. They asked for you in particular.' He looked uncomfortable. 'Have you seen the front pages of the newspapers this morning?'

Richard frowned and shook his head. 'Do I need to see them?'

'I think you should, before you speak to the people waiting. The front pages have the murder splashed across them with some pretty lurid sketches of what they think happened to the girl in the moon. The headlines are very creative.' The constable swallowed. 'Sir.'

'Creative?'

'Yes, sir.'

'Where are the newspapers?'

The constable winced. 'In the waiting room, sir.'

'Who put them in there?'

'I'm sorry, sir, it was me. It's just that Sergeant Fellowes said it's my job to make sure the waiting room is comfortable for visitors...and I thought, well, newspapers...people like to read them, don't they?'

Richard momentarily closed his eyes and let out a long breath. 'Right, Field. Go into the waiting room and retrieve said newspapers and bring them into my office. I'll have a look at them before I speak to whoever is waiting to see me. Do we know what they want to see me about?'

'A missing person, sir.' Richard inclined his head towards the waiting room and waited for the constable to bring the newspapers into his office.

'Here we are, sir,' said Field, placing the newspapers in front of Richard.

Richard nodded and glanced at the front pages, sifting through them and sighing. It wasn't just the sketches that were lurid. The headlines also took some beating. Some competitive and ambitious reporters had had a field day with the tragedy.

One of the headlines read...**Hey Diddle Diddle, The Police Force Just Fiddles, A Girl Found Dead in The Moon.**

Another read....**The Café Bonbon Makes a Killing as Murdered Girl Leaves Scotland Yard Moonstruck.**

Richard threw the newspapers across the desk.

'Blast!' he cried, then remembered there were people waiting for him to enquire about a missing person. 'When will this ever end?' he said under his breath, knowing with some certainty that crime in London was there to stay.

The people waiting for him were a woman and a girl. The woman was stout in build, her face set in an expression of 'don't mess with me'. The girl was slight with a worried look on her face. Both wore clothes that had seen better days and shoes in need of a polish. The girl's nails were bitten to the quick, something she tried to hide by stuffing them into her palms.

'You wished to speak with me, madam?' Richard said as he entered the waiting room.

The woman stood and folded her arms under her bosom. 'Me girl's missing.'

'Your girl?'

'Me daughter, Charlotte. She goes orf sometimes, but I was expecting her back yesty and she d'int turn up. That's right innit, Brenda?' She turned to the young girl who also stood and moved closely beside the woman, nodding. 'She was due back at ours to start a new job in the bettin' shop on the Latchmere Road in Clapham, but they sent a message sayin' she 'adn't turned up. I waited and waited, fought p'raps she'd gone orf the idea but she d'int come 'ome niver.'

Richard nodded, an uncomfortable feeling settling about his solar plexus. 'Your daughter, Madam. Would you describe her please?' He indicated for them both to sit down again.

'She's about my height, with dark brown hair. She's pretty like. The boys like 'er. She's got a shape if yer know what I mean.' Unfortunately I do, thought Richard.

'Could she have gone off with a boyfriend...or just a friend, someone you're familiar with?'

'A boyfriend?' the woman exclaimed. 'My Charlotte don't 'ave no truck with boys. Sensible she is, got 'er 'ead screwed on.' Not anymore if my hunch is correct, thought Richard.

'How old is Charlotte, Mrs...?'

'Baynes. Me names Sarah Baynes. She's eighteen, just a babe really, but course they grow up so quick these days, they fink they know everythin' don't they, these girls? This is Lucy, me youngest. She's firteen.'

Richard nodded and indicated for the woman and her daughter to sit in the waiting room for a moment longer. 'I won't keep you long, Mrs Baynes. I need to discuss something with one of my officers and I'll be back soon. Would you like a cup of tea? I'm sure one of the constables can rustle one up for you and your daughter.'

Sarah Baynes nodded. 'That would be very nice,' she said, smiling. 'And a biscuit would go down a treat too.' Richard pulled a small smile thinking she might change her mind once she'd tasted the stale offerings he and Camille had been given that morning.

Richard went back to his office and mulled over what Sarah Baynes had told him. He knew he now had the unpleasant job of telling her a girl matching Charlotte Baynes description had been found murdered at the Café Bonbon, a task he knew every officer on the force hated.

He picked up the receiver from the telephone on his desk and asked to be put through to the mortuary. He needed to organise a visit for Sarah Baynes to identify the body of a girl lying on a trolley with her neck broken. He hoped it wasn't Charlotte, but his policeman's instinct was telling him otherwise.

'At least we have a name,' he said under his breath. 'At last we know who that poor girl was.'

Chapter 28

When Sadie Murphy left Scotland Yard after her interview with Richard, she cut through Derby Gate onto Parliament Street, which took her to Great George Street, then onto Horse Guards Road. She walked quickly, her hat trembling on her head as she hurried. Her destination was St James' Park where she had arranged to meet Millie Spencer near the drinking fountain where there was also a tea stall, somewhere they could sit and discuss what had happened during their interviews and what had been said. Sadie spotted Millie sitting on one of the seats near the stall. She looked pale and dejected and hadn't bothered to get herself a cup of tea in all the time Sadie had been at Scotland Yard.

'D'int yer get yerself any tea, Millie?'

Millie shook her head. 'D'int feel like it. D'int want to have tea on me own. Thought I'd wait fer you to arrive.'

'D'yer want one now?'

'Yes please.' She fumbled about in her bag for some coin but Sadie didn't wait, and went directly to the stall where she ordered tea and cakes for two. She waited for the stallholder to pour the tea and put the cakes onto a pretty plate before taking them over to the rather wobbly wrought iron table where Millie was sitting. 'My treat,' she said, smiling at the younger girl. 'You look proper pale, Millie. Buck up now. Get this down yer.'

'I dunno about eating cake,' said Millie. 'I feel proper sick,' she cried. 'It was 'orrible bein' in that room with a flippin' Chief Inspector and the other one, bein' asked questions like that. 'E 'ardly gave me time to answer a question before he fired another one at me. I felt like a criminal.'

Sadie picked up her cup and took a careful sip of the hot liquid. 'What did 'e ask yer,' she asked Millie, staring at her over the rim of her cup.

Millie shrugged. 'I 'spect 'e asked you the same fings, about Emma, where did I think she'd gone...who did I think would 'ave killed 'er. That kind of thing.'

'And what did you say?'

Millie looked at Sadie, her eyes filling with tears. 'That I d'int know nuffink, cause really I don't, do I? I don't know where Emma is. I thought she was at the Café Bonbon same as us.'

'Did yer know 'er friend?'

Millie shook her head. 'No, did you?'

'No...I didn't, but I just don't understand why Emma didn't tell us she was goin' to ask the girl to stand in fer 'er. That's the trouble with Emma...too many bloody secrets. She couldn't even be honest wiv us. Pain in the bloody arse. I reckon she's orf wiv some bloke somewhere. I'll 'ave 'er when I get me 'ands on 'er. She still owes me five shillings. Like I can afford fer 'er not to pay me back.'

'What did they ask yer?'

Sadie frowned. 'Who?'

Millie glared at her. 'Yer know who, the police, that Chief Inspector bloke, the one what looks right through yer as though he can see right inside yer.'

'Same as you.'

'What did yer say?'

'Same as you I expect.'

Millie picked up her cup and sipped the cooling beverage. 'And what was that?'

'Bloody 'ell, Millie, you're beginning to sound like the police.' Millie slammed her cup down onto the saucer, rendering the tiny piece of crockery in two. 'Now look what you've done,' spluttered Sadie. 'We'll 'ave ter pay for that now. Well, you can. You was the one what broke it.'

'What did yer say to 'em, Sadie?' cried Millie, ignoring the broken saucer. 'I need to know. If we told 'em somethin' different they'll be after us and I can't go through it again. I was nearly sick on the desk I was that frightened.'

'I dunno what you're gettin' like that with me for,' Sadie cried, looking cross. 'It ain't my fault.'

'Ain't it, Sadie? Then tell me whose fault it is.'

Sadie leant forward and snarled at Millie. 'We d'int kill the bloody girl. We d'int murder 'er did we?'

'No, we didn't, but the police don't know that. Until they find out who did they'll be watching us. They're prob'ly watching us now.' Millie looked over her shoulder and shivered. 'I din't know it was going ter be like this. I thought it would be easy, but it's all gone wrong.' She looked back to Sadie. 'It weren't werf it. I wish I'd never got involved. And what I 'ad ter do, God,' she closed her eyes and swallowed hard, pulling a face of disgust, 'it were bloody 'orrible. And it weren't even 'er were it? It were some girl who we don't even know. What was the point of it, Sadie?'

Sadie placed her cup carefully on the saucer and sat back in her chair, folding her arms across her stomach. 'There was every point, Millie,' she said, her voice hard. 'There's always a point.'

'But I didn't know what the point was,' Millie cried through a fresh fall of tears. 'Nobody told me.'

'That's cause yer didn't ask the right questions. You just accepted it. You had the money didn't yer, bird? You took it and asked nothing.'

'I need it for me Ma. She's got nothin' and all those mouths to feed. I didn't have a choice. I never 'ave a choice.'

Sadie shrugged. 'Well, there you are then. You were satisfied, and if it 'ad gone to plan we'd be laughing now, and stuffin' our face with tea and cake with not a care in the world. Sometimes things go wrong, but they can be rectified.'

Millie swallowed hard and wiped her eyes with the back of her hand. 'Rectified? What does that mean?'

'It means we keep goin' until the job is done.'

Millie shook her head. 'No...not me. I'm done. I'm not doin' this again.'

'Yer 'ave to finish the job, Millie. We was given a job ter do and we must finish it, otherwise it won't just be the police on yer tail.'

'Will 'e come after us?'

'Sure 'e will, as sure as eggs is eggs. He'll want 'is money's worth, will he not? Wouldn't you if you'd paid someone ter do a job. Yer'd want the job done wouldn't yer? You're frightened of the police. They're nothing compared to 'im.'

Millie moved to the edge of the chair, her expression desperate, her eyes roaming across Sadie's face. 'But...but I did me job. I did what was asked of me.'

Sadie leant forward and patted Millie's knee. 'Yes, yer did, and you was very brave, but the job ain't finished. You was given a lot of money for a girl of your age.' She sat back. 'Sorry, Millie, but you're in this right up ter yer neck, so you are. There's no way out of it.'

'Will we go to the noose if they think it was us? We will, won't we? We'll be hanged as murderers and my Ma and the kids will end up dying of starvation. It'll be all my fault.'

Sadie shrugged. 'I don't know what will happen. All I know is she 'as to be got rid of.'

'Another murder?' Millie whispered. Sadie nodded her head once.

Millie bowed her head and allowed the tears coursing down her face to drop onto her hands that were knotted together in her lap.

'What do we have ter do, Sadie? 'Ave yer spoken to 'im?'

'That I have. He knows it wasn't our fault it didn't go as planned.'

'Why can't 'e just forget about it? What difference will it make?'

Sadie pursed her lips. Her patience with Millie was wearing thin and she couldn't understand why the girl was asking so many questions.

'Look, 'e means something to me all right?'

Millie frowned. 'What d'yer mean, he means something to yer?'

'Him and me. We've got an understanding.'

'Yer never said.'

'I don't 'ave ter say. It's my business and none of yourn.'

Millie shook her head, thinking she was being enveloped in whatever Sadie had in store for her and she didn't want to be. She wanted to go back to being the moon girl like she was before, just giving her Ma what she earned and forgetting about it. Life was so much easier. The money she had been given for the part she'd played in whatever Sadie and her bloke were up to hadn't been worth it. She had hoped with all her heart the girl had been killed by mistake, but as time went on her confidence had been shaken and she felt increasingly it had been part of the plan, the part she hadn't been party to.

Sadie had clearly kept it from her...deliberately, she had no doubt. Millie's eyes flicked towards her, acknowledging at last this was a woman she could not trust.

'And what if I say I don't want ter be part of it anymore...that I want out?'

'Yer can't.'

'Why?'

'Still got the money 'e gave yer 'ave yer. You'll need ter give it back.'

'But I did what 'e asked. And the money's gone to me Ma, yer know that.'

Sadie stood and brushed cake crumbs off her skirt.

'D'yer know what, Millie. I wish you 'adn't been part of it an' all. You're proper getting' on my nerves wiv yer constant complaining.' She leant forward at the waist, her hands on her hips, her mouth pulled into a snarl. 'You'll do as yer told, d'you understand?' Millie nodded, her face the picture of misery.

Sadie left her and walked out of the park, making her way to their lodgings. She shook her head, then kicked a stone at a bird in her annoyance with the girl, wishing she'd not involved her. She did it out of the goodness of her heart, knowing the girl needed money for her family. She tutted with annoyance.

'Yer just can't 'elp some people,' she said under her breath.

Chapter 29

'What did 'e say, Madam? Chief Inspector Owen? Did 'e 'ave anythin' to tell yer about the case?'

Cecily hung up Camille's duster coat in the wardrobe after giving it a brush, and stowed the matching shoes in the box at the bottom amongst all the other boxes. Camille sat at her dresser and removed the pins from her hair, then lit a cigarette and relaxed back into the chair.

'He did indeed, Cecily. And some rather surprising information too.'

Cecily sat on the ottoman, waiting for Camille to pass the information on, her hands between her knees in her default position which always made Camille smile.

'The missing girl, Emma, is Louise Clemence and Monsieur Gaultiere's daughter.'

Cecily gasped. 'Was they married, Madam?'

'They were.'

'So what 'appened?'

Camille drew on her cigarette and frowned, looking into the distance. 'I'm not sure we know that yet.'

'So why didn't they tell Chief Inspector Owen before?'

Camille shrugged. 'Who knows. It was Aaron Kaplan who told Chief Inspector Owen.'

Cecily shook her head. 'Goodness.'

'Also, the murdered girl was pregnant. Chief Inspector Owen got a report from forensics this morning.'

Cecily's hands flew to her mouth, her eyes filling with tears. 'Oh, Madam, no. How terrible. Both of 'em dead. Who would do such a thing?'

'That's what we aim to find out, Cecily.' Camille stubbed her cigarette out in the ashtray and leant towards Cecily. 'I told the chief inspector about our idea and he has agreed.'

Cecily nodded, still overcome by the news that the murdered girl was pregnant.

'I think it's the only way, Madam. We know that don't we? We've done it before. The only way to get to the truth is to get inside what's 'appening. Get in amongst 'em. Someone will let something slip.'

'I wish it was you who was to be the new Emma, Cecily. Elsie can be so erratic sometimes.'

'But Mrs West looks the part, don't she, Madam? I mean...' she looked down at her chest, 'with the best will in the world, and even with a few socks shoved down there, I don't think I could carry that off. And me face ain't right neither.'

Camille tutted. 'No, you've got a point. Elsie's decolletage should have a square named after it, it is so prominent. And with her lustrous blonde hair she could pass as Emma, although she'll have to do some work with cosmetics. Emma is only nineteen. I think Elsie's teenage years are way behind her, although I won't tell her that. We need her to do this for us. Flattery goes a very long way with Elsie.'

'It's nice to see yer, Camille,' said Elsie as she brought in a tray of coffee and some petit fours made by her cook. 'Cookie made these,' said Elsie, cramming one into her mouth before offering one to Camille. 'My Rose loves 'em. So do I.'

'So I see,' said Camille, chuckling. 'You're lucky you don't have to watch your figure with the fondness for sweet things you have.'

Elsie chuckled with her. 'I let others watch my figure, Camille, if yer know what I mean.'

Camille did. 'How *is* Nathanial Fortesque-Wallsey? I haven't seen him recently.'

'He's all right. Gettin' deeper into 'is politics now he is. Makes me proud, it really does. I've bin there a few times yer know, to the 'Ouse. We go in the bar after all the talkin' what they do, and mix with the toffs. Nathanial says we 'ave to circulate and make friends so when he puts up an idea for 'em all to consider they all vote in the way 'e wants. It's 'ow it works apparently.'

'So they don't vote for something because they think it's the right thing to do. More because they like the person who mooted the idea?'

'Exactly.'

Camille frowned as she sipped her tea. 'That doesn't sound right.'

Elsie shrugged. 'It's 'ow it works, ducks. It's called netting. You 'ave ter get them into yer net, then they can't get out and they 'ave ter vote for yer, otherwise *you* don't vote for *them* when they put up an idea. Nat says it 'appens all the time. And...I've got some customers from there an' all.'

Camille looked astonished. 'From the House?'

'Oh yes. They're exactly the clientele I want on my premises. They've got money and they know 'ow to be'ave,' she pursed her lips, ' well, mostly. We 'ave 'ad a few instances, but they're few and far between.' She looked at Camille. 'D'int come in yer car then? Yer got a cab I see.'

Camille smiled. 'Darling, you know what it's like in Bucks Row. I'd leave the car outside then discover in the time it's taken for us to have a cup of tea and a biscuit the wheels have gone, along with the steering wheel, the windscreen wipers and anything else they could unscrew. Please don't be offended.'

'Oh, I ain't. I know what they're like around 'ere. I live 'ere don't forget.'

'Have you ever thought of moving somewhere more salubrious?'

Elsie raised her eyebrows. 'I can't can I? Me business is around 'ere. Everyone knows where I am.' She took a sip of tea. 'There's a brothel in Duke Street yer know.'

Camille looked astonished. 'Really?'

'Course. There's probably one in every street in Fitzrovia and beyond. It's the most subscribed business in the city, and it makes the most money...for the country an' all. I pay me taxes, and anything else I'm expected to pay, and if the other brothels are run prop'ly they're doin' the same. It's why a lot of 'em don't get closed down. Make too much money, see.'

'Did Nathanial tell you that?'

'Yes, 'e did. 'Im and 'is mates in the 'Ouse know where all the brothels are. They make it their business to know.'

Camille rolled her eyes. 'I bet they do.'

'Anyway,' said Elsie, helping herself to a handful of petit fours. 'You din't come 'ere to talk about brothels. What d'yer want?'

Camille pulled a sardonic smile at Elsie. 'There's nothing like getting to the point, darling.'

'No there ain't. I know 'ow much you 'ate comin' 'ere so let's get our cards on the table. You want me ter do something for yer don't yer?'

'It's not just for me.'

'No, it'll be fer 'is nibs an' all won't it? Your Chief Inspector. All right, what's it about?' Camille reminded her about the murdered girl who was found in the moon at the Café Bonbon and the fact that Emma was still missing.'

Elsie frowned. 'So what do yer want *me* ter do?'

'Pretend to be Emma.'

Elsie's eyes widened. 'But you said she's nineteen. I ain't nineteen, nowhere near. Can't yer get your Cecily ter do it?'

Camille looked discomfited. 'As much as I think the world of Cecily, and her sleuthing skills are second to none, she doesn't have the right...' she thought of what Richard had said, 'bone structure.'

Elsie eyed her, then narrowed her eyes when it dawned on her what Camille meant. 'Do yer mean bosoms?'

Camille shrugged. 'I suppose I do, but it's not just that. You're a very attractive woman, Elsie. You have the ability to attract people, men, who will hopefully talk to you, particularly when they've been drinking. We need someone to start talking...about what happened at Café Bonbon, and who they think might have done it. We need to find out why Emma was missing and why the girl who was pretending to be Emma was killed.'

Elsie's mouth dropped open. 'She was pretending to be Emma? And she was killed? And it's what you want me ter do? Don't yer care I might be killed too?'

'Of course I care, and you won't.'

'How do yer know that?' Elsie cried.

'Because you'll be watched and protected...by police officers standing around the club looking like guests, and by me and Richard and Cecily. We'll all be there, making sure you're all right.'

'Bloody 'ell, Camille. You've asked me ter do some things in my time but this takes the cake.' She breathed out a long breath. 'I'm a mother yer know. I've got Rose. She comes first in everything.'

Camille nodded. 'I know.'

'I don't do these things for glory. Cause there ain't no glory. I've yet to receive a medal for anythin'.'

'I know.'

'And if it weren't fer you I wouldn't do it. It's only because yer me friend.'

'I know.'

'Know a lot don't yer?' Camille stayed quiet. 'What's in it fer me?'

Camille thought, scratched her head which she had always told Ottilie not to do because it wasn't ladylike, then thought some more.

'Two tickets on a ship bound for New York. One for you and one for Rose. And a hotel stay in Manhattan.'

Elsie's mouth dropped open and her eyes widened. 'Are you serious?'

'Never been more so. It's our next trip. I'm taking Ottilie. I promised her the trip of a lifetime and I'm terribly curious about America. It seems so...so full of everything. It would be lovely if you and Rose could come.'

'Done.' Elsie held out her hand to Camille. Camille took it and they shook on the deal. 'You tell me what yer need me ter do and I'll do it. My Rose is goin' ter be a travelled woman. I can't believe it. America! When? When will we go?'

'Have you plans for Christmas?'

Elsie pulled a face. 'None I can think of.'

'What about Nathanial?'

"E don't like Christmas, well, 'e's not that bothered by it. Jewish remember. It ain't really on their calendar.'

'I rather thought Christmas in New York would be lovely.'

'Oh, I can't wait,' Elsie cried, clapping her hands. 'Christmas in New York. Ooh, Camille, thank you.'

Camille smiled warmly at her friend. 'It's the least I can do. Are you all right about what I've asked you to do?'

'All right's a bit strong, but...yeah, I'm all right with it? Is there a uniform? I do like a uniform.'

'Yes, and we'll need to tell the owners of the Café Bonbon what we're planning. They'll need to be in on it and approve it.'

Elsie frowned. 'But what if they *are* in on it, properly I mean? What if *they* killed the girl for some reason? It'll tip 'em off.'

Camille sighed. 'I know. I had thought of that. But something's telling me they're not part of it. Louise Clemence is an American businesswoman who has her head on perfectly straight. I just can't imagine she would do anything to harm her business. And Emma is her daughter. Louise was raised in an entrepreneurial family; her father owned clubs and restaurants in New York, and some in London. She works hard and wants Café Bonbon to be a success. I don't think she would do anything to harm its prospects.'

Elsie nodded. 'Is she married? You said she was married to the chef.'

'Not anymore. They divorced but we don't know why. The man she is now married to...Ivor Clemence. Hmm, not sure about him.'

'D'yer want me to work on him?'

It suddenly dawned on Camille. 'Will he not recognise you? You said you thought he was a visitor here.'

Elsie nodded. 'He is, if it's the same person, but 'e goes to Marcie. Says he likes the dusky girls. Bloody creep.' She blinked at Camille. '*You* want ter watch 'im, that's fer sure. I've only met 'im briefly ter tell 'im off about the way he was treatin' my girls, so I reckon there's no danger there. An' what if 'e does recognise me? Don't see why it would matter. Marcie takes his money. I wonder if his wife knows about 'is little trips to Bucks Row? She sounds like the sort of woman who would 'ang 'im up by the balls if she found out.'

'Yes, I believe she would, and who could blame her?'

'When is all this going to happen?'

'We thought tomorrow evening. Are you free?'

'I'll make meself free.' Elsie inclined her head in thought. 'Is Ivor Clemence a partner in the Café Bonbon?'

'I think so.'

'So not in his interests to give the club a bad name then, although men and girls,' she shook her head, 'ain't a good mix in that h'environment. Sometimes men lose control when there's girls about, in more ways than one, 'specially when they're wearing nothing more than a smile and an 'Owdedo. I've seen it wiv me own eyes.' She nodded, more to herself than Camille. 'I'll work on 'im, get 'im talkin'. If 'e does know anythin' I'll find it out. I 'ave means.'

They grinned at each other. 'Oh, I know you do,' said Camille. 'I truly believe you're the only person who could do this. You're my go to for being someone you're not. I don't know what we'd do without you.'

Elsie nodded, smiling. 'I 'ave my uses…and my talents. Ask Nathanial.'

Chapter 30

The Café Bonbon was full to bursting point. News of the murder and the subsequent disappearance of Emma had circulated far and wide thanks to the newspapers who were falling over themselves to come up with the most creative headlines, and those people with a dramatic penchant for lurid details of a macabre nature in their personality, wanted to see exactly where the dead girl had been left.

Richard had despaired when he'd seen the increasingly sensational headlines and had flung the newspapers across his office where they'd hit the door and fluttered like dead moths to the floor. Poor Constable Field had been frightened to show him the latest news. He'd chosen a moment when Richard was out of the office before leaving them on his desk.

'What is wrong with these people?' Richard had cried to no one in particular. 'Isn't it enough that a poor girl has lost her life through no fault of her own? No, it isn't enough. Someone has to make money out of it. I've a good mind to confront the editors of these rags and ask them what the bloody hell they think they're up to. It's just macabre.'

'Any more news?' Camille asked him as they sat at the table which had been earmarked for them so they could see everything going on around them.

Richard pulled out her chair for her, and then one for Cecily before answering. 'Yes, we've had a positive identification of the girl.'

Camille stared at him. 'How on earth did that happen.'

'The other day when you came to Scotland Yard, a Mrs Sarah Baynes was waiting to see me about a missing person, her daughter, Charlotte. She was supposed to begin a new job but hadn't turned up. The owner of the business had contacted Mrs Baynes to find out where the girl was.'

'And the girl in the morgue is Charlotte Baynes.'

'She is indeed.'

'How old?'

'Eighteen, soon to be nineteen. They were planning a birthday surprise for her, nothing too much, her mother said, just a little cake with some candles, and a few friends.' Richard shook his head. 'It was difficult. Extremely difficult. Mrs Baynes had to be taken home in a police car. She could barely stand.'

'Did Mrs Baynes know Emma?'

'No...and said her daughter was an angel and never, and I quote, "had no truck wiv no boys".'

Camille bit her lip. 'Oh dear. She got that wrong didn't she, poor woman?'

'Indeed, and we really need to know who the father is.'

'I suppose it could be significant.'

'It's definitely significant. If the father had found out about Charlotte's pregnancy perhaps he did not approve, wanted out of the situation. It's happened before and I've no doubt it'll happen again.'

Camille closed her eyes momentarily. 'The world is a very wicked place sometimes.'

'Yes,' agreed Richard, but we must also acknowledge there is good in the world too. Whether it's equally balanced I wouldn't like to say, but one hopes it leans towards the good side, that people's finer natures take precedence.'

'Mm. I certainly hope so.' Camille looked across to Cecily. 'You look beautiful tonight, Cecily.'

Cecily blushed. 'Thank you, Madam.'

'Is Constable Lewis here?' Camille asked Richard.

'He is, in the shadows somewhere, keeping an eye on Mrs West.'

'One could hardly miss her,' chuckled Camille. 'I think the uniform Louise Clemence gave her is slightly too small. You can imagine how she looks I expect.'

Richard smiled. 'I don't have to. She's advancing on us as we speak.'

Camille glanced up and there was Elsie in all her glory, the uniform usually worn by a teenage cigarette girl straining across her embonpoint.

'Look at this,' she said, pulling at the tiny blouse. 'One false move and I'll pop out of it. Those girls must be so skinny.'

'You're not exactly big yourself, Elsie,' said Camille. 'Apart from the obvious of course.' Cecily was trying hard to stifle a laugh without much success.

'No, but I've obviously got more than they've got. I reckon I 'ad more than them when I was twelve. Bloody ridiculous.'

'How are you getting on?' asked Camille, eager to move the conversation on.

'Well, apart from muddling up the prices of the cigarettes and cigars, all right.' Camille winced. 'The blokes don't seem to mind I got the prices wrong, and it's usually blokes what come over for cigs. Women don't bother.' She glanced at Richard. 'You interested, Chief Inspector?' Richard blinked at her. 'In me cigarettes, Chief Inspector. Nuffin else. Naughty, naughty.' She shook an admonishing finger at him. Now it was Richard's turn to blush. 'None of that now. Reckon Camille would scratch me eyes out, wouldn't yer, Camille?'

Camille didn't have time to answer as Ivor Clemence approached Elsie and asked her to go to a table where there were diners who wanted cigars. 'No peace for the wicked. Any'ow, I'm gonna start talking to the staff, see if they can throw any light on what 'appened 'ere. Someone must know somefink.'

'I agree,' said Camille. 'Someone knows something. Perhaps we haven't asked the right people.'

Richard shook his head. 'We've interviewed everyone who was on duty that night...apart from Gregory Northcutt, also known as, to me anyway, Miceli Tiseu.'

Camille blinked at him. 'You haven't questioned him?'

Richard shook his head. 'He's been hauled back to prison. So much for giving someone another chance and turning over a new leaf. Sometimes prison doesn't work.'

'I'm not sure it ever does, particularly with people like him. What will you do now?'

'I have to go to Pentonville to question him. Just because he's been sent back to prison, it doesn't mean he wasn't involved in Charlotte Baynes murder in some way.'

Camille nodded. 'I wonder what he did. And he could be working with someone else? Someone who works here?'

'I would say it's almost a given. To set things up the way they were, someone must know something.'

'I hope Elsie is able to find something out, jog a memory perhaps, even that would be helpful. Perhaps someone was here that night who had forgotten something and seeing Elsie in the uniform will help them remember.'

'Hmm. I think seeing Mrs West in the uniform might send someone into shock.'

Camille shook her head. 'She is so game for everything. I cannot fault her, although the offer of two tickets to New York at Christmas might have convinced her.'

Richard stared at her. 'You're going to New York?'

'I promised Ottilie...and Rose would be such good company for her. New York...Manhattan was next on my list. America sounds so exciting don't you think?'

Richard nodded. 'It does. I've always thought so.' He frowned. 'Takes a while to get there.'

'Yes, but it will be part of the adventure. Ottilie gets a long Christmas holiday from her school in Hampshire so I thought I would make the most of it.' She stared at him. 'Why don't you come too?'

Richard swallowed hard. How he'd wanted her to ask him, but he wasn't sure, after the news he'd given her about his past, if she would be willing to overlook it.

'And what about what I told you the other evening, about my father and his associates.'

Camille pursed her lips. 'I'm not asking your father to come to New York, or his associates. I'm asking you. Will you?'

'I have some holiday owing.' He nodded. 'I would love to accompany you.' He smiled. 'Anyway, a woman like you shouldn't travel alone. Too many cads about.'

Camille giggled. 'Cads. Gosh, that's an old fashioned word. Well, yes, I'm sure there will be men who think unaccompanied women are an easy target. Obviously Cecily will come with me. I cannot go anywhere without my wonderful lady's maid...and partner in crime.' She glanced at Cecily who smiled. 'And there will be Elsie of course, and her daughter Rose. We'll make a fine party don't you think?' Richard nodded, a surge of warmth going through him.

'I've been watching Mrs West, Madam,' said Cecily. 'She's been speaking to the staff. Most of them have shaken their heads after she's spoken to them, so I don't think she's found much out. Looks like she's gone into the foyer with someone, Mr Clemence I think. She was talking to him last.'

Camille frowned. 'Are there police constables manning the doors.'

Richard got up from the table and went to the concierge's desk.

'Where did the cigarette girl go?'

Yvette, the girl at the desk frowned. 'I think she went out into the foyer with someone. Perhaps she needed to refill her tray. The girls do it sometimes if a customer asks for a brand they've run out of. The refills are in a locked cupboard in the office. Why?'

'Richard didn't answer her but went immediately out to the foyer, and then into Ivor Clemences office where he and Louise were going over an account book.

'The cigarette girl. Did she come through the foyer?'

'She was there with someone. They were talking for a while,' said Louise Clemence, 'then it went quiet. I thought she'd gone back into the club.'

'Do you know who she was talking to? Was it the doorman?'

'The doorman goes off duty when the guests have arrived. As you know we lock the doors when the last guest on the book arrives. We never leave the door unlocked. People wander in thinking we're a public house and get upset when we refuse to serve them drinks.'

'So you don't think they went outside?' He didn't wait for them to answer but went to the double doors and tried them. They were open. Louise and Ivor Clemence came out of the office. 'They're open,' Richard said.

Louise looked shocked. 'But how? We have the only key.'

'What about the doorman?'

'No, never. We would never give our doormen keys. We see them out. I believe they go to a café down the street. Some of them go home if they live near enough.'

'So it's not the same one every evening?'

'No, we have two and they split the evenings between them,' answered Ivor Clemence. 'We're not worried about who works which night as long as there's someone there.'

'Do you know all the doormen?'

'We know the ones we personally took on.'

Richard frowned. 'I'm sorry, what does that mean?'

'We took on two doormen for security, but if they want to have a night off for some reason we expect them to find someone else. We don't actively employ them. They're sent to us from a company called,' he frowned and tutted, 'what are they called Louise?'

Louise Clemence ran into the office, then brought out a file, leafing through it with swift fingers.

'FailSafe,' she cried, holding up a contract. 'We chose the first two doormen they sent for an initial interview with the proviso that should they be unwell or could not attend for any reason, they would send another in his place. The company motto is, "We will never fail to keep you safe."'

Richard nodded. 'But that would mean you wouldn't necessarily know who it was they sent in the original doorman's place.'

Ivor Clemence and his wife looked at each other. Clemence shuffled his feet and looked unperturbed. 'It's how these things work, Chief Inspector. We pay the company to provide security. It's what we pay them for, to oversee it so we don't have to.'

'Which means you don't know who is on your door from one night to the next.'

Ivor Clemence looked annoyed. 'We know it's an employee from FailSafe. That's all we need to know.'

Camille and Cecily joined Richard in the foyer. Camille looked worried. 'Where's Elsie?'

Richard turned and stared at her. 'I wish I knew. It seems she was asked to come into the foyer by someone, probably under the pretext that someone wanted cigarettes. Mr and Mrs Clemence heard her speaking with someone. Then nothing.'

Camille thought hard then something occurred to her. 'She knows one of the doormen, doesn't she? She was speaking with him the other evening, don't you remember? It's why she didn't join us at the table for some time.'

'Yes, I do remember,' nodded Richard. He frowned. 'But did she not say they were friends? Surely he can't be mixed up in this?'

Ivor Clemence interjected. 'This, being what?'

Richard looked at him, his eyes narrowing. He began to recall what Aaron Kaplan had said about him, that he didn't trust him and thought he was a buffoon.

'Mr Clemence,' Richard said in a firm voice. 'You have had a murder on your premises this week. Your original cigarette girl, Emma,' he turned to Louise Clemence, 'who I understand is your daughter, Mrs Clemence, he turned back to Ivor Clemence, ' is missing. And now another woman has gone missing, seemingly in Emma Gaultiere's stead.'

Louise gasped. 'You know about Emma?'

'Yes, Mrs Clemence. I know that Emma is your daughter, and that Monsieur Fabian Gaultiere is her father.'

'What difference does it make?' asked Ivor Clemence in a querulous voice. 'So the Frenchman is her father, so what?'

'It makes all the difference in the world, Mr Clemence,' replied Richard, a hard edge to his voice. 'It means she is in danger. Think about it. One girl murdered because she looked like Emma, another missing who was also dressed and made to look like Emma.' He stared at them both. 'You need to tell me everything, Mr and Mrs Clemence, and Monsieur Gaultiere also. Someone is out to get Emma...and perhaps I should repeat this, although I don't know why I should bearing in mind you have kept information from me throughout this investigation. She is in danger. Your daughter, Mrs Clemence. Her life is in danger.'

'It is not,' said Louise Clemence, her voice low and quiet, as though she were very tired, almost to the point of exhaustion. 'She is safe, Chief Inspector.'

Richard's face darkened. 'In the office...now,' Richard commanded. 'And I want to know everything. No lies, no subverting, no leading me in the wrong direction. You have undermined this investigation for the last time. I want the truth.' The Clemences turned to go into the office.

'Where's Millie?' Camille asked, looking up to the moon which was still suspended above their heads. 'Should she not be in the moon?' They all raised their faces to look up.

'Switch on the lights,' cried Richard. 'Quickly now.'

'But, Chief Inspector,' cried Ivor Clemence. 'The ambience, the atmosphere, the mood. All will be lost once the lights go on. You know this. It changes everything. We will lose custom. The guests have come here because of the notoriety, the drama. Can you not see that?'

'I don't give a damn about the ambience, your guests, or the drama they'll miss out on, Mr Clemence,' shouted Richard. 'I want this place sealed off now. No one is to leave until I say so.'

Camille and Cecily stood silently while Ivor Clemence went to a board behind the curtain and switched on the lights. There was a roar of annoyance and disappointment from the nightclub. The guests, who were just finishing their entrée, had had a rude awakening.

'Camille, Richard said. 'Please go to the kitchen and fetch Monsieur Gaultiere. Bring him here. He has questions to answer.' Camille nodded and left the foyer, heading for the kitchen. 'Cecily.' Cecily looked up at him, bright eyed and happy she would at last have something to do to help with the investigation. 'Go into the nightclub and ask Constable Lewis to instruct the other constables to make sure no one leaves the nightclub without permission, then ask him to join us in here.'

Cecily nodded. 'Yes, Chief Inspector.'

She went into the nightclub and found Russell Lewis where he had been standing all evening, noticing he was wearing a rather good suit. His shirt was pristine white, and his collars were beautifully starched. Force of habit meant she couldn't help but look down at his shoes. They gleamed. She took in a breath and stepped towards him.

'Chief Inspector Owen wants you to join him in the foyer, Constable Lewis.' Russell Lewis nodded and followed Cecily into the foyer where Camille and Monsieur Gaultiere had already arrived.

'Lewis,' cried Richard when he saw him. 'Help me get the stepladder from behind this curtain.' he beckoned Lewis over to where the stepladder was kept, and between them they dragged it across to the moon. Once it was set up Richard instructed Constable Lewis to climb up.

'What are we looking for, sir?' Constable Lewis asked Richard.

'You'll know when you get up there, Lewis.' Richard nodded. 'It might be nothing.'

'Yes, sir.'

Russell Lewis climbed the tall stepladder, hoping with everything he had he could face whatever he found there without making a fool of himself. As a young constable his experience in policing had been more of an administrative nature, pushing pieces of paper around various desks, rewriting reports for some of the inspectors and detectives whose handwriting was practically illegible, and adding punctuation where it was required because the upper echelons of the police had either seemingly forgotten it, or never been taught.

Occasionally he had gone out on the beat with another officer. As yet he hadn't been allowed to go alone. One of the other officers had said he had the complexion of a girl and wasn't safe to be out alone in the big wide world. The other officers had laughed. Some might have been offended, but Russell Lewis had taken it in good part and laughed along with them, which had endeared him to his fellow officers.

He had been fortunate to have gone to a good school in Hertfordshire where his parents lived, and been grateful for the sacrifices they had made so he could chase his dream of becoming a police officer at the famous Scotland Yard. What he hadn't bargained for was that he would be called upon to spend an evening in a rather seedy nightclub, then climb up a less than stable stepladder to look into a moon suspended from a ceiling. He took each step slowly, acknowledging to himself he was reluctant to get to the top because of what he might find, but Chief Inspector Owen had put his trust in him, and for that he was grateful.

When he got to the small platform at the top of the stepladder, he peered inside. There was a piece of crumpled fabric, a thin bedspread he thought, edged with tassels and embroidered with roses. Constable Lewis pulled the fabric back. Below it was the body of a thin, pale girl whose watery blue eyes were still open, an expression of shock crossing her face as she stared at nothing at all. Her hair was still in a chignon and tied into a pre-Raphaelite style, beautiful, Russell thought, yet sadly macabre. In her hand she clutched a champagne glass, the contents of which had spilt and soaked her dress. The smell of cheap alcohol sickened him and he began the descent into the foyer.

Chief Inspector Owen put a hand on his shoulder. 'Well, Lewis?'

'There's a girl up there,' Russell Lewis said, momentarily placing a hand across his mouth. 'She's dead, sir. I reckon it's that Millie what was interviewed.'

Camille and Cecily gasped and Louise Clemence cried out. 'Is it Millie? Oh, please Lord, don't let it be poor little Millie.'

'Describe her, Lewis,' said Richard as he drew in a deep, wobbling breath.'

'Fair hair, tied up around her head with various coloured ribbons. Pale skinned, very pale, sir, thin, too thin.' He shook his head. 'Her eyes are open. They're blue, light blue, pale, almost see through.'

Richard sighed and squeezed Russell's shoulder. 'First dead body, son?'

Russell nodded. 'Yes, sir.'

'Go outside for some air. Cecily, would you accompany Constable Lewis to the entrance please and allow him to get some air. Allow no one in or out. Do you understand?'

Cecily nodded. 'Yes, Chief Inspector Owen.'

Richard smiled at her and winked. 'Good girl.'

He beckoned Ivor Clemence over to the stepladder. The man reluctantly joined Richard under the moon. 'Up you go, sir.'

Clemence looked exasperated. 'Me?'

'Yes, sir, you. We need a positive identification before I call the forensics team in to remove the body.'

'But...but, why me?'

'Mr Clemence...are you refusing? I will wonder why if you do. You are the proprietor here and Millie Spencer's employer.'

'For God's sake, Ivor, just do as the Chief Inspector asks,' cried Louise Clemence. 'There are more important things going on here than your pathetic feelings.'

Ivor threw Louise a hard look then began to climb the stepladder. He wobbled slightly when he got to the top, reluctantly glanced into the suspended moon, then began the descent back down the stepladder. When he got to the bottom he pulled his jacket into position, swallowing hard, then rubbed his hand across his face.

'Well, sir?' Richard asked, his face devoid of emotion.

Ivor Clemence nodded. 'It's her.'

Louise Clemence let out a scream of utter horror and looked close to collapse. Fabian Gaultiere went to her aid, supporting her as he led her into the office, whispering comforting words to her as he sat her behind the desk. Ivor Clemence looked on, his face a picture of annoyance, then dismissiveness.

'Presumably this means we must have your men here again, Chief Inspector,' he said. 'How long will they be here?'

'As long as it takes, Mr Clemence. I suggest you make an announcement to your guests that they must remain in their seats, that you will provide any refreshment they need, and it is likely they will be questioned with regard to the finding of a body on the premises.'

'And what good will it do? I thought you had already decided it was not a guest at the club who was involved in these crimes.'

Richard gritted his teeth. Ivor Clemence was deliberately standing in his way to do his job, and he resented it. The newspapers had already accused Richard and his colleagues of dragging their feet over the original murder, saying that the word plod was not a misnomer, but perfectly described the speed at which the investigation was moving along.

'If one of the guests was here the night the body of Charlotte Baynes was found, he...or she...will be a person of interest and will be someone we will want to interview again.' Richard drew in a breath. 'I will not tolerate any obstruction, Mr Clemence.'

'Easy for you to say, Chief Inspector. You don't have your savings tied up in the Café Bonbon, the business of which has been severely disrupted over the last week.' He sighed and spoke in a quieter voice. 'I'm sorry if I seem hardened to what has happened to the girls, of course I'm upset, particularly over Millie, but I'm concerned for the future of the nightclub. I can't help feeling all of this is being done deliberately to destroy what Louise and I are trying to build.'

Richard nodded. 'I hear what you're saying, Mr Clemence, but I'm afraid I don't believe these murders are being carried out to bring you and your wife down. At least, not the lone reason. Rather, I think there is another reason entirely.'

Ivor Clemence looked surprised. 'You do?'

'Indeed. Now I must telephone Scotland Yard and arrange for our forensics team to collect the body of Millie Spencer, and for enough detectives to question everyone here. The sooner I am allowed to do it the sooner things can get back to a semblance of normality for Café Bonbon. With your permission I'd like to use the telephone in the office.'

Ivor Clemence inclined his head. 'Of course, Chief Inspector. If you need to use the office for your own use, Louise and I can find somewhere else to conduct business.' Richard thanked him, thinking it wasn't before time that Ivor Clemence backed down and admitted he and his wife needed to cooperate.

Outside the Café Bonbon, Constable Russell Lewis sat on one of the steps leading up to the clubs entrance with his head in his hands. Cecily sat beside him, quiet, thinking that silence was probably best for him to come to terms with what he had seen. He had vomited into the gutter which had clearly embarrassed him, and was now wiping tears away from his cheeks with a large, white handkerchief. After a while he spoke.

'You can go in if you like. It's gettin' a bit chilly out here.'

'No, it's all right. Chief Inspector Owen didn't want you to be on your own.' Russell nodded and sniffed. 'It's a shock, isn't it, seeing a dead body for the first time?' He nodded again. 'It don't get any easier, niver.'

He glanced up at her and frowned. 'How many bodies 'ave you seen then?'

'A few. Me and Lady Divine, we sometimes help with investigations. She's like a private investigator, and I'm 'er assistant.'

'I thought you were her maid.'

'I am. I look after 'er, 'er clothes and things, make sure she ain't late for anythin', do 'er 'air, 'elp her with her cosmetics. Do a bit of cleaning an' all if I 'ave time. I don't mind. Duke Street is a lovely 'ouse, an' it's my 'ome too, so it's in my interests to keep it nice. I also run 'er guest book for her little beach house in Brighton.' Cecily smiled to herself. 'She lets it out, see, to people what want a holiday down there. It's a lovely place, although the last time I saw it was near Christmas, and it was bloody freezing.' She startled, remembering she wasn't speaking to Knolly or Phillips. 'Sorry.'

'What for?'

'For swearing.'

Russell chuckled in spite of the way he was feeling. 'That's nothing. You should 'ear 'em down at the station. The words they use. It would turn yer face puce, believe me.'

'D'yer like bein' a police officer?'

He sniffed again, then wiped his nose on the huge handkerchief. 'I did, but today...well, weren't expecting it was I?'

'D'yer think Chief Inspector Owen made you go up the stepladder for the purpose, ter get yer used to it like?'

Russell nodded. 'Yeah, I think 'e did. 'E's a good'un 'e is. Really encouraged me. Let me sit in on interviews and everythin', and even asked for my opinion. No one's ever done that before. I want to be a detective, or a Chief Inspector like 'im one day. It's my ambition, to do well.'

'D'yer think yer'll stay at Scotland Yard then?'

He turned to look at her and smiled, nodding. 'Yeah, I think I will.' He stared off into the distance. 'I like London. I've 'eard it called the arse 'ole of England cos of all the crime and whatnot, but there's crime everywhere, not just London.'

Cecily nodded. 'I know. There was crime when we went to Brighton...and when we went to Paris. Terrible it was.'

He smiled at her again, wondering if he should say what he had wanted to say since he'd first met her. 'Chief Inspector Owen says you 'aven't got a beau.'

Cecily widened her eyes, her mouth forming a perfect 'O'. 'Oh, did 'e now. 'E's a cheeky one. Fancy 'im tellin' yer that.'

'Well, 'ave yer?'

She frowned. 'Ave I what?'

Russell sighed. 'Got a beau.'

Cecily shrugged. 'No, I 'aven't.'

'Would you like one?'

She pursed her lips. 'I dunno. No one's ever asked me.'

He drew in a breath. 'Well, *I'm* askin' yer. Will yer be my girl?'

Cecily raised her eyebrows, flushing slightly, but then gave him a sideways coy look. 'All right.'

'So you're my girl?'

She grinned. 'Yeah.' She fluttered her eyelashes like she'd seen the movie stars do. 'I s'pose I am.'

He reached for her cold little hand and she slid it into his warmer one. They stared off into the night, both thinking that sometimes good came out of bad things. He gave her hand a squeeze and she giggled.

'You all right now?' she whispered.

He turned his head and smiled at her, his eyes twinkling. 'I've never been more all right in my life.'

Chapter 31

Richard waited for Louise Clemence to compose herself before asking the questions he needed to ask. A surge of anger went through him because he knew in his gut that Louise and Ivor Clemence had pulled the wool over his eyes. He was not happy. He also knew people made mistakes and made decisions, the wrong decision as it often turned out, when they were under pressure. First he needed to discover where Emma Gaultiere was, and second what her connection was to the murdered girl, Charlotte Baynes.

'Are you feeling better, Mrs Clemence?' he asked her. They had found chairs; Richard and Camille sat opposite Louise Clemence, while Ivor Clemence took his usual position of leaning up against the wall with his hands in his pockets and his legs crossed at the ankles, rather arrogant, Camille thought, as though he were waiting for a bus. He was clearly irritated with Richard taking control of proceedings, but it's what they were there for, and as far as she, Camille, was concerned, both Ivor Clemence and his wife had lied by omission.

'I'm better, Chief Inspector,' answered Louise Clemence as she took a sip of the brandy Fabian Gaultiere had poured for her. He was sitting next to Louise, more concerned for her welfare, it seemed, than her husband. 'I apologise for the hysterics. I was deeply shocked. Poor Millie. Such an innocent. Why the hell would anyone want to kill her?'

'To keep her quiet I would imagine,' Richard said airily, glancing first at Ivor Clemence, then back to Louise.

Louise frowned. 'To keep her quiet?' She shook her head. 'To keep her quiet about what? She is harmless, an employee. She doesn't know anything.'

'It is what you assume, Mrs Clemence, but in my line of work one should not assume anything. I believe Millie does…did…know something, and she was killed because of it. Before I explore that line of questioning further, I wish to ask you about your daughter. You said she is safe, so with that in mind you must know where she is.'

'We do know where she is.'

'I don't,' said Ivor Clemence, his jaw hardening. 'I barely know the girl. Don't drag me into this.'

'Where is she, Mrs Clemence?' asked Richard.

'In New York. Or soon will be. Fabian and I put her on a ship headed for New York. She will stay with a friend of mine who lives there.'

Richard frowned. 'Why?'

Louise Clemence opened a drawer in her desk and removed a sheaf of papers, placing them in front of Richard. 'Because of these.'

'What are they?'

'Threatening letters, all saying the same thing.'

'Which is?'

'That Emma is in danger. That we will pay for our misdemeanours with her life.'

Richard began to read the letters, handing each one to Camille when he had finished. He glanced up at Louise Clemence. 'What do they refer to?'

Louise shrugged. 'I wish I knew. When we left New York we settled immediately in London, made a home here,' she shrugged, 'a kind of home, not the home we really wanted.'

'You wanted to be in Manhattan.'

'It's the place I've known all my life, Chief Inspector. You can take the girl out of Manhattan, but you can't take Manhattan out of the girl. It feels as though I have been planted in the wrong soil, Emma too in a way, although she had been to school in both England and France.' She reached for Fabian Gaultiere's hand. 'Fabian wanted her to have a rounded education and it is what she received. She is clever.'

'So why was she a cigarette girl? Not much of an ambition for someone who had the education your daughter was given.'

'It was temporary...a way of earning a little pocket money. She's a young girl, she wants the good things in life; nice clothes, a motor car, her own home one day. She's ambitious.' She frowned to herself. 'We thought if she stayed with us in London those things would be available to her, but then we began to receive the letters...sometimes every day a new letter would turn up.'

'So you have an enemy.'

'It would seem so.'

'And do you have any idea of what the misdemeanours are?'

'None.' She glanced at Fabian Gaultiere. 'Apart from the fact there was an accident in the restaurant where Fabian was chef...the oysters. A girl's life...yes, it was awful. Absolutely awful, and Fabian has suffered terribly ever since, with remorse and guilt. Sometimes I thought he would take his own life. The person writing these letters cannot possibly know what he has been through.'

'Clearly the person who wrote these letters knows where you are now. Were they sent to your home address or to the Café Bonbon?'

'Here.'

'So it's quite likely they don't know where you're living.'

Louise Clemence drew in a deep breath and closed her eyes momentarily. 'I certainly hope not.'

Camille eyed Fabian Gaultiere's hand which was still covering one of Louise's. 'Why did you divorce Monsieur Gaultiere, Mrs Clemence?'

'So I could marry Ivor.'

'But not for love.'

'No.'

Camille smiled to herself. She had already worked it out. It was the thing that had been sitting in her mind ever since she had meant Louise and Ivor Clemence. There was no love between them, no affection. If anything they were curt with one another, dismissive, almost businesslike.

'For money,' she said. 'And for residency.'

Louise Clemence nodded. 'Yes, Lady Divine. You have it in one. Ivor wanted to stay in New York, and the only way he could do it was by getting married. We went through all the right channels, blood tests and whatnot, jumped through the hoops. We married. The Café Bonbon in New York was struggling because of the protection rackets; it wasn't just one outfit. There seemed to be so many of them, all grubbing around trying to get our money, money we had made honestly. And we weren't the only ones. Many businesses went to the wall, or the proprietors got beaten up regularly. It was a dreadful situation.

'When the club began to fail and I couldn't pay them they got nasty. The money Ivor gave me for enabling his residency had almost gone. It was then I made the decision to come to London. Of course, there was no way

I would leave Fabian to the wolves in Manhattan. I insisted he came with us, and Emma was desperate for him to accompany us. Yes, we had divorced, regrettably, which I think we have both now acknowledge was a mistake. As soon as we can, and with Ivor's agreement, we will rectify it. I felt the racketeering in London wasn't so bad as in New York, and I was right. We have had approaches from various outfits, have paid one or two, but it has been minimal compared to New York. Instead we've been thrown into this situation.'

'Why didn't you inform the police, Mrs Clemence?' Richard asked her.

Louise shook her head, but Camille answered for her. 'You were frightened for your daughter weren't you? I understand, Mrs Clemence. I have a daughter. I would do anything to protect her. Perhaps I can give you some advice. Work with Chief Inspector Owen now. If we don't find out who is behind the threats, the letters, and the murders, you will live your lives in fear. And so will Emma, and I'm sure you don't want that for her. Were you threatened if you made contact with the police?'

Louise Clemence nodded. 'Yes, we were. The letters warned me off the police, saying the consequences would be fatal if I involved the police...or told anyone what was happening. All I could think about was getting Emma to safety, which was why I sent her away.' A tear trickled down Louise Clemence's cheek. 'I miss her. So much.' She glanced at Fabian Gaultiere. 'We both do. We want to be a family again, like we used to be when she was small. We were so happy.'

Fabian Gaultiere spoke for the first time.

'Until the unfortunate incident at Le Petit Champignon.' He shook his head sadly. 'I feel responsible. Emma is everything to us, so I understand the poor girl's family needed someone to blame. They blamed me, went public. The newspapers had a field day. I was branded as the wicked chef, the monster who had killed a girl with cheap food for profit. Customers dried up and the owners of Le Petit Champignon asked me to leave. I had to leave. I could do no other. Circumstances at the restaurant could not continue, for them or for me. But even with advertisements in the newspapers saying the restaurant had a brand new chef it was too late. Le Petit Champignon closed three months later.' He closed his eyes and shook his head. 'That little plate of oysters took everything from me; my reputation, my livelihood, my belief in myself, and my confidence. And a girl lost her life.' He opened his eyes and gazed at Richard. 'The smallest thing can change one's life, Monsieur Owen, and often not for the better. I have lived to regret it ever since.'

Richard turned his attention to Ivor Clemence.

'What is your take on all of this, Mr Clemence?'

Clemence pushed himself away from the wall and stood in front of them, his arms folded. Camille knew she disliked the man. There was something about him. Was he the protagonist in everything that was happening to Louise Clemence and Fabian Gaultiere? Stranger things had been uncovered in her other investigations. She knew people would do whatever they could to get what they wanted. What did Ivor Clemence want? Would he go so far as to kill two girls to get his own way and keep someone quiet? She stared at him for a moment, waiting for his answer.

'I don't have a take on it, Chief Inspector. It is how Louise says. It was a marriage of convenience. We both knew it. I wanted to stay in New York and Louise needed the money to keep her business going. My life in England was over, or so I thought. However when things got a bit sticky in America we decided to come here. I know London like the back of my hand, so I knew where would be a good place to open a new nightclub. There's money around here...our prices aren't the cheapest, but I knew if we gave the rich of London a good time they would come back again and again. And we were doing it until everything went wrong.'

'The money you put into the club in Manhattan, Mr Clemence?' Ivor Clemence nodded. 'Where did the money come from?'

Clemence look annoyed. 'I don't think I have to answer that. Why would you ask a question like that? It's no one's business.' He looked uncomfortable.'

'No,' said Richard, 'you don't have to answer it, but I can guess.'

'From the insurance payout after your wife's death was it not, Mr Clemence,' Camille said, disliking the man even more. 'It takes a lot of money to keep a business afloat, particularly if it is in debt.'

Clemence shrugged. 'I don't see what difference it makes where it came from. It was my money to do with it what I wanted. I thought it was a good investment.' He turned a sour face towards Louise Clemence. 'Unfortunately I was wrong. I didn't lose everything...we used what was left to start up the Café Bonbon here.'

'And what of Charlotte Baynes?' asked Camille. 'You knew her didn't you?'

Clemence shook his head. 'No, but Louise did. Tell them Louise.'

Louise Clemence nodded. 'Yes. She came here for a job. Wanted to be the moon girl but I could see she wouldn't be right for it. As soon as I met her my mind was made up. She was the image of Emma, although a brunette. I knew with a blonde wig she could be Emma.'

Camille sighed with annoyance. 'Did it not occur to you that you were putting Charlotte Baynes in danger?'

'No.' Louise shook her head. 'I hadn't thought that far. I panicked. I just wanted to get Emma out of the country with no questions asked.'

'And the girls who shared rooms with her?'

'Wouldn't have known. Emma stayed with me until she sailed. I told Charlotte not to speak to Sadie or Millie, to keep her distance because of course they would have realised she was not Emma. It was fortunate that both Millie and Sadie work the foyer, and rarely need to go into the nightclub. In fact I told them if I saw them in the nightclub they would be fired. Already they take too much time in the restroom and go together, even though they were requested not to.'

'Where is Sadie Murphy this evening?' asked Richard.

'She sent a message saying she was sick. We covered it.'

There was a noise in the foyer. Camille got up to investigate and found Cecily and Constable Lewis locking the front door.

'Are you feeling better, Constable Lewis,' Camille asked him.

'Much better, thank you, Lady Divine.'

She nodded, then turned to Cecily. She was about to say something to her then stopped in surprise. Cecily positively glowed. Her eyes sparkled in the overhead chandelier. She seemed totally relaxed, rather dreamy Camille thought.

'And how are you, Cecily,' she asked her maid, smiling. Something has happened, she thought. I've never seen Cecily look so...contented.

'I'm very well, Madam,' Cecily answered. 'What will happen now?'

'The guests are being questioned by detectives and are being allowed home, table by table I believe. The premises are being searched for Elsie, but you and I are very much aware that men, including police constables I'm sorry to say, are not particularly good at looking for things. You and I will make our own search, Cecily. So far no one can remember seeing her, and certainly not after she left the nightclub to go into the foyer.'

'This evening, Madam?'

'Yes, it must be tonight. It's quite possible Mrs West has wandered off with a friend, perhaps the doorman she said she knew, but my instinct is telling me the opposite. I want to satisfy myself she is not here and the only way to do it is by searching myself.'

'Of course, Madam. Russell will come with us, won't you, Russell? We need someone to keep us safe.'

Camille raised her eyebrows and blinked. 'Russell? No formal title this evening, Cecily? Is Constable Lewis not on duty?'

Cecily looked embarrassed. 'Er, er, I meant Constable Lewis.' She flushed bright pink.

Camille nodded and smiled warmly at Cecily, doing her best to stifle a giggle. 'As long as Chief Inspector Owen doesn't need him for anything else, yes, I think it's a good idea.'

Chapter 32

By the time Camille, Cecily, and Russell Lewis began their search for Elsie the nightclub had been emptied of guests. Richard was with the forensics team from Scotland Yard in the foyer. They had retrieved the body from the moon, Millie Spencer a different prospect in size to Charlotte Baynes, and had placed her on a stretcher.

Louise Clemence had stayed in the office with Fabian Gaultiere, not wanting to witness the young girl's body being examined by forensics and the police. She cried silent tears wondering what an earth she had done to warrant such awful things happening. The only thing she felt she could be happy about, if happy was the right word, was that Emma was on her way to New York and would soon be with her friend who had agreed wholeheartedly for Emma to stay. She missed her daughter already, they were close, as much friends as mother and daughter, but Louise knew the sacrifice would keep her daughter safe. She swallowed hard when she heard Richard and one of the doctors conversing in the foyer.

'Well?' asked Richard. 'Is it the same as last time?'

'No.'

Richard looked surprised. 'Really? What's your verdict?'

'She's been suffocated, probably with that tasselled blanket.' He pointed to the blanket which covered Millie Spencer's body. 'There are fibres at the entrance to the nostrils and the capillaries in her eyes are prominent.

Clearly there will need to be more tests, but if you're asking me now,' the doctor grinned, 'which of course like all policeman you are,' that's my verdict. There doesn't seem to be any broken bones, although the girl is so undernourished I should think her bones would crack if someone blew on her.'

'She's very thin, isn't she?'

The doctor shook his head. 'It's the kind of thing we see when we're examining someone from the old rookeries. Most of the inhabitants have the diseases of the undernourished and uncared for. Some of the children are so thin they can barely stand. I would say this girl fits very nearly into the same category. If someone hadn't made the decision to take her life she certainly wouldn't have made old age, unless of course someone had changed things for her and taken care of her. Her stomach is concave, not good for a young woman of her age.' Richard sighed and shook his head. 'How old is she?'

'Twenty...or close to, I think.'

'She has the body of a twelve year old. I thought she worked here?'

'She does?'

'So she must be paid.'

'Yes.'

'Well she's not spending it on food that's for sure. Her fingernails are brittle and bitten down to the quick.'

Richard blew out a breath. 'Poor girl.'

'Think you could have two killers on your hands, Chief Inspector Owen. Killers usually employ the same method to rid themselves of their victims. The modus operandi for this girl is entirely different to the killing of Charlotte Baynes.

Chapter 33

Camille, Cecily and Constable Lewis searched every inch of the Café Bonbon. In her heart, Cecily had been doubtful they would find Elsie within the premises. She tried to put herself in the shoes of the abductor, which she grimaced at, but was sure she would not have remained on the premises with her victim.

'Don't fink she's 'ere, Madam,' she said to Camille. 'I can't say I'm surprised. We've searched every office, cupboard, alcove, and storage area and there's no sign. I don't think she's 'ere.'

'Nor me,' sighed Camille, 'but there is somewhere we have yet to search. That door,' she pointed to the door which led to the storerooms and Aaron Kaplan's living place, 'leads to the basement. If the door is unlocked I think we should venture down there. I know we've been asked not to go down there again, but if I were the abductor I would take my victim somewhere unobtrusive.'

Constable Lewis gazed at Camille askance. 'But Mrs West was last heard of in the foyer, Lady Camille, not in the nightclub. The abductor would have had to drag her through the nightclub in front of the guests, and the constables who were stationed at various points to get her through the door. I can assure you it did not happen.'

'I know,' sighed Camille, 'and of course you're correct. If she's in the basement they didn't come this way, but I think it's worth a look, just to put my mind at rest.'

Constable Lewis nodded and he glanced at Cecily. 'As you wish, Lady Divine, but I'll go first. If the abductor is down there he will have heightened sensitivities and I have been trained to repel an attack.' Cecily's expression warmed and she gazed at Russell with pride.

Camille acquiesced. 'Of course, Constable Lewis. I will bow to your more experienced judgment.'

They made their way across the nightclub floor to the door over the other side.

'It might be locked, 'specially after we were told not to go down there,' whispered Cecily.

'Then I think it will rather decide for us don't you, but I'm hoping because Aaron Kaplan has made his home in the basement it has been left unlocked so he may come and go as he pleases. I'm assuming he is not a prisoner.'

Camille was correct in her assumption the door would be left unlocked. As Russell pushed the handle down the mechanism gave a satisfying click. He turned and grinned at Camille and Cecily.

'We're in,' he said triumphantly. 'Don't forget, ladies, you must let me take the lead.' Both Camille and Cecily nodded. Cecily accepted his instruction without question. Camille raised her eyebrows and knew if push came to shove she would do what she had to do, regardless of how dangerous. Elsie's life was in danger, and she couldn't help but feel more than a little guilt she had encouraged her friend to take the place of Emma Gaultiere. She thought of Rose and what would happen to her without her mother, of the dreadful way in which Charlotte Baynes had died. No, she could not think like that. She had to believe that Elsie was still alive and as feisty as ever.

Russell switched on the light and Camille and Cecily followed him down the stairs into the musty, dust covered basement. Camille shivered, wondering how Aaron Kaplan could possibly live in such a place. She made up her mind in an instant to change his situation. The Clemences may have offered him somewhere to stay, but in her opinion, the air outside was cleaner.

'Where is Mr Kaplan's area?' asked Russell. He frowned. 'Surely he doesn't live down here all the time?'

'Lives and works down 'ere,' said Cecily. 'Poor bloke. If Knolly saw this she'd be in floods, I know she would.'

'Knolly?'

'Mrs Knowles, Lady Divine's cook. She knew Mr Kaplan from years ago, but he was a very different man then.'

'Yeah,' Russell nodded, 'Chief Inspector Owen explained. He was questioned about his wife's murder weren't 'e?'

'He was,' said Camille, 'but completely exonerated. I do believe the man does not have a violent or unkind bone in his body.'

'Does your Knolly know about it?'

Camille shook her head. 'No, and I'm not looking forward to being the one to tell her.'

They walked in single file along the corridors where the walls were swathed in cobwebs, like eerie bunting, holding the remnants of myriad flies that had been caught up within the threads.

'Oh, Madam,' cried Cecily. 'I don't know why, but it seems even worse than before.'

'I know what you mean, Cecily,' agreed Camille. 'Gosh, this is an awful place.'

They shuffled along the corridor until they got to an area used for storage. The racks lining the walls were still empty which Camille found strange.

'I can only assume the Clemences are operating the club on a shoestring,' she said. 'Where are all the bottles for the bar, the equipment one would need to run such a place? One wonders what they do when they run out of anything.'

'Is that where Mr Kaplan stays?' asked Russell, pointing to a shabby, seemingly swiftly made bed and a small cabinet on which there was a bottle of whiskey, half full and a greasy glass. There was an old lamp with a lightbulb in the top, but no shade. Aaron Kaplan was nowhere to be seen.

'Yes, this is where he lives,' answered Camille. 'Gosh, one wouldn't keep a dog down here. This is awful. Something must be done.'

They stood by the bed surveying the scene. Russell stood with his hands on hips, wondering how anyone could be expected to live in such dire circumstance. Cecily wiped away the tears that had settled on her cheek, biting her lip to stop herself from sobbing. Camille's face had hardened with anger that anyone could be treated in such a way through no fault of their own.

'There's no one here,' said Russell. 'Are you sure this is the end of the corridor.' He pursed his lips, wondering why the corridor didn't go further. 'Did you not say Mr Kaplan was the caretaker of three premises? If that's the case, how does he get to the other two?'

Camille stared at him. 'You're absolutely right.' She bent and switched on the lamp on Kaplan's bedside table. 'There must be a way through to the other basements. The Clemences would certainly not want him wandering through the nightclub. Is there a door we've missed into the other corridors?'

'What's that over there,' said Russell, pointing to an alcove, deep in shadow now that the bedside lamp had been switched on.

'It looks like a bookcase,' said Cecily, "cept there's no books on it.'

Russell went towards it, peering through the shelves. He put his hand on the frame and pulled it back.

'It's moving,' he said. 'It's on hinges. Oh, that's clever, a bookcase hiding an entrance.' He turned to look at Cecily and Camille, smiling. 'I think we've found it, ladies,' he said. 'This is how Aaron Kaplan gets to the other premises. He simply pulls back the bookcase and goes down the corridor.'

'Is that what we're going ter do?' asked Cecily.

'Certainly,' said Camille. 'We've come this far. We must not be deterred now.'

'Oh, Madam,' cried Cecily, her hands shaking as she brought them up to her face in distress. 'I've just thought of somethin' 'orrible.'

'What, Cecily?'

'You don't fink it's 'im do yer, Madam?'

Camille shook her head, frowning. 'Think it's who, Cecily?'

'Aaron Kaplan. Do you fink it might be 'im what's doin' all this stuff, the murders, the abduction. Oh, please, God, don't let it be 'im. Knolly will never get over it.'

Camille stared into the dark corridor. It had not occurred to her that Aaron Kaplan might have been involved all along. But what would have been the motive? Isn't it what Richard always says, she thought. There must be a motive?

'But what would the motive be, Cecily?' He surely has no connection with the Clemences.'

'We don't know that, Madam. All we know is that Knolly knew him once, in another life, in another time, and his wife was murdered. Where's he bin since then? He could have gone to America in all that time. We don't know 'im do we? We don't know what he's done.'

Russell lit a match from a box in his pocket and they made their way down the filthy, musty corridor.

'I wonder which premises this leads to?' asked Camille. 'My sense of direction has been thrown completely out of kilter down here. I couldn't tell you if we were going left or right.'

'Nor me, Madam,' said Cecily, holding onto the back of Russell's jacket.

'We're going to the right of the Café Bonbon,' said Russell. 'That's the restaurant isn't it?'

'Yes,' nodded Camille. 'Where Fabian Gaultiere gets the food to feed the guests. No wonder the Clemences have no money. It must be costing a fortune.'

They continued down the corridor for another hundred yards. At the end was a grating, the size of a door.

'Reckon we need to go through there and it will lead us to the restaurant basement,' said Russell. He suddenly stopped and put his finger against his lips. 'I can hear voices,' he whispered. They waited as they tuned their ears into a voice coming from a few yards in front of them. Russell blew out the match, flinging it onto the cobbles below, then slowly opened the grating, gingerly pulling it towards him, praying the hinges would not squeal. He pulled it far enough back so that they could all squeeze through the opening. When they were all inside a brick arched, white-painted room housing storage shelves full to bursting with packets of ingredients, bunches of root vegetables, and dozens of eggs, and a cold room with a metal door, new and well-cared for, they squatted down behind a preparation table, listening to a lone voice which was doing the talking. There was strip light on the ceiling which threw out a cold, almost bluish light. It flickered annoyingly and made a clicking noise.

'Do you recognise the voice, Madam?' whispered Cecily.

Camille shook her head. 'It's an American accent,' she said. 'A man's voice, obviously.' She squinted her eyes and tried to make out what he was saying. The voice suddenly changed and another voice could be heard. Cecily's mouth dropped open.

'That was Aaron Kaplan,' she whispered. 'Oh, no. Oh, no. He *is* involved.' Camille's heart sank to her fine leather shoes. So Cecily had been right yet again. How she had hoped for once she had been wrong. She knew how finely tuned Cecily's instincts were, but it seemed she, Camille, had been wrong about Aaron Kaplan.

'Get up!' they heard the American voice command.

'Don't speak ter me like that,' came an indignant woman's voice. 'I ain't a child, and I ain't your bloody prisoner, niver. Ain't yer got no manners? An' yer can leave the old bloke alone an' all.' Camille put her hand across her mouth to stop herself from guffawing. It was Elsie, and she didn't sound happy. 'And yer can take that gun out a me face, mister. I've seen it all before, yer know. 'Ave yer any idea who I am?'

'I don't give a damn who you are. Where's Emma Gaultiere?'

'How the 'ell should I know. I don't even know who she is.'

'I don't believe you. 'You're dressed to look like her. I thought once we'd got rid of the other one they would have realised I won't give up. I will never give up.'

'If I knew what you was talkin' about I'd 'elp yer, course I would, but I don't. And while we're on the subject, let this old bloke go. He ain't done nuffin wrong, as 'e.'

Camille and Cecily looked at each other. 'Aaron Kaplan,' said Cecily, smiling. 'Thank goodness.' Suddenly she sneezed. The look on her face was one of complete horror. 'Must 'ave bin the dust,' she whispered. 'I've always 'ated dust. It was so dusty in Ma and Pa's place. 'As a bad effect on me.'

Camille, Cecily, and Russell Lewis looked up at the same time to see the long barrel of a gun hovering above their heads.

'Now what do we have here?' said the owner with a sarcastic tone and a grin in his voice. 'More lambs to the slaughter. Go and join the flock.' He waved the gun towards Elsie and Aaron Kaplan. Camille got up first, followed by Constable Lewis and Cecily. 'This is turning into quite a party,' the man said. 'Sit with them and don't do anything unless I tell you to.'

'Who are you?' asked Camille. Constable Lewis threw her a look as if to say let me take the lead, but Camille returned it with one of her own and he looked away. Russell Lewis was a young man who had just joined the police force and certainly had no experience of what they were facing. Camille knew he wanted to impress Cecily, but this was neither the time nor the place.

'It matters not who I am, but what you're doing here...' he glanced at Elsie. 'But I'm kinda thinking you're looking for your servant.'

Elsie reared up. 'I ain't no one's servant, mister. You need to get yer facts straight.'

Cecily narrowed her eyes and stared at the man brandishing the gun. 'You're Louise Clemence's brother ain't yer, the one she ain't seen since she got married. Yer look like 'er.'

'At last, someone who possesses a brain. I am Louise's brother, you're right. But honestly, none of this has anything to do with any of you. I need to able to finish what I came here to do. What I want to know is...where is Emma?'

'Somewhere well away from here and out of danger,' said Camille. 'What is it you want, Mr Bruce?'

Suddenly a door opened in the basement underneath the restaurant, allowing a flow of warm air to permeate the cold basement. Footsteps could be heard padding over the cobbles beneath the restaurant.

'Sadie,' Ronnie Bruce called out. 'Sadie, we have visitors.'

Sadie Murphy came through one of the brick arches, surprise written across her face, which turned into a grin once she saw Camille and Cecily.

'Oh, dear, Ronnie. What have you done? she said in a broad Irish accent. 'This lady,' she pointed to Camille, 'is Lady Camille Divine, a Lady of the Realm. Think we could be in trouble, lover.'

Bruce shrugged. 'It means nothin' to me, darlin', but Emma is not here.'

'Who's that?' asked Sadie, pointing at Elsie. 'Why's she all done up, now, like Emma? Why do they keep doing this?' she stamped her foot in frustration. 'We'll never get this finished. They must think we're stupid if they think she,' she pointed her finger at Elsie, 'looks anything like Emma Gaultiere.'

'She does look like her,' said Ronnie, 'from a distance. I was fooled by the deception, Sadie, but I haven't seen Emma since she was a young girl. I knew she was blonde and full figured like you told me. The other one looked like her too if your description of Emma was accurate. Of course I was mistaken. You know her better than I do.'

'Of course my description was accurate, spoilt brat so she is. I lived with her for two months, I should know, and all her dirty habits. Anyway it makes no matter. One of these is going to tell us where Emma is.' She glared at Ronnie. 'Have you worked on the old guy?'

'Not yet.' Camille's breath caught up in her throat. Surely they weren't going to hurt Aaron Kaplan.

Ronnie Bruce bent down and grabbed Aaron Kaplan by the front of his shabby coat, and pulled him to his feet.

'Now, old man. I know you're the caretaker here, which to my mind means you know everything that's going on in these places.'

'Clearly not,' replied Kaplan, his gravelly voice wobbling. 'I didn't know about you, Mr Bruce.'

'So you don't know where Emma is?'

'I do not, why would I? I'm the caretaker who lives in the basement. Why would your sister tell me anything?'

'Because you and she are close. I've heard you talking through there.' He pointed to the Café Bonbon's basement. Ronnie Bruce laughed. 'Yep, didn't know I was listening, did yer? And she didn't know her baby brother hadn't gone back to the states after the sham of a wedding with a plan up my sleeve. I've been working in this restaurant for the last six months. Couldn't believe my luck when Louise and her money man opened the nightclub next door. Who'da thunk it? It fell right into my lap.'

'What did,' asked Camille, hoping to take Ronnie Bruce's attention away from Kaplan.

'The plan to secure the rights to run the Bruce empire. Dear Pa left her everything. There's a house in The Hamptons, a boat in the harbour, but my darling sister is not allowed to touch any of it until she makes a profit in the Bruce business. I don't blame dear old Dad. He was always like that. He reckoned because he started with nothing she has to do the same. He made a name for himself, and she'd have done it in Manhattan too if it hadn't been for the gangs of protectors running around the streets. She thought it would be easier here. She's got no chance. Not while I'm around.'

Camille frowned. 'But why would it concern you whether she makes a profit or not?'

'The will gave her six years. Six years to make a go of it, then, when she fails, it's all turned over to me. Didn't tell yer that, did she?'

'She had no reason to, but why are you after Emma?'

'She's the heir, and the apple of her Mama and Papa's eye. She has a claim, and I ain't watching what is rightfully mine to go to some snot-nosed kid. Louise wanted her to be a partner in the business...to further her education,' he said mimicking a French voice.' He snorted. 'Over my dead body. If she makes her daughter a partner it sends me further down the hierarchy. I ain't having that. And I ain't waitin' six years. I want it now. I was his son. It should have gone to me.

'If I have Emma and threaten her life I know Louise would turn it over. She said the girl meant everything to her, so this is her chance to prove it. I just need to get hold of the girl.'

Camille turned to Sadie.

'And what about you, Sadie? I thought you were Emma's friend.'

Sadie's expression turned into an ugly scowl. 'Friend! That's a joke so it is. Why would she be my friend? Her father killed my daughter. She's no friend ter me. I'd see her dead in a heartbeat.'

Camille and Cecily turned to one another, Cecily's mouth dropping opening in shock. 'Your daughter,' cried Camille. 'Your daughter was the girl who died from food poisoning?'

'That's right. We went for a birthday treat. Just fifteen she was. I'd saved for it for weeks, dinner at Le Petit Champignon. She chose the restaurant; said she'd looked in the window loads of times on her way home from work.' Sadie sat heavily on top of a potato sack. 'She was so excited...we all were. Even her father had made the effort to turn up which was unlike him.' She shook her head. 'But then it all went wrong. The oysters. They were tainted. She'd never had oysters before. She said she didn't like them. Said they tasted funny. And they did, but not because they were oysters. It was because there was something wrong with them.

'That idiot of a chef had served us bad oysters. We all became ill. Everyone in the restaurant who'd had the oysters got sick. It was terrible, so it was. Awful. We all recovered, but she didn't. It took her, her little body too weak to fight it.' Sadie released a sob and got up from her seat on the potato sack. 'Why should they have their daughter when I don't have mine?' she cried, copious tears running down her face. 'There's no justice. All they got was a fine, even though a girl had lost her life. My girl. My wee one who never did anyone any harm.'

'You were in America?'

'Sure...went there for a better life. Some life. Then I hear the chef had come to England, so I followed. Had to do things I would never do just to get the fare. Thems have ruined me, them Clemences, with their money, and their properties, and their daughter,' she cried.

'Destroying the Clemences won't bring your daughter back, Sadie,' Camille said softly. 'And what happened wasn't Emma's fault. It was an accident.'

Sadie gritted her teeth and walked towards Camille, kicking Camille's feet hard as she stood in front of her. 'And what would you know, yer high and mighty bitch? You're just like them. You know nothing of how real people live, what they have ter do.'

Camille winced as Sadie kicked out at her, rubbing her ankle where Sadie's Mary Jane shoe had made contact.

'I have a daughter, Sadie,' answered Camille. 'I can't imagine what you're going through, I don't ever want to, but it was an accident. Monsieur Gaultiere is a good man with a daughter of his own. He would never have hurt yours intentionally. He is mortified at what happened. It has affected his whole life. He can no longer do his work, nor have the confidence to even attempt it.'

Sadie threw her head back and laughed. 'Oh, deary me, what a shame.' She bent towards Camille, snarling again. 'Well, that's just too bloody bad ain't it? I'm glad it's affected his whole life. He wants to spend a day in my shoes to see how my life has been destroyed.'

Camille nodded, knowing she could not really know how Sadie felt. Then a thought occurred to her. 'But you have a son, Sadie. Isn't he worth living for?'

She saw Sadie bite her lip. The thought of her son had clearly affected her. 'You leave my son out of it. 'E's got nothin' ter do with this. 'E's just a poor little mite who was brought into the world at one the saddest times of my life. *He* has saved me. No one else. He and I look after each other. We don't need no one else.'

'Who's his father?' asked Richard.

Sadie glared at him, turning her attentions away from Camille.

'And that's your business because?'

'Because I think his father is Mr Bruce.' He turned his gaze on Ronnie Bruce who was still wielding the gun. 'Isn't that right, Mr Bruce?'

Ronnie Bruce looked perplexed. He shrugged and shook his head. 'I have no idea, and frankly I couldn't care less.'

Sadie glanced at him. 'Let's face it, Ronnie. You care about no one but yourself.'

Ronnie Bruce returned her glare. 'Is he my son? It could be anyone's though couldn't it? You've never been that particular about who you associate with.'

'I wasn't bloody well particular when I associated with you, that's fer sure.' Camille glanced at Richard, understanding what he was trying to do. Gradually he was turning Ronnie Bruce and Sadie against one another. Divide and conquer. She remembered how it worked.

Ronnie Bruce shook his head as though trying to rid himself of the thoughts invading his mind. He had enough to worry about without thinking about a boy he was sure he had no connection to.

'What are we gonna do with them?' Bruce asked Sadie. 'We can't leave them here. One of us will have to stay and make sure they don't leave. I'm going to the Café Bonbon to speak with Louise and we'll both need a gun. I have the only one.'

Sadie gaped at him. 'You're going to tell her it was you?'

He shrugged. 'Why not? We're getting nowhere and I'm getting impatient.'

'But that ain't a good idea, Ronnie.'

'Do you have a better one?'

Sadie said nothing, but then her eyes widened. 'We can shut them in the cold store. You can't unlock the door from the inside. I know that because there's one in the kitchen of the Café Bonbon.'

Ronnie Bruce grinned at her. 'At last, Sadie,' he cried. 'You're using your head.' He nodded. 'Yeah, we'll shut them in there until we've finished with the Clemences.'

Camille and Cecily glanced at each other, both filled with fear, both knowing this was one of the most dangerous situations they had found themselves in. That Ronnie Bruce was quite mad was obvious. All he could see was that he felt he had been overlooked a father whom he clearly adored; looked up to, admired, yet was scathing about him. Did he love his sister, Louise? Camille could not tell, but the fact he intended to take a gun with him when confronting her did not bode well.

'Mr Kaplan will die if you subject him to something so dangerous, Mr Bruce,' she said. 'In fact what Sadie has suggested could kill all of us. You have committed murder twice that we know of, and I'm guessing you're assuming to kill others will not change things, but it will change the lives of those who love us, and it will change the sentence you'll receive when you're caught.'

'I don't intend to get caught, Lady Divine,' he said, a smirking grin on his face. 'That's the first thing you've got wrong. The second is that I have not killed two people. I mistook the first girl for Emma. She struggled, kept screaming, so I had to put my hand over her mouth or we would have been discovered. She would not stop struggling so I twisted her neck. I did not intend to kill her, but in my haste and concern I may have used too much force. If she'd have come quietly she'd still be alive.'

'And when you discovered she was in fact not Emma?' Bruce shrugged. 'And what about Millie, an innocent girl who has also lost her life.'

He shrugged again. 'You'll need to speak to *her* about what happened to the girl in the moon.' He lifted his chin to Sadie.

Camille turned to look at her. 'You killed Millie?' she cried. 'Why? What on earth had she done to make you take her life?'

'She lost her nerve.'

Camille frowned. 'Her nerve? But...but she wasn't involved in any of this.'

'Yeah, she was,' sneered Sadie. 'The stupidity of the police, and you, Lady Divine. I'm surprised to be honest. You seemed really smart, but even you didn't work it out. Did you really think someone lugged that heifer of a girl up to the moon in the time between all the guests had arrived at the Café Bonbon and when Millie found her?' She threw her head back, enjoying taking the floor in front of the unwanted guests. She bent towards Camille from the waist, her hands on her hips. 'She was already there and had been since the morning. Millie laid on top of her when all of you were swanning into the nightclub. She just pretended it was like any other evening. She was paid well for her act. The dead girl was above your heads and you didn't even know it.' She laughed again. 'Genius.'

'You paid her to pretend the girl had been put there in between the time we arrived and when you and Millie came back from the bathroom.' Sadie nodded, grinning. 'So why did you kill her if she'd done what you asked?'

'She got jittery when I told her it hadn't worked and we would have to try again. The aim was to take Emma and then decide what to do with her. I was all for getting rid of Emma but Ronnie wanted to use her as a bargaining chip.' She glanced at Ronnie Bruce. 'We need to find her.'

He nodded. 'We will find her. Louise will tell me where she is. I'll threaten to take out her beloved French chef.'

Camille wasn't about to let Sadie get away with what she'd done. 'So you suffocated Millie? I thought she was your friend.'

Sadie turned her attention to Camille once more. 'Yeah. I used that blanket she carried about with her all the time. She said it reminded her of home.' She shook her head. 'Didn't even struggle. I reckon she'd given up on living.' She pulled a face. 'I think I did her a favour. And I don't 'ave friends, Lady Divine. Don't trust anyone enough for friendship.'

Camille glanced at Elsie who had gone uncommonly quiet. 'Are you all right, Elsie?'

Elsie swallowed hard. 'Just thinking about my Rose and what I would do if anything happened to er.' She glanced at Sadie then leant towards

Camille. 'I would feel the same,' she whispered. 'I can't blame 'er for 'er grief.'

'I understand, but you wouldn't kill someone,' Camille whispered back.

Elsie went quiet and looked morose. 'No, no I wouldn't. I couldn't do that, especially not a young girl with 'er whole life in front of 'er.' She glanced up at Sadie who was talking to Ronnie Bruce. 'Somethin's gone wrong there. Do yer think they'll do what they said? I 'ate being cold.'

Camille nodded. 'I think they will. I don't see how else they'll keep us confined.'

'What about 'im?' Elsie inclined her head towards Aaron Kaplan who was slumped against the wall, his eyes heavy lidded and half-closed. ''E looks about done in. Don't think 'e'll survive it.'

Camille sighed deeply. 'Neither do I. Perhaps I can persuade them to take him with them. He might not survive that either, but he won't be shut up in a cold room. Louise Clemence will take care of him.'

Ronnie Bruce turned to them and told them to get up. His eyes seemed wild, too bright, too blue and his movements were erratic.

'Absinth,' whispered Elsie. 'Seen it all before. It does that to yer. He'll be goin' into the bar in the Café Bonbon soon for another slug. It's prob'erly what keeps 'im goin'.'

'There might not be any absinth on the premises. It's like a drug isn't it?'

Elsie nodded. 'Yeah, and I'm sorry, Camille, but there's absinthe under the bar. I saw it when Ivor Clemence was showing me around. 'Bet 'e knows where it is an' all,' she said, indicating Ronnie Bruce.

Camille decided to confront him.

'Mr Bruce. Is it still your intention to shut us up in the cold room?'

'Yep,' he said, pushing them in a huddled group towards it with his gun.

'Mr Kaplan?'

'What about him?'

'He won't make it, Mr Bruce. He is an elderly man with health issues. Could you not take him with you?'

'Nope.'

'Why not? What harm can he do?'

'He and my sister are close. She looks after him, more than she ever looked after me. No...he goes with the rest of you.'

'So you'll have another death on your conscience.'

He laughed. 'I ain't got a conscience, Lady Divine. It's not helpful in my line of work.'

'Which is?'

'Getting people to do what I want when I want them to do it. And what I want you to do now is shut your trap and get into the cold store.' Camille closed her eyes momentarily, frightened of what could happen to them all.

'You tried,' whispered Elsie. 'At least Cecily's got her bloke with her.' They both turned to see Russell Lewis with his arms around Cecily, comforting her and telling her everything was going to be all right.

'You know?' Camille frowned.

'Yeah...obvious weren't it? I could tell 'e fancied 'er.'

Camille shook her head in astonishment thinking she must have missed out somewhere. 'Hopefully we won't be in there too long.'

Elsie gave her a long stare then smiled. 'If I'm going to be frozen to death I couldn't have chosen a better person to be with, my best friend, Camille Divine.' They hugged and waited for the inevitable.

Chapter 34

Richard looked at his watch. Nine-thirty. He sighed and took a bite of the sandwich he had bought at a stall on the corner of Bear Street, knowing it would likely be the only sustenance he would get that evening. For the second time he had been deprived of a sumptuous dinner at the Café Bonbon, seemingly almost at the point of putting the food in his mouth. He chuckled. It hadn't been quite like that, but it felt like it.

He had returned home to get changed into one of the suits he usually wore for work at Scotland Yard. Fastening his tie over the pristine white shirt, he shrugged on his jacket, dreading the next few hours. The powers that be at Scotland Yard had secured him an interview with Gregory Northcutt, insisting to their powers that be at Pentonville Jail it was an emergency; absolutely imperative that their investigating officer, Chief Inspector Richard Owen be allowed to interview Gregory Northcutt, known to Richard as Miceli Tiseu, one of his father's old associates.

He shook his head in frustration. He had tried to shake off his tenuous association with his father and his criminal exploits, but this particular investigation had proved how difficult it would be, simply because he, Richard, had chosen the profession he had, the one diametrically opposite to his father's.

Hearing an engine rumble outside his house he pulled back the curtain slightly. It was the car Scotland Yard had insisted he take, complete with driver. He hoped it was Russell Lewis. Richard hadn't seen him after he had left the Café Bonbon and he could only assume it was because he had escorted, Camille, Cecily, and Mrs West home, which of course was the correct thing to do. His hope was to be dashed however when he got into the front passenger seat.

'Where's Constable Lewis?' he asked the unknown constable.

The constable shrugged. 'Don't know, sir. He hasn't returned to the station with the others.' Richard frowned, wondering why Lewis hadn't returned to Scotland Yard to be debriefed. 'All right. You know where we're going, constable?'

'Yes, sir. Pentonville.'

Richard nodded. 'Put your foot down, constable. I'd like to get home before midnight if at all possible.'

His Majesty's Prison Pentonville was situated north of the River Thames on the Caledonian Road, a hop, skip, and jump from Islington, and a little further on from Regent's Park. It was an austere building, one would have expected nothing less, with the appearance of a Victorian workhouse. As the motor car approached the entrance Richard felt his stomach roll. He was transported back in time to when his father would be ensconced in a place that almost became his second home; less frequently the older he became. He had learnt how to dodge the authorities and whose palms he had to grease to stay out of prison.

As they went through the entrance, Richard showed his identity card to the prison officer on duty.

'I'm expected,' he said. The prisoner officer simply nodded and waved them through.

'Ever been here before, constable?' Richard asked the young driver.

'No, sir. I haven't.'

'There's no need for you to come inside. Park over there and wait. I'm hoping not to be too long.' Richard acknowledged to himself with a sigh it was an understatement.

The gate slid open, then was locked again by a prison warder who led Richard down a starkly lit corridor towards a door at the end. There was an odour in the corridor which had hit Richard as soon as he had entered the prison; boiled cabbage, nicotine, and unwashed bodies. Richard swallowed his nervousness, reminding himself he was an experienced police officer and it didn't matter who the prisoner was, he would be required to approach the interview like any other.

'This is the interview room, Chief Inspector Owen. The prisoner is not handcuffed, but please sit on the opposite side of the table at all times, and do not lean towards the prisoner. There will be two prison warders standing by the door should you need assistance and I will be positioned outside.' He opened the door and allowed Richard to go through.

Miceli Tiseu was seated at a table in a room with few windows, a hardwood floor, and walls adorned with flaking paint. The windows in the room were high up the walls so one could not see outside which made no difference to the ambiance of the room, and brought no light inside. It was already dark outside.

Richard pulled back the chair on the other side of the table and sat down, facing the prisoner, the one he knew so well.

'Mr Tiseu.'

Tiseu inclined his head once. 'Chief Inspector.'

'You know who I am?'

Tiseu chuckled. 'Of course I do. You're the disappointment of a son your father had to endure, the one who betrayed him.'

'I think I was a bit young for that.'

'You betrayed his memory by becoming what you are.'

'And of course, you didn't betray him, did you?' Richard's eyes narrowed as he observed Tiseu whose face darkened.

'It was an arrangement; one you would never understand.'

'You're damned right about that.' He shook his head. 'I never understood any of you, but I say it with some relief.'

'I know why you're here.'

Richard leant back in his chair and crossed his arms. 'If you know anything about the murder of the girl you are duty bound to tell me.'

'Duty?' Tiseu guffawed. 'Don't speak to me about duty. Where was your duty to your father.' Richard ignored the comment.

'A girl was murdered, Miceli,' Richard said, softer now, thinking that using the man's Christian name might appeal to his better nature. If he had one.

Tiseu nodded. 'I know.'

'She was an innocent, pulled into something that put her in danger. If you have any information, please, help me prevent any more killings.'

Tiseu inhaled a deep breath. 'What's in it for me?'

'What are you in for this time?'

'Receiving stolen goods.'

Richard shook his head. 'Why, Miceli? You had a chance at something. To change your life.'

'Old habits die hard.'

'But you didn't need to do it. The Clemences had given you an opportunity when you came out of prison.' Tiseu shrugged, looking bored with the subject.

'What do you know?'

'About what?'

'The girl.'

'Nothing.'

'Come on, Miceli. If there's trouble you're usually in the thick of it.'

'Not this time.'

'But you know something?' Miceli shrugged.

'If you know anything...tell me.'

'I repeat...what's in it for me?'

'A reduced sentence.'

'I have your word on that.'

Richard nodded, hating he had to give this vile man anything for him to help to prevent the murder of another girl, probably Elsie West if Constable Russell had not found her.

'I've been given authority from the powers that be to reduce your sentence if you can supply me with information.

'I'll give you a name.' Richard nodded. 'Ronnie Bruce.'

'Louise Clemence's brother?' Richard said frowning. 'But he's in the States.'

'You think he is. You'll find he isn't.'

'Did you help him?'

'I unlocked a door and lowered the moon. I didn't ask why. It's all I did. Nothing more.'

Richard's face darkened. 'He knew you had criminal past.'

'It takes one to know one.'

'Where is he?'

Tiseu shifted his position. 'Let's say he's taken a liking to a certain restaurant lately, one that couldn't get closer to the Café Bonbon.'

Richard rose to leave.

'Before you go.' Richard lowered himself onto the seat wondering what was coming next. Miceli Tiseu put his hand in his pocket and pulled out a green jade buddha. 'Give it back to Mrs Clemence. She is better than the man she calls her husband...a better person. I couldn't help taking it. It wasn't screwed down. People shouldn't leave things lying around.' He shrugged and passed the buddha to Richard who palmed it, shaking his head.

Chapter 35

Richard returned to Scotland Yard. It was nearly midnight. The lights from some of the offices still burned brightly, as would his when he got inside, realising he very likely would not see home that night. As soon as he entered the foyer, one of the constable on duty collared him.

'Sir?' Richard frowned and lifted his chin. 'There's been a telephone call from...' he looked down at a notebook...'a Mrs Knowles. She said she was expecting a Lady Divine to have returned home by now but there's been no sign of her. Apparently she's with a Miss Cecily Nugent.' Richard looked contemplative, then made to go to his office. 'Oh, and, sir.'

'Yes?'

'Constable Lewis, sir. He was supposed to return here after leaving the Café Bonbon but he hasn't returned.'

Richard nodded. 'Thanks, constable.' He rubbed his chin. 'Round up some of the officers. If we don't have enough here stir them from their beds. Ten should be sufficient. Tell them to meet me in the foyer in half an hour.'

'Yes, sir.'

'And if you want some excitement you come too. Get someone else to man the desk.'

The young constable looked pleased. 'Yes, sir. Thank you, sir.'

Richard drove himself to the Café Bonbon. He had become increasingly worried at the non-appearance of Camille and Cecily in Duke Street. He knew she had deliberately told Mrs Knowles she would not be late home that evening. It was a good ploy. Mrs Knowles had done the right thing in contacting Scotland Yard. The fact that Constable Lewis had not reported back to Scotland Yard increased his concern. Something wasn't right.

He thought back to earlier that evening. He had been speaking with the forensics team in the foyer, when Constable Lewis had approached him, saying Camille and Cecily had decided to look further into the disappearance of Elsie West, and he thought it would be best if he accompanied them. Richard had nodded his agreement. In his heart of hearts he knew he hadn't given the request enough attention, so taken up had he been with the discovery of another body. As he drove through the now quiet streets, he tutted to himself. He should have paid more attention.

Camille and Cecily were sensible of what they could achieve by investigating themselves, of that he had no doubt, but they were missing, he could not deny it. They and Elsie West had possibly had something befall them they could not get out of. It made sense. Camille…and he had to admit…Cecily, were astute, clear in their thinking, and often came up with ideas that escaped him. They were inventive in their ordering of events, and Richard could only hope that whatever had befallen them was temporary, a situation they could get themselves out of. If not, he knew time was of the essence. It was imperative he found them, and fast.

His mind then went to Miceli Tiseu. His conversation with him had been uncomfortable in the extreme. He was a man Richard had hoped would never cross his path again. He shook his head and tutted, his eyes narrowing at the brightness of the streetlamps shining through the windscreen. Life had a strange way of organising things so the very thing one didn't want to happen, did. And yet he had to admit if it wasn't for Tiseu telling him about Ronnie Bruce, he would have less information about who he thought was probably holding the women and Constable Lewis.

He drew up outside the Café Bonbon just as the other motor cars drew up behind him, three in all. As the constables left the vehicles, Richard held a finger to his lips. He wanted there to be an element of surprise. No good would come of Ronnie Bruce knowing they were there. If he was an agitated sort of man, he may do something they would all regret. Richard stepped towards the double doors at the front of the Café Bonbon and put a gentle hand on the door handle, pressing it down. The door clicked open. Someone had gained entry.

Richard lifted his chin to his men who formed a semi-circle around him. They all carried regulation police truncheons and looked ready for a fight if needs be. Richard pushed slowly on the door. Again he raised his finger to his lips. He could hear voices, coming he thought from the office. There was no electric light emanating from the room, but the glow of a candle flickering shadows against the walls.

'Tell me where she is,' he heard someone say. It was not a voice he recognised, male with an American accent. This was Ronnie Bruce; Richard was sure of it. Then, a female voice, supporting him in his demands.

'Just tell 'im, Mrs Clemence, or Gaultiere will get 'is 'ead blown off.'

'I don't understand, Ronnie,' he heard Louise Clemence say, her voice wobbling in fear. 'What have I ever done to you?'

'Ah, shut up, Louise. You know damn well. You were always the favourite, even though I was the son. Everything should have come to me, the house in the Hamptons, the boat, and now, because of you we'll both lose out. You've made a hash of things. If the money had come to me I would be making a profit right now, and not in this dirty hole of a place. The Café Bonbon should have stayed in Manhattan.'

Richard moved slowly and quietly into the foyer, beckoning three of his men to join him. Quietly and with not even a scintilla of noise, the three men followed him into the foyer, their eyes on Richard, waiting for his command.

'We couldn't stay in Manhattan,' cried Louise. 'You know why. The protection rackets. We were giving them everything we earned.'

'And that's not the only reason,' said the female voice. 'What about 'im? He killed my daughter.'

Richard heard Louise Clemence gasp. 'Your daughter? The girl who died was your daughter?'

'She was only fifteen, a child, my child. Why should you have your child when I can't have mine. She was taken away from me.' The female voice descended into a sob. 'I'll never forgive you,' the woman cried. 'There cannot be forgiveness. You must learn how it feels to lose the one thing that means everything.'

'Sadie, I'm so sorry. I am so sorry for your loss, but trust me my dear, it was not Fabian's fault.' Richard's eyes widened in astonishment. So the woman's voice was Sadie Murphy's.

'Of course it was 'is bloody fault. He dished the oysters up. Could 'e not tell there was something wrong with 'em?'

'It was a new supplier,' said Gaultiere, his voice barely audible. Richard surmised he was being held. 'I promise you we would not have taken such a chance if we had had an alternative. Our regular supplier could not be relied upon. I'm so sorry, so very sorry.'

'Don't give me that,' cried Sadie. 'I ain't interested in your sorries.' There was a pause. 'Just shoot 'em, Ronnie,' she cried. 'Let's get this over and done with. If they won't tell us where Emma is then they're the next best thing. Get rid.' Another pause. 'Gimme the gun. I'll do it,' she said impatiently Richard nodded to his men and they ran from the foyer into the office. Richard followed, ready to disarm whoever had the gun. As the constables and Richard rushed the office, Sadie turned and fired.

Chapter 36

'How is he? Camille asked Cecily as she knelt down to look at Aaron Kaplan.

They were sitting on the floor of the cold room waiting to be liberated. Camille hoped with all her heart that it would be Richard. She had instructed Knolly that if she and Cecily hadn't returned by eleven o'clock she was to telephone Scotland Yard. She took a breath in, thanking her lucky stars she had thought to speak with Knolly before they left for the Café Bonbon, but she knew it in no way would ensure their safety.

'He's not too bad, Madam. Me and Russell are sitting close to 'im to keep 'im warm,' she wrinkled her nose,' but 'e does 'um a bit. Reckon he needs a bath,' she whispered.

'How about you, Elsie? Are you all right?'

Elsie raised her head. 'Yeah, I'm all right, Camille. Remind me not to offer to 'elp you ever again.' She smiled wearily at Camille and sighed. 'I just want ter get 'ome to my Rose.'

Camille sat on the floor next to her and slipped an arm through one of Elsie's. 'I know you do. And for what it's worth, I'm sorry. In my wildest dreams I did not think we would end up like this.'

'I know yer didn't. I'm glad yer came lookin' for me, though Camille. I thought everyone 'ad given up on me. That bloke, what's 'is name...Ronnie something…reckon e's a madman. Got a real funny look about 'im, and it ain't just because of the absinthe niver.'

'I think you're right. Whatever it is that's upset him has very much got to him.' Camille shook her head. 'So many odd people in the world.'

Elsie chuckled. 'Me and you bein' two of 'em.' Camille smiled and nodded as Elsie shuffled onto her other buttock. 'God it's uncomfortable sitting on this floor. And I thought it would be colder an' all. I mean, it's cold all right, but it ain't freezin' is it?'

Camille glanced at her. 'I turned the dial on the outside of the cold room as we were pushed inside. It was lucky I wasn't seen. I didn't know if I'd made the cold store colder or turned it the way we needed it to increase the temperature. I thought either way it would give us a chance to survive being shut in here.'

Elsie stared at her. 'You're so clever. I'd 'ave never thought of doin' somethin' like that.' She glanced at Aaron Kaplan. 'Good job yer did. 'Don't reckon 'e would be 'ere now if you 'adn't.'

'No…and I wish this was over. The man needs medical attention. I'm not sure even now he's going to make it.'

'It won't be them what lets us out of 'ere, Camille.' She shook her head. 'Don't reckon they care whether we live or die. No…it'll 'ave ter be 'is nibs. And I fer one will be very glad to see 'im.'

Chapter 37

'Where are they, Miss Murphy? You know where they are don't you?' Richard asked Sadie Murphy. She had been forced onto one of the chairs in the office with her wrists handcuffed behind her. Richard had questioned both her and Bruce for the last two hours, hoping they would let something slip regarding the whereabouts of Camille and the others.

'I might do, but I dunno why you think I would tell you. Yer keep askin' me the same questions and I ain't told her yet. Why should I make it easy for yer? No one makes it easy fer me.'

'Because it'll be worse for you if you don't.'

'Is 'e dead?' She lifted her head to Ivor Clemence who had been hit by the bullet released from the gun when Sadie had fired.

'No, fortunately for you. It's a superficial wound, but your sentence will be a lot less if you help me out now.'

'I doubt it.'

Richard's face darkened. 'Why do you say that?'

"Cos I'll more than likely face the hangman's noose won't I, so it don't matter how many people I take with me.'

'Why do you say that? How many people have you killed? I thought Mr Bruce was responsible.'

'He were, for the girl what 'e thought were Emma.'

Richard reached into his jacket pocket and pulled out a packed of cigarettes, lighting one from a box of matches on the desk. He eyed Sadie Murphy with disgust, wondering how a young woman could get so hardened.

'You killed Millie Spencer.'

"At's right. I did,' she sneered.

'You seem almost proud of it, Miss Murphy.'

'It ain't a question of bein' proud. I did what I 'ad ter do. No one means anything anymore, not now my girl's gone.'

'What about your son?'

Sadie pursed her lips. 'He'll be looked after.'

'By whom?'

She grimaced cockily at him. 'The workhouse prob'erly.'

'And it doesn't concern you that he'll be brought up in such a place, a boy of only two?'

'It ain't that bad.'

Richard raised his eyebrows. 'You've had experience of it?'

'I have, Chief Inspector. I got by d'int I. He'll do the same.'

Richard was feeling desperate. He had already questioned Ronnie Bruce, but the man was clearly not in his right mind and nothing sensible could be obtained from him.

'Miss Murphy. Sadie. Wherever they are, there are two mothers there, Lady Divine and Elsie West. They both have daughters too. Would you punish those girls in the way you're punishing yourself? They could lose their mothers. What happened to your poor daughter is not their fault. Please, I'm asking you not to punish them.'

Sadie glared at him. 'What makes you think I'm punishing meself?'

'Parental guilt. Doesn't everyone feel it? No matter how hard you try, no matter what you do, in some way you'll feel you've let your children down?' Sadie nodded. 'The love you have for your daughter is clear to me, Sadie. She meant everything to you. Please, help yourself, and your son. I'll put in a good word for you. Wouldn't it be better for the mother he has come to love to raise him rather than some anonymous person who doesn't care about him and will never provide the love and care you could?'

Sadie glanced up at him, her eyes filling with tears. She sighed in submission, shaking her head as though she'd given up.

'They're in the cold store in the basement under the restaurant. You can get to it from the door in the nightclub. The corridor is behind a bookcase. That's where you'll find them.'

Richard swiftly instructed two of the constables to take Sadie and Ronnie Bruce to Scotland Yard. If they didn't face the hangman's noose they would both be locked up for a long time. He had appealed to Sadie's mothering instincts, and Richard was relieved it had worked.

He and another constable ran into the nightclub where Louise Clemence and Fabian Gaultiere were sitting, holding hands in the darkness.

'Where's the door leading to the basement,' he asked them.

Louise pointed to the other side of the nightclub floor. 'Over there, Chief Inspector.'

'Don't leave, Mrs Clemence, or you Monsieur Gaultiere.' He motioned for two of the constable to sit with them.

He made for the door and shoved it open with his shoulder, running down the spiral staircase until he got to the bottom. Following the crumbling corridor he realised when he had reached the area that Aaron Kaplan had made his home. Poor man, he thought. Living like this is no reward for a man of his age. Richard wondered where Aaron Kaplan was as he looked for the bookcase.

The bedside light had been switched on, so someone had come past quite recently. Then he spotted it, a bookcase that had been swung into the corridor at the back of the bed. The alcove was in darkness. Richard flicked on a small torch he'd taken from his pocket, one that had accompanied him on every investigation since he'd been a constable, and made his way down the corridor.

He followed it until he got to a wrought iron door.

'Is that it,' said the constable who had accompanied him.'

'I think that room is the basement under the restaurant. Now all we have to do is find the cold store.'

Richard opened the wrought iron door and stepped into the restaurant basement, thinking how different it was from the one underneath the Café Bonbon.

'It's at least a comfort to know the restaurant take cleanliness and tidiness seriously,' he breathed as he squinted around the room. 'This place is a different prospect entirely from where Aaron Kaplan lives.'

'I think that's the cold store, sir,' said the constable, pointing to a square white box on the right hand side of the room. 'Look there's a dial on the outside of it.'

'Very modern,' said Richard. 'Someone's making money.'

He stepped towards it followed by the constable and depressed the handle. The door swung open. Inside were five people lying on the ground. Richard's breath hitched up in his throat and his stomach rolled. Had the cold store turned into a tomb?

Chapter 38

Cecily and Russell climbed out of the cold store with shaking limbs, with Aaron Kaplan supported between them. Elsie and Camille followed, holding each other up.

'Mr Kaplan will need an ambulance,' said Richard, as the older man stumbled between Cecily and Russell. He indicated for the constable to organise one. 'Is anyone else in need of medical assistance?' They all shook their heads.

He went towards Camille and Elsie, offering his arms as support.

'Let's get you upstairs into the nightclub. I think a brandy wouldn't go amiss. Was it very cold in there?' He frowned. 'I must admit I thought it would be colder.'

'Camille turned the dial round,' said Elsie, her voice hoarse with dryness. 'She's a genius, ain't she?'

Richard turned to Camille, his eyes soft and warm. 'Well done, Lady Divine. I think you've saved your lives, particularly that of Mr Kaplan. I'm quite sure he wouldn't have survived if you hadn't been so quick thinking.'

Camille grinned. 'The thing is I didn't really know what I was doing. I've never seen anything like it before, it's really quite new, but I decided either way it would give us a half chance of it going the way we needed it to.'

'Thank goodness it went the right way,' breathed Richard. 'A brandy for you all, then home. I'm sure you can't wait.'

'How did you know where we were, Richard?' asked Camille. 'Elsie was quite sure neither Ronnie Bruce or Sadie Murphy would have released us. She was hoping you would appear as our knight in shining armour on your white charger to save us.'

'And there you were, Chief Inspector. Just as I predicted,' said Elsie, 'but without the 'orse. I said, di'nt I Camille, 'is nibs will find us. 'E always does, and there you were. I just 'ope we don't make an 'abit of it, all this getting' abducted and locked away. My throat feels like the bottom of a birdcage.'

Richard pulled a knowing face at Camille and they both laughed, knowing that Elsie was looking forward to her brandy.

'Old habits die hard,' she said with a giggle.

Richard nodded and drew in a breath. 'It's the second time I've heard that said today.'

Camille and Richard, Cecily and Russell, sat with Louise Clemence and Fabian Gaultiere in the nightclub, all nursing brandies, all relieved the worst was over.

'Are we safe now, Chief Inspector?' asked Louise. 'Is Emma safe?'

Richard nodded and took a long sip of brandy. 'Yes, Mrs Clemence. Your brother is in police custody, as is Sadie Murphy. I think I should tell you that Sadie Murphy killed Millie Spencer.'

Louise gasped. 'What? No.' Why?'

'Millie knew about what was going on, but because Mr Bruce killed the wrong girl Sadie insisted she play her part. She had apparently been paid for what she did.'

'What did she do?' asked Fabian Gaultiere.

'Charlotte Baynes' body was in the moon before the club opened. Ronnie Bruce had already killed her. Millie had to lie on top of her body to pretend all was as it usually was, until she and Sadie got back from the bathroom. That is when they claimed the body had been placed there, when they had left the foyer.'

Louise Clemence put her hands over her face. 'Oh, no, no. How could they do such a thing to that poor girl? She was so quiet, so innocent. And of course she would have accepted any payment offered to her. She was struggling, as was her mother and her children. I used to slip a bit extra in her pay packet to help her out. That poor, poor girl. Such wickedness.' Louise Clemence burst into tears as Fabian Gaultiere shook his head with sadness.

'So much death, so much sorrow. And to such young people. It is wicked indeed. Life...can be so hard.'

It was after four in the morning. Knolly had been pacing the hall floor along with Phillips, waiting for Camille and Cecily to return home. When the front door had opened and she could see Camille and Cecily were unharmed, she had instantly gone into the kitchen to put the kettle on to boil and made tea for everyone, then taken herself, and Cecily, who was utterly exhausted, upstairs. She put Cecily to bed and went to her room where she thanked the Good Lord for returning her beloved Lady Camille, and her so much loved and almost adopted daughter, Cecily, to her. There had been no questions asked, no enquiries as to the condition of Aaron

Kaplan. There would be time for it the following day, but right now, Mrs Knowles, affectionately known as Knolly was the happiest she'd ever been.

Chapter 39

Camille and Richard sat in her living room sipping tea. A small fire had been lit, the early mornings were chilly, and Camille sat with her legs pulled up onto the sofa underneath her. Richard watched her as she leant against the arm of the sofa, her beautiful dark hair shining in the glow from the fire. She sighed with pleasure and glanced up at Richard, a smile appearing across her face.

'I can't tell you how glad I am it's over, Richard. This was a difficult one wasn't it?'

'I can't argue with that. And for a moment there I thought something had happened to you. I wouldn't have put it past Ronnie Bruce. He is an unwell man.'

'It's strange what jealousy can do to a person. He was clearly incandescent he was not the main heir, not that I think it will make a difference. Louise Clemence doesn't have long to make a profit does she? I wonder what will happen to the house and the boat if she can't achieve it.'

'Richard shook his head. 'Who knows. A long-lost member of the family perhaps. If I were Louise Clemence I think I would ask for a stay of execution. Let's face it, she's had a lot to deal with.'

Camille nodded. 'She has, poor woman. At least Emma will be safe. Do you think she will go back to New York?'

'I'm sure Louise will, but perhaps not with Clemence. Not much love lost there. It's quite likely Fabian Gaultiere will go with her. They seem to have reignited their affections for each other.'

'Not a bad ending for them,' said Camille, staring into the fire. 'Not a good one for those poor, poor girls.' She yawned, covering her mouth with her hand.

'You're tired,' said Richard, standing to leave.

Camille glanced up at him. She put her teacup on the occasional table and reached for his hands.

'This all began with you trying to tell me about your past,' she said softly. 'Or at least...your father's past.'

Richard looked embarrassed. 'I felt I had to before Lord Divine did it for me. I felt sure he would discover who my father was, and the first person he would tell would be you.'

Camille nodded. 'He did tell me, but it was after our conversation at the Café Bonbon.' Richard startled and Camille gripped his hands. 'The thing is Richard, he told me because he wanted to bury the fact he was planning to marry again, to soften his words, to make it seem he was protecting me, when all the time he was just breaking the news to me that on his marriage I would have to relinquish my title. He is extremely astute, and rather cunning. I've learnt that about him.'

'He warned you off me.'

'Yes, he did. Or at least...he tried to.'

'And your answer?'

'My answer was that if he had the option to choose whomever to be by his side, then I had the same option without recourse to anything he may think or feel. I will not be told who I can and cannot have in my life.' It went quiet as the fire crackled. 'And I choose you. I don't care what your father did, or that your mother was not faithful. I do care about you and that you are the most honourable man, apart from my own father, I have ever met.'

Richard gazed down at her, his eyes growing warm, and crinkling at the sides as his face broke into a smile.

'I'm very relieved to hear you say that, Lady Divine,' he said with a sigh. He bent his head and placed his lips against hers. She returned his kiss, leaning against him, revelling in his warmth and the leanness of his body. Richard Owen was a handsome man, an honest and honourable man. She knew she would not find another who outshone him.

Their lips parted and they smiled at one another.

'One day, Camille,' he whispered. 'One day.'

Camille leant her head against his chest and closed her eyes. 'When I'm truly free, Richard. You have my word.'

Chapter 40

A quiet, rather hoarse voice explained Aaron Kaplan's situation and his change of circumstance. He, Knolly, Cecily, Camille, and Phillips were sitting around the huge pine table in Duke Street, each nursing a hot cup of tea and nibbling at the cakes Knolly had baked for the occasion.

Aaron Kaplan looked very different from the man Camille and Cecily had first met, the one who lived in the filthy basement of the Café Bonbon. When he had left hospital, Camille had immediately taken him under her wing, insisting he allow her to help him. She had given him a room at Duke Street so he could recover in comfort, then, when he was better, had taken him to be fitted for new clothes, but not before she had suggested he make a trip to the barbers. His hair and beard were now trimmed and clean. He wore a navy blue suit with a light blue tie, and a pristine white shirt. He looked a different person, a much happier, more relaxed person. He even had a twinkle in his eye which Camille was overjoyed to see.

'I tried to love my wife,' he admitted as he laid his cup down on the saucer with a chink, 'but she was highly strung. I admit, I did not love her. Please understand I never felt any ill will towards her. She was my wife, an arranged marriage it's true, one neither of us would have chosen, and we tried to make the best of it. She did not love me either, a disappointment I did my best to bear.

'Of course, when someone is murdered as she was, the blame is always planted onto the nearest person. That was me. I was questioned by the police for hours, many, many hours, but I had an alibi…firm and true. I was at my gentleman's club with my brothers the evening she was killed. Then the police suggested I had arranged her killing because I wanted her money, and that of her family. Again, that came to nothing. I had money, my family were wealthy, wealthier than hers, so the accusation did not stick. It was one of the most frightening times of my life. If I had been charged with her murder and found guilty I would have been hanged.'

He took another sip of tea. No one said anything.

'It changed me, frightened me. I found I could not cope with ordinary life. I worried about everything I did and said. My wife's family said it was because I was guilty of killing her, or of arranging her killing and I was being punished for my sins. My family tried to help me, but I thought I had brought shame on them. I ran away, began to live rough, on the streets, in sheds, on doorsteps, under bridges. It was the only life I could live.'

He lowered his head, and Camille's heart dropped with sorrow for this poor man. What a dreadful thing to happen to someone so innocent, and so bereft of the tools one needed to get through a life that had become so unfortunately difficult.

'Who took her life, Aaron?' Knolly asked him, placing a hand over one of his. 'Yer don't need ter answer if you'd rather not.' He glanced at Knolly, his eyes warm, and Camille could see real affection there, an affection which had survived the years.

'A burglary, one which had gone very wrong. They thought the house was empty, but of course it was not. My wife was there on her own. The police finally discovered that the garden door had been broken into. They took money, silver trinkets. They were discovered when some of those trinkets appeared in a pawn shop in Covent Garden. The owner remembered who had brought them in. They were arrested and charged and went to the gallows, two young men who had wasted their lives, ended another, and ruined mine, for a handful of trinkets.' He shook his head and Knolly squeezed his hand. He straightened up, took a deep breath and turned to Camille.

'Lady Divine, you are an angel.' Camille flushed but accepted his compliment. 'You have taken care of me when no one else would. I cannot thank you enough, but I think it is time for me to move on. One cannot let the grass grow under one's feet, and I have imposed on your hospitality for too long. I will leave today so your household can return to what is usual. An elderly man you hardly know living in one of your sumptuous rooms is not.'

Knolly frowned, her eyes troubled, her lip almost quivering. 'But where will you go, Aaron? Do you have somewhere to be?'

'Not yet, but I have spent most of my life on the road. Caretaking was a lucky find. It provided me with shelter, food, and an income of sorts, but Mrs Clemence and Monsieur Gaultiere are returning to New York. The restaurant has found another caretaker in my absence, so I must look for different employment.'

Camille sat forward and put a hand on Aaron's arm. 'Mr Kaplan, you are welcome to stay here. Phillips would like some help, I'm sure. He has taken on an allotment near one of the parks to grow vegetables for Knolly's kitchen, and of course, there is the maintenance of this house which is ongoing.' Camille nonchalantly reached for another lemon tart. She wanted everything to be calm, wanted Aaron to know she wasn't offering charity. 'What are your thoughts, Phillips?'

Phillips nodded. 'It'd be good to 'ave another man about the 'ouse. I've always felt ganged up on by the ladies.' They all laughed. 'Yes,' he nodded again, 'I would appreciate the 'elp.'

Camille glanced at Knolly who she thought was going to cry with gratitude. Instead she leant across to Phillips and kissed him on the cheek.

'You're a fine man, Phillips. And yes, you've needed 'elp for ages, 'cept yer wouldn't admit it.' She glanced at Aaron. 'Aaron, will yer stay, dear?' she asked him softly.

Aaron placed his hands together as if in prayer and closed his eyes. He took a breath then looked at Phillips. 'Mr Phillips, I don't want to intrude on your position.'

Phillips smiled. 'You ain't intruding. If Lady Divine wants yer to stay it's good enough fer me. Anyway it'll be nice to 'ave some company.'

Aaron smiled and his eyes twinkled once more. 'Thank you, Lady Divine. I accept...with great thanks and gratitude. To be part of a family again, even one that isn't my own, is the greatest gift you could have given me. Thank you. Thank you with all my heart.'

Cecily, Knolly and Camille glanced at one another with relief. Knolly sighed with happiness, Cecily giggled, thinking about her planned evening with Russell.

And Camille...

Camille glanced around at the family she had put together. They were people she had chosen, or they had chosen her which seemed to be more accurate, and she felt truly honoured. Her thoughts went to Richard and she smiled to herself. In him she had found her soulmate, the most wonderful man, kind and true.

She could only wonder what the future had in store for them all.

A Note from the Author

Hello,

Thank you so much for choosing the fourth book in The Camille Divine Murder Mysteries Series. I hope you enjoyed it.

I am overwhelmed by your unwavering support and enthusiasm for the Camille Divine Murder Mysteries Series. Your dedication to following Camille's adventures through the intricate web of mysteries and intrigues fills me with immense joy and inspiration. You feedback and encouragement are the lifeblood that fuels my passion for storytelling, and for that, I am deeply thankful.

For those who have embarked on the journey with Camille Divine from the very beginning, from the snow-covered streets on Christmas in London, through the quaint streets of Paris to the sun-kissed shores of Sicily, your loyalty knows no bounds..

To those who have just discovered Camille's world with this latest instalment, I extend a warm welcome and invite you to delve deeper into the series.

As you immerse yourselves in the twists and turns of Camille's investigations, I hope you find solace in the pages of these mysteries; a temporary escape from the chaos of the world around us. I urge you to revisit the earlier books in the series, to unravel the clues and mysteries that have shaped Camille's journey thus far.

And for those eager to uncover more secrets, rest assured Camille's adventures are far from over. From THE CHRISTMAS TREE MURDERS to THE SICILIAN MURDERS, each instalment offers a unique tapestry of suspense, intrigue, and unforgettable characters.

Once again thank you for your continued support, and for joining me on this thrilling odyssey. Your passion for mystery and your love for storytelling inspire me every day, and I cannot wait to share more adventures with you in the future.

Warmest regards,

Andrea Hicks

Author of the Camille Divine Murder Mysteries Series.

OTHER BOOKS WRITTEN BY ANDREA HICKS

99 Nightingale Lane – The Complete Saga

The complete series Books 1 - 8
London, Christmas 1914

Eighteen-year-old Carrie Dobbs has a secret. When her parents discover her condition, Carrie's mother, Florrie takes matters into her own hands and arranges a marriage with Arnold Bateman to get Carrie out of Whitechapel and away from the gossips. He is a man Carrie could never love, the opposite of Johan, the young man she adores. Arnold has been posted to India and expects her to go with him and be the wife he needs to further his promotion and position in the army. India is a country she only knows from an atlas and she is terrified she will never see her family and her beloved best friend, Pearl again. Feeling she has no choice, she travels to India with a heavy heart, wondering if she will ever return to the place she calls home? India is a mystery to her, but this strange and vibrant country gets under her skin, and when someone she admires from afar is kind to her, Carrie wonders if she will find love again.

Join Carrie in her spell-binding journey into love and independence, and discover the consequences when she makes a decision that will change all their lives!

Books in the 99 Nightingale Lane Series
MRS COYLE'S COOKBOOK

INSPIRED BY STORIES FROM 99 NIGHTINGALE LANE and to accompany the popular series.

Stories and recipes from 99 Nightingale Lane from Ida Coyle

'I do believe I was born thinking about food, which didn't do me much good seeing as we didn't have much of it. I know I'm lucky compared to many who had it harder than me...I've worked at 99 Nightingale Lane for most of my life, taken in by the family who lived there before the Sterns when my Ma was killed by The Ripper. They were an old London family, not that I would have taken any notice then. I was just a smidgen of a girl, one of many who worked here, nearly as many as the fleas on a dog's tail. And...this is one of the things I learned from Mrs Brimble, the cook who taught me everything I know.

'When I think about where I was born, where we lived over the tanners shop, and what my Ma had to do to put food on the table,' I shook my head, 'she wouldn't believe that I stood there in that grand room, amongst all those beautiful things. And now I'm here in this kitchen with you, cooking the Hamilton's luncheon. I so wish she could see me now.' Mrs Brimble put a hand on my arm. 'She is watching, Ida, and I know she'd be proud of how well you've done and how hardworking you are, but not because of who you work for. She'd be proud because of who you are, the type of person you've become. That's what's important, ducky, not money and things what can be bought. Not tables of silverware and fruits from the continents or gowns from the salons of Bond Street. You're just a little'un really, still young, but you will learn about what's important, and there will be more laughter and smiles and happiness below stairs around our simple table when we have our Christmas dinner than there will be in that beautiful room, you mark my words.' She lowered her voice. 'Y'see, Ida, they haven't learned how to count their blessings. This is just another day to them. They see rooms like that all the time so they've forgotten how to be swept away by it. Do you think Lady Davinia will go into *that room and widen her eyes in wonder like you did? Do you think Mr and Mrs Hamilton will take much notice of the table that the upstairs maids and the footman worked so hard to make look lovely? They'll give it a glance only to find an imperfection. It's how they are. They have plenty, they definitely do, but none of them appreciate it.'* She stared at me. *'And that's for your ears only,'* she whispered.

You see. I had the best teacher. This is my story, of when I was a girl starting work at the age of thirteen and how I fought my way through the ranks below stairs to become cook at 99 Nightingale Lane. And I've brought my favourite recipes with me, documented in MRS COYLE'S COOKBOOK for you to make yourself for you and your family to enjoy.

I hope you love my story and my recipes. It means so much to me that I've been given the opportunity to share them with you.

Warmest wishes from your friend, Ida Coyle, Cook at 99 Nightingale Lane'

Books in the Lily Pond Victorian Murder Mysteries Series

THE CURIOUS LIFE OF LILY POND

THE DORSET STREET MURDERS

Romantic Comedies

CHRISTMAS AT MISTLETOE ABBEY

A charming-to-read Christmas romance novella to snuggle up with under a tartan blanket, sipping a glass of spicy mulled wine. Enjoy! 'An enjoyable read that was entertaining from start to finish. It was simply delightful, and I highly recommend Christmas at Mistletoe Abbey.'
'From the first page to the last, this fun romance novel kept me hooked. A real page-turner I couldn't put down!'

THE CHOCOLATE SHOP ON CHRISTMAS STREET

The sweetest Christmas Romance to cuddle up with!

Standalone Novels

THE GIRL WITH THE RED SCARF

Tom Alexander has no memory of his life at House in the Hills orphanage on the outskirts of Sarajevo, or of his birth parents, the ones whose faces he wants to see, but doesn't remember. When he receives a letter from ChildAbroad, the agency that arranged his adoption in 1994, he is offered the opportunity to search for the boy he once was, Andreij Kurik—if he returns to Sarajevo. With Sulio Divjak, the driver and interpreter Tom befriends, he searches the derelict orphanage and discovers he has two siblings, one who was also at House in the Hills. Sulio uncovers a faded photograph in Andreij's file of a girl wearing a red scarf. She looks like Ellie; the girl Tom fell in love with at first sight in a café in Regent's Park. Devastated when he realises what it could mean, Tom goes back to the UK to get some answers. Accompanied by Ellie he returns to Sarajevo to find his birth parents, only to receive news that destroys everything he thought he knew about Tom Alexander—and Andrej Kurik.
A young love forged at the height of war, a chance meeting, and a collision of faded memories and half-truths, The Girl with the Red Scarf will appeal to fans of historical, women's and romantic fiction.
From the author of The Other Boy, shortlisted for the Richard & Judy Search for a Bestseller

THE OTHER BOY

Their new home promises so much, an idyllic life in the countryside, a peaceful existence outside the busyness of London. She'd dreamt of it. A forever home. But something happened there, a heart-breaking tragedy infused in its walls. The history of the old house returns to haunt her, and when the memories she had buried return she isn't the only one who fears them.

Before you hide the truth, make sure the dead can't give up your secrets. If you love gripping, ghostly psychological thrillers that you can't forget, make a big pot of coffee - THE OTHER BOY won't let you go.

Find out why Amazon reviewers are saying, "Unputdownable and heart-breaking. Not just a psychological thriller, not just a ghost story, but so much more"…*Birdie Advanced Copy Reviewer*

"The Other Boy is beautifully written, as always. I expect nothing less from the author. This story is a revelation. By blending stunning writing with a heart-breaking ghost story and a psychological twist she had me captured from the very first moment." *MW Advanced Copy Reviewer*

'It's the other boy in the basement,' said Tobias. 'The other boy telled me.'

DESTRUCTION OF BEES

The Year 2030

Embark on a gripping journey into the unknown with DESTRUCTION OF BEES – a heart-pounding thriller that will have you on the edge of your seat until the very last page.

When Nina Gourriel is rushed to hospital after a terrifying collapse, little does she know it's just the beginning of a harrowing ordeal. Instead of receiving medical care, she finds herself ensnared in a web of conspiracy and intrigue, whisked away to a clandestine government facility.

As Nina grapples with the mysterious tests forced upon her, she crosses paths with Cain, an enigmatic scientist who reveals the startling truth: she's being hunted for something she doesn't even know she possesses. With each passing moment Nina's world unravels further, plunging her into a deadly game of cat and mouse with multiple adversaries closing in on her. She doesn't know who to trust.

Is she a beacon of hope or the harbinger of destruction?

If you crave a pulse-pounding narrative that will haunt your thoughts long after you turn the final page, DESTRUCTION OF BEES is a must-read. Join Nina as she navigates a treacherous landscape where danger lurks at every corner, and the fate of humanity hangs in the balance.

Printed in Great Britain
by Amazon